SECRET UNDERTAKING
The Seventh Buryin' Barry Mystery

"The story's resolution is satisfying on many levels. de Castrique draws the reader into his protagonist's world with consummate grace."

—*Publishers Weekly*

"Buryin' Barry" unearths a corrupt plot in his sleepy North Carolina town....The hero's easy charm in his seventh case makes the reader feel like a longtime Gainesboro resident and a sleuthing sidekick."

—*Kirkus Reviews*

RISKY UNDERTAKING
The Sixth Buryin' Barry Mystery

"De Castrique's latest mystery continues the irreverent wit and independent spirit that has marked the series thus far. The focus on the beautiful setting of western North Carolina and its Cherokee traditions is well crafted. ...This is a complex and well-executed police procedural as well."

—Library Journal

"De Castrique's engaging sixth mystery featuring funeral director and deputy sheriff Barry Clayton...offers insights into the political, economic, and cultural ramifications of Indian casinos, along with a large cast of believable characters with a wide emotional range."

—Publishers Weekly

FATAL UNDERTAKING
The Fifth Buryin' Barry Mystery

"...de Castrique gives readers a tantalizing mystery full of humor and eccentric characters, along with a nice dollop of current social issues."

—*Booklist*

"De Castrique writes complicated mysteries that lead his sleuth on journeys of self-discovery while unwrapping the motivations behind murder. Here the focus is on how greed warps the human spirit. De Castrique's unassuming but commanding prose style is comparable to James Lee Burke and Margaret Maron."

—*Library Journal* (starred review)

FINAL UNDERTAKING
The Fourth Buryin' Barry Mystery

"De Castrique offers original plots, strikingly human characters, and a heartwarming portrait of American culture. His writing is to be savored."

—Library Journal (starred review)

"The fourth entry in the Undertaking series, featuring North Carolina undertaker Barry Clayton, offers further evidence that funeral parlors provide rich material for offbeat fiction....Barry uncovers a far-reaching fraud scheme, but his biggest problem may be Deputy Hutchins, who is doing every nasty thing he can to ensure that Barry doesn't solve the case. Strong characters and an engaging setting add up to a thoroughly enjoyable yarn."

—Booklist

"...de Castrique has married the complexity and fast pace of a police procedural with the folksy setting and lovable characters of a cozy."

—Publishers Weekly

FOOLISH UNDERTAKING
The Third Buryin' Barry Mystery

"As important and as impressive as the author's narrative skills are the subtle ways he captures the geography—both physical and human—of a unique part of the American South."

—Dick Adler, *The Chicago Tribune*

"De Castrique returns with his third adventure featuring undertaker Barry Clayton. When his father was stricken with Alzheimer's, Barry left a police career in Charlotte to return to his tiny Appalachian hometown of Gainesboro, North Carolina, to help run the family funeral business. Barry's loving, respectful relationships with his parents and uncle are part of what makes him such a compelling protagonist: family loyalty is the driving force in his life. In this adventure, Barry is preparing for the funeral of Vietnamese Y'Grok Eban. Y'Grok was part of the Montagnards, a fiercely loyal resistance group who helped save the lives of countless Americans during the Vietnam War—including that of Gainesboro sheriff Tommy Lee Wadkins. When someone attacks Barry and steals Y'Grok's body, the likable undertaker has more than embarrassment to worry about.... Another stellar entry in an outstanding series that deserves wider recognition: the family focus and rural North Carolina setting make it a natural for Margaret Maron fans."

—*Booklist* (starred review)

"...a fabulous thriller that grips the audience from the moment the corpse is purloined and never slows down..."

—*bookcrossing.com*

GRAVE UNDERTAKING
The Second Buryin' Barry Mystery

"It's not every day that the second entry in a series trumps the debut—but de Castrique accomplishes just that with this follow-up to *Dangerous Undertaking*....The plot is nicely layered with suspense...but what really stands out about this series is de Castrique's rich yet respectful portrait of life in the Appalachians...a first-rate installment in an excellent series."

—*Booklist*

"Realistic and sensitively drawn characters, including Barry's Alzheimer's-afflicted father, together with a neat plot that builds to a powerful ending...lift this poignant novel…"

—*Publishers Weekly*

DANGEROUS UNDERTAKING
The First Buryin' Barry Mystery

"I really enjoyed this book. Mark de Castrique writes with an authentic insider's voice. He clearly knows and loves these mountains and he respects the people who live there."

—Margaret Maron

"Adept at both the grizzly and the graceful, de Castrique has produced a marvelous mystery you won't want to put down."

—*Publishers Weekly*

Secret
Undertaking

Books by Mark de Castrique

The Buryin' Barry Series
Dangerous Undertaking
Grave Undertaking
Foolish Undertaking
Final Undertaking
Fatal Undertaking
Risky Undertaking
Secret Undertaking

The Sam Blackman Mysteries
Blackman's Coffin
The Fitzgerald Ruse
The Sandburg Connection
A Murder in Passing
A Specter of Justice
Hidden Scars

Other Novels
The 13th Target
Double Cross of Time
The Singularity Race

Young Adult Novels
A Conspiracy of Genes
Death on a Southern Breeze

Secret Undertaking

A Buryin' Barry Mystery

Mark de Castrique

Poisoned Pen Press

Copyright © 2018 by Mark de Castrique

First Edition 2018

10 9 8 7 6 5 4 3 2 1

Library of Congress Control Number: 2018935809

ISBN: 9781464210358   Hardcover
ISBN: 9781464210372   Trade Paperback
ISBN: 9781464210389   Ebook

Poisoned Pen Press
4014 N. Goldwater Blvd., #201
Scottsdale, AZ 85251
www.poisonedpenpress.com
info@poisonedpenpress.com

Printed in the United States of America

For Linda

Chapter One

"I want you to put me in jail." Archie Donovan, Junior, sported a wide smile as he made the request.

I stared at him in disbelief. "What?"

The two of us sat in the back booth of the Cardinal Café where Archie had urgently summoned me for a mid-morning cup of coffee. He'd walked from his insurance office and I'd strolled the few blocks from our funeral home, wondering with each step, what harebrained scheme he would propose. It looked like I wasn't going to be disappointed.

"Yes, Barry. You're a deputy sheriff."

"Part-time."

"Well, it's still official when you're on-duty."

"I'm not now."

Archie shook his head. "I don't want you to arrest me now. It will be at the parade."

I slid farther back in the booth, glancing around to see if anyone was overhearing our ridiculous conversation.

"Archie, you want to give me more background before I say no?"

Archie and I had known each other since grade school and in those years we'd been as compatible as oil and water. In junior high, Archie had dubbed me "Buryin' Barry" because my family lived in Gainesboro's one and only funeral home. The name had stuck through high school, and even today a former classmate might rib me in public. In short, Archie could push all my buttons without even trying. Now that we were both in our mid-thirties, I'd come to realize he wasn't mean, he was just tone deaf to the impact of what he said. That never stopped him from talking.

He leaned across the table. "Now, you support the Boys Club and Girls Club of Gainesboro, right?"

"Yes." I recognized his strategy of getting me to start saying yes before the poisoned-pill question was sprung.

"And you agree that they help mold young lives so the kids don't wind up in your jail?"

"Of course. Just get to the point."

"I want to raise money to help them. Through the Jaycees float in the Apple Festival Parade."

"By being arrested?"

Archie's eyes gleamed. "By being bailed out. Everyone thinks it's a great idea."

I restrained myself from asking who everyone might be.

Archie took a sip of coffee and then pushed the cup aside. "All right. Let me start over. I'm chairman of the Jaycees charity committee that's responsible for raising money. You know, like the annual haunted house."

"Bad example," I said. One year, at Archie's insistence, I'd lent the Jaycees a casket for the Halloween fundraiser, only to have a man murdered in it.

He shrugged. "Well, then not like it. Everything will be out in the open. The float will feature kids from the Boys and Girls Clubs and I'll be on it, standing in a mock jail, wearing one of those old-timey striped prison suits. The lettering on the float will say 'Free Archie and help our kids.'" He spread his hands as if the beauty of his proposal was now self-evident.

"I get it. People raise your bail for charity. How much?"

"Ten thousand dollars."

I whistled softly. "I don't know, Archie. That's a lot of money. How long can you stay on the float?"

"Just for the parade. Then I'll go to your jail. I'll post pictures on Facebook. I bet Melissa Bigham and the *Vista* will want to follow my progress. Every morning the paper could run an update." His eyes brightened even more. "Maybe list donors and corporate sponsors. How much will the funeral home kick in? It's great publicity."

I signaled time-out. "None of this is my call. You can do what you want with your float, but the jail's another matter. Tommy Lee has say over that, not me."

"But the sheriff listens to you. And he's always doing outreach programs. It's a win-win, a no-brainer."

Both expressions grated on my ears. "Win-win" reduced everything to a game, and "no-brainer" meant some decision was being made by someone without a brain. I took the easiest exit I could find.

"All right. I'll ask Tommy Lee, but no promises." I made a show of looking at my watch. "Sorry. I've got to go. Appointment at eleven."

Archie's smile vanished. "Someone die?"

"No."

The smile returned. "Good. I was afraid it was one of my policyholders. When they die, they stop paying their premiums."

I wondered how much money could be raised to keep Archie in jail.

As I neared the funeral home, I spotted a silver Mercedes parked in one of the handicapped spaces near the ramp to the front door. My eleven o'clock appointment had arrived early. Normally, this wouldn't have been a problem because my partner, Fletcher Shaw, would have covered for me. But young Fletcher had taken the week after July Fourth for a vacation in the Bahamas with his girlfriend. He'd confided that he hoped to bring her back as his fiancée.

I quickened my stride and looped around the lot to come in through the back porch of the old antebellum home. Mom stood at a counter in the kitchen, wearing an apron over one of her Sunday dresses, arranging an assortment of cookies on a china plate. A tray with service for coffee was on the kitchen table.

"There you are," Mom said breathlessly. "Mrs. Sinclair showed up thirty minutes early. I was still in my housecoat."

My mother lived upstairs, where she and my father had raised me, their only child. After Dad died, I tried to convince Mom to move to a retirement community but she would hear nothing of it.

She set the cookies on the table with the coffee. "Fortunately, Wayne was still here and took her into the parlor."

Her brother, my Uncle Wayne, had moved upstairs a few months ago after selling his home in the county. If anything offered the possibility of encouraging Mom to join a retirement community, it was being under the same roof as Uncle Wayne. Although they loved each other dearly, they clashed over everything from politics to which blossoms made the best funeral arrangements. Mom was short, round, and cheery. Wayne was tall, slim, and skeptical. He was mid-seventies; she mid-sixties and forever the little sister. The only thing they shared in common was a headful of curly, cotton-white hair. And the belief that I was the smartest son/nephew in the world.

"Is he still with her?"

Mom rolled her eyes. "If he hasn't run her off." She lifted the coffee tray. "Bring the cookies and we'll see."

I followed her out of the kitchen and down the hall to the parlor. Before we were halfway there, I could hear Uncle Wayne speaking at the decibel level common to those who are hard of hearing.

"It's a crime, I tell you. I just don't want you shocked when you hear how much."

I tensed. Uncle Wayne must have jumped to providing cost information, something that was supposed to be left to Fletcher or me. My uncle quoted prices from memory—from 1975. And he apologized for them. I wondered how much damage I'd have to undo and whether Mom's homemade cookies would make our guest more amenable to whatever adjustments would be necessary.

"Barry's here," Mom called, as she crossed the threshold. "And I brought coffee." She set the tray on the table in front of our guest who sat on the sofa. Uncle Wayne was in a wingback chair angled across from her.

Mrs. Sinclair looked grateful for the interruption. She wore a gray skirt and a white blouse with a small rounded collar. The top two buttons were unfastened to reveal a pearl pendant hanging from a delicate gold chain. She started to rise, but I shifted the cookies to my left hand and offered my right.

"Please don't get up, Mrs. Sinclair."

"Janet, please." She stood anyway.

Her grip was firm.

"And thank you for the coffee. Black will be fine."

I set the cookies on the table and stepped back so Mom could pour.

"We were just getting started," Uncle Wayne said. "I was telling her how outrageous it is what the newspapers charge for an obituary. I mean when someone leaves this Earth, that's a news event. The family shouldn't be expected to pay for it any more than a sports team should pay to post the score of a game."

Janet Sinclair looked bewildered by the comparison, and I worried if she envisioned her loved one sandwiched between a stock car race and the local shuffleboard tournament.

"Wayne, can you help me in the kitchen a moment?" My mother wrapped her demand in the veneer of a question, but even Wayne understood he had no other option.

"Certainly, Connie." He stood and gave a slight bow to our

guest. "A pleasure to make your acquaintance. Barry will take good care of you."

I remained standing until they left and then took the chair my uncle had vacated. Janet Sinclair took a sip of coffee and I took the chance to examine her more closely.

She appeared to be in her mid to late forties. Her pale skin had a hint of blush on her cheeks. Her black hair was cut short and a stark contrast to bright blue eyes. Those eyes were free of crow's-feet. If she'd had cosmetic surgery, it was excellent. The only discernible indications of age were lines along her neck where the skin wasn't as tight.

Unlike so many bereaved who came to our funeral home, Janet Sinclair gave no sign she'd been crying—no running mascara, no tissues clenched in tight fists. All she'd said when she'd spoken with my mother earlier was could we meet at eleven. Her early arrival suggested an urgency that hadn't come through her initial request.

"I'm sorry to show up a half hour before our appointment," she said. "I was to meet our insurance agent, but he'd evidently been called out of the office."

Archie, I thought. He'd been so excited about his parade appearance that he'd skipped out on a client.

"That's all right. Any questions about what my uncle might have told you?"

She smiled. "No. He was waiting for you. He was lamenting the cost of obituaries because I asked if you handled them."

I made a mental note to tell my mother that Uncle Wayne hadn't strayed off the reservation after all.

"Yes, we can coordinate that for you. Has there been a death? I'm sorry but I don't know the circumstances of your visit."

"I guess you could call this fact-finding. I'd like to make preliminary arrangements for my husband and me."

I eyed her more closely. She looked healthy. Perhaps her husband was gravely ill and she wanted to make suitable plans for both of them.

"Why don't you describe what you and your husband think you would like? Then I'll know what suggestions might be appropriate."

She nodded. "Is our conversation privileged?"

"Privileged?"

"Like with a lawyer or a priest."

In my years in the funeral business, no one had ever asked me that question. My father had told me he had met a few terminally ill husbands who wanted to keep their conditions from their wives as long as possible, but Dad told them he'd never lie if asked directly.

"There's not legal protection," I said, "but we do adhere to a strict level of confidentiality. If for some reason I had to appear in court under oath, I would have to reveal the substance of our conversation."

She pursed her lips, not happy with my answer.

"That will be the same for any licensed funeral director," I added. "But we don't gossip. As long as you're not requesting anything illegal."

She arched an eyebrow. "Illegal? Like what?"

"Well, like a burial on land not approved for cemetery use. One man loved to hike and wanted to be interred at an overlook in Pisgah Forest. Sprinkling ashes is one thing but a grave and headstone is something else."

"Nothing like that," Janet Sinclair said. "But we will be going back north to a cemetery outside of Paterson, New Jersey."

"If you'll give me the name of a local funeral home you'd like to use, we'll be happy to coordinate."

"No."

Her emphatic tone surprised me.

"Well, we can step out of the picture and you can deal directly with the Paterson funeral home for transportation."

"No, just you. I can give you the name of the cemetery so that you can contact them directly."

I sat quietly for a moment, trying to figure out why she'd avoid a local funeral home in New Jersey. And why she wanted this conversation to be privileged.

She sensed my reluctance. "My husband, Robert, wants us to be buried with his parents, but there's a family rift. We own our plots outright so there's no legal issue." She gave a humorless laugh. "His siblings never visit the graves, so they may never even know we're there."

"Okay. I understand." I told her that, but I'd never known a family feud to be so vehement that it extended beyond death.

"Wonderful, Mr. Clayton. It will be a comfort to my husband."

"How's his health?" I asked. "Was your visit today prompted by a medical condition?"

"No." She hesitated, weighing a decision whether to say more. "I was reviewing our life insurance and that just got me thinking. If you would go ahead and give me an estimate, I'd appreciate it. I'll give you the address of the cemetery, but please don't contact them yet. Put in what you think will cover everything. For both of us."

"But I don't know what they'll charge for opening a grave."

She tapped her foot nervously on the carpet. "Then make a general inquiry. Tell them you have clients thinking about burials there, but that you're going to be handling everything. When the time comes, either my husband or I will give you full instructions." She paused as her voice choked. "Or if both of us were to die in a car or plane crash, our attorney will send the information."

"All right."

She relaxed. "And then would half up front be sufficient?"

I smiled. "That's not necessary. We don't encourage prepayment plans. I recommend you set the money aside in your own account. Let's hope it will be there a long time."

Her eyes teared. "I wouldn't count on it, Mr. Clayton."

Chapter Two

The Paterson cemetery bore the bucolic name of Forest Glen. My knowledge of New Jersey conjured up "Turnpike Glen" as probably being more appropriate. I found the number online and called. The phone rang and rang. I was surprised that no answering machine picked up, especially if the office staff was at lunch. After what must have been twenty rings, I lowered the receiver toward the cradle. A voice sounded just in time for me to snatch the phone to my ear.

"Hello? Hello?" a woman repeated.

"Yes. This is Barry Clayton with Clayton and Clayton Funeral Directors in Gainesboro, North Carolina."

"Give me your number. I'll call you back this afternoon. Things are crazy at the moment."

Having no other choice, I did as she asked. Business in New Jersey must be good. Cemeteries weren't known for crazy times.

I drew up an estimate of our charges including transportation, an overnight in the city, and embalming. Cremation would have eliminated all these costs but Mrs. Sinclair had said neither she nor her husband wanted that option. I would have expected that response to come from our local mountain people who weren't big on turning their loved ones into ashes, but, as Northerners, the Sinclairs could have preferred the growing trend for cremation.

When I'd estimated a cost for every item except for Forest

Glen's charges, I closed the computer file and turned my attention to my first problem of the morning—Archie.

Although his plan for raising funds for the Boys and Girls Clubs was admirable, Archie had a talent for snatching defeat from the jaws of victory. His exploits were well known to Tommy Lee, and I felt confident the sheriff would nip this jail-bail escapade in the bud. I dialed his direct line.

"Sheriff Wadkins' office."

I recognized the voice of Marge Colbert, Tommy Lee's administrative assistant.

"It's Barry. Is the High Sheriff of Laurel County in?"

"Early lunch. I expect him back in about twenty minutes. Can I give him a message?"

A message describing Archie's idea wasn't one I wanted floating around the department.

"Twenty minutes, you say? I'll come in if his calendar is clear."

"It's a slow day in paradise," Marge said. "But I thought you were off-duty this week?"

"It's a slow day here at the gateway to paradise. See you in a few. You know you can't get along without me."

Marge laughed and hung up.

I grabbed a quick lunch with Mom and Uncle Wayne at the kitchen table. My favorite. A peanut butter and jelly sandwich. I'd probably had ten thousand so far.

"So, did you get Mrs. Sinclair straightened out?" Uncle Wayne asked.

"More or less. They want to be buried back in New Jersey, but they want us to handle everything up to the cemetery there."

My uncle set down his glass of milk and cocked his head. "No local funeral home?"

"No. Maybe she thinks we'll be cheaper even with traveling to New Jersey."

"Could be. God only knows how much them big city funeral homes charge. A thousand dollars for saying, 'Sorry for your loss.'"

I laughed. "Maybe. I've got a call into the cemetery. So, if someone phones with a New Jersey accent, get the charge for opening and closing a grave."

"The husband must be sick," Uncle Wayne said. "The wife's too young to be finishing up naturally."

"They may just want to have their affairs in order," Mom said.

"Of course she could be one of them trophy wives," Uncle Wayne said. "And the old man's friends are dropping like flies. He probably doesn't even know she was here."

"Maybe he just doesn't want to talk about it," I countered.

Uncle Wayne took a deep drink of milk that left a white mustache. He licked it clean and then clicked his tongue. "Well, we all have to talk about it someday, don't we? Sooner or later, everybody in Gainesboro comes through our doors."

I swallowed the last of my sandwich, chasing away thoughts of the day I'd have to face the death of my uncle or mom.

The temperature for this second week in July threatened to top eighty-five with high humidity—a heat wave for our mountain town. I decided my earlier walk to meet Archie was enough outdoor exercise so I drove my jeep to the Sheriff's Department behind the Laurel County Courthouse.

When I entered the bullpen of cubicles, I heard the click of keyboards, but didn't bother to see which of my fellow deputies were in. I went straight to Tommy Lee's office and knocked on the jamb of his open door.

He wheeled around from his computer screen and gave me a wide grin, a grin that wasn't impaired by the scar running from underneath the black patch on his left eye and across his cheek to his jawline. The disfigurement was a permanent display of his courage in Vietnam when he'd led his platoon through a firefight despite a shrapnel wound that took the eye and part of his face.

"What the hell are you doing here?"

I slid into the chair opposite him. "Nice to see you too."

"So...what? Things too quiet at the funeral home?"

"With Uncle Wayne living there now?"

Tommy Lee laughed. "I get it. Feel free to hide here all you want, but I don't have the money to pay you for more than your part-time hours."

"I'm not here to go on-duty. I'm here to discuss a problem. Archie's got a proposal."

Tommy Lee let out a long groan and shook his head. "What is it this time?"

I told him Archie's idea, expecting the groans to continue. To my dismay, I could see Tommy Lee giving the fundraising gimmick serious consideration.

"I'm just telling you because I promised Archie I would," I said in desperation. "I didn't think you'd want to turn the jail into a circus."

"Both my kids grew up in the Boys and Girls Clubs. I coached the softball teams."

Tommy Lee's son and daughter were now grown, but the nostalgia in his voice was unmistakable.

The sheriff rubbed his chin. "And I've got some additional funding for our Junior Deputy program in the elementary schools this fall. The parade could be a good kickoff. Maybe we partner with the Jaycees on the float."

The annual Apple Festival Parade was held every Labor Day weekend, right when school was getting underway. Had I crossed into an alternate universe where Tommy Lee thought Archie had a good idea? The prospect was unnerving.

"What about me arresting him?"

Tommy Lee gave a hearty laugh. "Hasn't that always been your dream?" He leaned back in his chair. "There is one thing that bothers me."

"What's that?"

"That the department doesn't have representation on the float." His grin turned wicked. "You know, an officer."

"The sheriff would be good."

"Oh, I always drive my patrol car as the lead vehicle. It's tradition. But, you, as the arresting deputy. Well, it's perfect. Archie in the mock jail cell, you standing outside holding a big key. We'll be the most memorable float in the parade."

"What about Archie coming here while the money's being raised?"

Tommy Lee shrugged. "We usually have a vacant cell. You don't have to stay with him. And there's the ten thousand-dollar bail. Archie might be here a while."

"He might," I agreed, and told myself I'd be doing it for the kids.

"So, tell Archie I approve on the condition that the Jaycees also include the Sheriff's Department in the float's signage."

"I can't believe you're making me do this."

He threw up his hands. "Hey, I'm not making you do anything. I'll be happy to tell the Boys and Girls Clubs you refused to help."

I shook my head. "Then how would you like me to wave? Like the Queen or the Pope?"

"Your choice. Now, I'm not such a hard ass, am I?"

"No. Just an ass."

Tommy Lee laughed and shooed me out of his office.

When I returned to the funeral home, Uncle Wayne met me in the hall.

"That lady called from the New Jersey cemetery."

"Could you understand her?"

"She spoke pretty good for a Yankee, but I don't know if she understood me."

"What do you mean?"

"I said we were asking for the cost to open and close a grave for the Sinclairs."

I realized with concern I'd neglected to tell Uncle Wayne that Mrs. Sinclair had asked not to be identified. That we simply wanted a quote.

"What did she say?"

"That her computer files showed no Sinclair plots. I thought maybe the name was pronounced differently in New Jersey. So, I tried Signcloor, Sinclayire, and every other way I could say those letters."

"That's strange. Mrs. Sinclair was very specific that it was her husband's family plot. Must be some computer glitch. Did you get a general price?"

My uncle folded his arms and leaned against the wall, self-satisfaction visible on his face. "Yep. Put the figures in the estimate myself."

"Thank you. But that wasn't necessary."

Uncle Wayne smiled like he used the computer every day. I'd have to check the form to make sure he didn't blow out any other data.

"And the lady asked me to give you her apologies for being so short with you when you called. They had a big graveside service going on and somebody fell out of a tree."

"A tree?"

"That's what she said. Guess they do things different in New Jersey."

I thanked my uncle again for getting the information, reviewed the estimate pleased to see he hadn't sabotaged any of the calculation formulas, printed the itemized figures, and dropped them in the mail to Mrs. Sinclair. I debated whether to inform her of the cemetery's mix-up with her husband's family, but to do so would have revealed my uncle had specified the name. Since there was no immediate need for a grave opening, I let the matter go. We could deal with it if and when the time came.

That night my wife, Susan, and I sat on the back deck of our cabin, enjoying a bottle of Chablis and sharing the stories of our day. Susan, a general surgeon with the O'Malley Clinic, had kept her last name, Miller. She'd performed appendectomy and gall bladder operations that morning, strictly routine and, in my mind, not as deserving of sympathetic comment as my Archie predicament. She was on-call so I'd stepped up to drink most of the wine. I'd just finished telling her about Uncle Wayne and Mrs. Sinclair when her cell phone rang.

"Ten o'clock. This can't be good." She answered it as she stood and walked back inside.

Five minutes later, she emerged in a change of clothes and with her chestnut hair gathered in a bun ready for her scrubs.

"Patient in the ER with a broken leg. Save my wine. I hope to be back by midnight." She eyed the bottle that was two-thirds empty. "And save some for yourself if you want to join me in a nightcap." She bent over and kissed me.

"Good luck. I'd say 'break a leg' but that would be in bad taste."

She laughed. "Taste never stopped you before."

I nursed my wine and listened to the crickets.

I awoke to our yellow lab Democrat barking a greeting. Then I heard the refrigerator door open and shut. Susan stepped onto the deck, Democrat at her heels and her unfinished wine in her hand.

"That was interesting." She slid into the chair beside me.

"Interesting case?"

"The man fell off his stepladder painting his ceiling. A simple, not a compound, fracture. So I was overkill. But, from the swelling and discoloration, it was obvious he'd delayed coming to the hospital for several hours. One of those macho-types who probably thought a shot of bourbon and an hour's rest would do the trick."

"Sounds like me. A real man's man."

"A man's man is a valet, and you whine about a hangnail."

"Well, they are annoying. So, was his tough-guy attitude what made the case interesting?"

"No. His name. Robert Sinclair."

I sat up straighter. "Really? Small world."

"Small town," Susan said. "With small-town coincidences."

Tommy Lee's voice rang in my head. "Never trust a coincidence."

Chapter Three

The summer season proved to be a boon to the Gainesboro economy. Low gas prices and high temperatures sent tourists into the mountains by the thousands. Summer residents complained the influx meant heavier traffic and fewer parking places, an ironic lament because the permanent locals had been saying the same thing about those same summer residents for years.

I was busy on both fronts—the funeral home and my deputy duties. The return of the snowbirds from Florida shifted our senior demographics upward and spiked funerals to at least one a week. An increase in population also meant an increase in traffic accidents and petty crime that stretched Tommy Lee's department to where my hours bordered on full-time responsibilities. My partner, Fletcher Shaw, had indeed returned from the Bahamas with a fiancée and was caught up in wedding plans. Still, being busy made the weeks fly by for both of us, and soon we were facing the reality of the Labor Day Apple Festival.

During the week leading up to the parade, decorations were hung from streetlamps. At the north and south ends of town, banners proclaiming "The 75th Annual Apple Festival" were strung over Main Street. The shops offered festival specials, and every sort of apple product, from cider to pies to dried carvings of animals, were for sale.

With all the hubbub, Archie grew more fixated on his pending role. He called me at least once a day with concerns ranging from whether he needed a PA system on the float to whether the Sheriff's Department had any chains left from the chain gang days. I could hardly wait to lock him in a cell.

Parade day dawned clear and cool. The temperature was predicted to rise, but the low humidity promised a hint of the approaching autumn. The organizational site for gathering marching bands, convertibles bearing local dignitaries, and floats was the Gainesboro High School parking lot and athletic field at the north end of town. Each unit had been assigned a number, and volunteers guided bands and vehicles into their proper positions. I saw Mayor Sammy Whitlock arguing with a parade official that his Mustang convertible should be right behind Tommy Lee's patrol car. His Honor, looking like a bowling bowl wrapped in a seersucker suit, was hopping up and down proclaiming he was the leader of the town and should therefore be the leader of the parade. Mayor Whitlock would be the kind of leader to take the whole parade down a dead-end street. The poor official, seeing me in uniform, waved me to come over. I mouthed "off-duty" and for the first time felt glad to be on a float rather than in the thick of traffic and crowd control.

I saw Tommy Lee standing by his car, talking to our Grand Marshall, North Carolina Commissioner of Agriculture Graham James. Mayor Whitlock, as usual, had tried to get Angelina Jolie, but her manager had again sent her regrets. We all suspected Whitlock just liked getting letters that he thought had been personally dictated by Angelina.

The parade participants had been cordoned off into designated areas: floats in one section of the parking lot, cars in another, and the marching bands on the grassy edge of the football field. The air was filled with the sound of brass instruments tuning and snare drums rolling in short bursts. Schools from Laurel and surrounding counties eyed one another suspiciously because the judging stand would name one of them Best of Parade, or as we locals called it, "Pick of the Crop."

The parade would undergo final formation as it began its route. It would be like shuffling three decks of cards together, each merging into its proper slot. The float for the Jaycees and Sheriff's Department was last. Archie took that as a compliment, like Santa Claus coming at the end of the Christmas Parade. Anything that followed would be anticlimactic.

I found him already on the float. He wore a black-and-white-striped prison uniform he'd ordered from an online costume store and he had loosely wrapped an iron chain around his ankles. I was supposed to handcuff him when the parade got underway.

He sat on a stool inside a fake jail cell constructed of cardboard tubing spray-painted black.

Surrounding the float were kids ages eight to fourteen who had been selected to ride. Adults tried to herd them into organized groups according to whether they wore a Girls Club or Boys Club tee-shirt.

The sides of the float were decorated in red and white crepe paper with gold letters spelling Gainesboro Jaycees and Laurel County Sheriff's Department.

I had to admit the whole design was impressive and if Archie raised the ten thousand dollars, I'd do the unthinkable—congratulate him on a good idea.

A small stepladder had been set up at the rear and I climbed it to join Archie.

"Oh, good, you wore your gun." He stood and pumped my hand like I was a dry well.

"Always, when I'm arresting a dangerous criminal."

He laughed and spread his arms. "What do you think?"

"Looks good." I saw bowls of wrapped candy sitting on the cell's floor. "You throwing that to the crowd?"

"Yeah." He bent down and retrieved one of the small packets. "Apple-flavored taffy. Try one."

I took the candy and read Donovan Insurance and Investments: Don't delay—Call today! "You couldn't get these with your picture?"

His expression grew serious. "I wanted to, but Gloria said I'd wind up in trash cans up and down Main Street. Not a good advertising environment."

Gloria was Archie's wife and always exhibited good judgment. But she'd married Archie. Ah, there was no explanation for the affairs of the heart.

"And I've been working on a routine with the kids," he added.

"What's that?"

"You have to wait and see."

We heard clicks of a camera shutter and turned to see Melissa Bigham of the *Gainesboro Vista* firing off a series of shots.

"Wait, Melissa," Archie shouted. "Get one of Barry putting the cuffs on me."

Melissa was the star reporter and photographer for our local paper. Only a few years younger than me, she'd received offers from much larger markets, but her love of the mountains trumped big-city bylines and bigger salaries. Her short blond hair, small stature, and cute looks caused politicians and corporate executives to underestimate her. They did so at their own peril.

Melissa lowered her camera. "All right, but then I've got to split. Mayor Whitlock is going to blow a gasket if I don't take a picture of him with the Commissioner of Agriculture."

I snapped one of the metal cuffs on Archie's wrist and then held the other poised above his free hand. The camera whirred.

"Got it." Melissa turned to go and then stopped. "Archie, how much money have you raised in advance?"

"Five hundred dollars. Only nine thousand, five hundred more to go."

Melissa winked at me. "So, you're confident you'll be out by Christmas?"

"Oh, with the friends I've got in this town, I'll be out by this time tomorrow."

I wondered if Tommy Lee would allow a Christmas tree in a jail cell.

Thirty minutes later, the parade got underway. As the last float, we were thirty minutes after that. The day had warmed, the children grew cranky and Archie and I were sweating through our clothes. But, a rousing cheer erupted when the tractor pulled us forward, and as we turned onto Main Street, Archie yelled, "Okay, kids, just like we practiced."

The left side of the float shouted, "Free!" The right side followed with "Archie!" The chant continued unabated. It was going to be a long parade route.

Archie turned to me and grinned. "Great, huh?"

"Yeah. Just great."

My prisoner bent to one of the candy bowls. "Barry, I can't throw the taffy in these handcuffs."

"You should have thought of that."

He lifted the bowl with his bound hands. "I'll hold and you toss. We can't disappoint the spectators."

So, I lobbed candy while "Free Archie" rang around me. We had traveled only three or four blocks when the float halted.

"What's the problem?" Archie asked.

"Maybe a band is performing at the judges' viewing stand."

"You think every band will do that?"

I shrugged. "They're not supposed to stop for more than a minute or two, but some of these band directors love to showcase their performance."

If a band was showing off, it was certainly taking its time. Ten minutes passed. The kids stopped chanting; I stopped throwing candy. Then I heard the wail of several sirens coming down Church Street, the road parallel to Main. I looked beyond the float in front of us and saw Deputy Reece Hutchins running between the parade and the spectators. Reece wasn't in the best of shape, and his red face told me he was winded.

"Something's wrong," I told Archie. I hurried to the front of the float and jumped to the tongue connecting it to the tractor. A second jump landed me on the pavement as Reece arrived.

"Barry," he gasped, "someone attacked the Commissioner of Agriculture." He gulped for air. "At Fourth and Main. Tommy Lee sent me—"

I bolted before Reece finished the sentence. As I ran down the street, I heard people call my name and ask what was happening. I ignored them because I had no idea. Who would want to attack the Commissioner of Agriculture? Why?

I neared the intersection and saw where police cars and an ambulance had arrived by the cross street. An EMT tended to Commissioner James, who had slipped off the back of the convertible and sat half in and half out of the rear seat. Tommy Lee stood with another EMT by the curb. The crowd had been pushed back. Two men lay on the pavement, one facedown and the other face-up. The man face-up was covered in blood. The man face-up was Uncle Wayne.

Chapter Four

Tommy Lee intercepted me as I ran toward my uncle. "He's alive, Barry." He glanced at the commissioner being treated in the convertible. "Wayne's the medics' priority. He's going to the hospital first and a second ambulance is en route for Commissioner James. He has a minor shoulder wound."

I pushed by the sheriff. "I need to see him."

My uncle's eyes were closed, but I saw his chest rise and fall with ragged breaths. His white shirt was soaked with blood, but I didn't see the source of the bleeding. I recognized the EMT. He was adjusting an inflatable neck brace. He must have determined there was some potential head or neck injury that required stabilization before Uncle Wayne could be moved.

"Is he conscious, Jake?" I asked.

The man looked up and shook his head. "But his pulse is strong. That's a good sign, Barry."

The rattle of a wheeled gurney signaled a third medic had arrived. I turned to see Lila Black, another EMT I knew, lowering the transport device till it was only six inches above the pavement.

"All right," Jake said. "Barry, if you and the sheriff want to help, let's keep him as level as possible. We'll lift on the count of three."

Jake took position at my uncle's head, Lila at his feet, and Tommy Lee and I on either side. Wayne groaned as we slid him onto the gurney.

"You want to ride?" Jake asked me.

"If there's room. I don't want to hamper whatever you need to do."

"Fortunately, we're only going a few blocks."

"Okay, then."

They ratcheted the gurney up to waist-height and I followed as they rolled Uncle Wayne to the rear of the ambulance.

"Barry! Barry!" Archie came running up, his hands still cuffed in front of him. His face drained of color when he saw Wayne. "Is he—?"

"He's unconscious. I'm going with him."

"Do you want me to get your mom?"

Archie's clear thinking surprised me.

"Yes. Try not to alarm her." I unlocked the handcuffs. "Just tell her Wayne's been hurt and that I asked you to bring her to the hospital. Tell her we don't know any more than that, because we don't." I climbed into the ambulance and Jake joined me. The doors shut and the siren wailed as the vehicle shot forward, a parade of one.

Jake and I sat on jump seats on either side of the gurney. I studied Uncle Wayne but saw no signs of additional bleeding. The medics must have staunched the flow. I remembered the third person, lying facedown near my uncle. No EMT tended to him. The deputy part of my brain told me he was dead. I wondered who he was and what had happened.

"Sounds like your uncle's a hero," Jake said.

"What?"

"I heard some of the people in the crowd talking to the sheriff. Toby McKay evidently charged the front of Commissioner James' car, firing a pistol. One bullet struck James' shoulder. Your uncle jumped from the curb and grabbed the gun. He and McKay struggled for it. It went off."

"Where was my uncle hit?"

"He wasn't." Jake waved his hand over Uncle Wayne's blood-soaked shirt. "The bullet must have hit McKay's aorta. This is his blood. Witnesses said they both fell and your uncle's head hit the pavement. I don't know if he has a fractured skull, a concussion, or both. That's why he's our priority."

Less than five minutes later, we pulled up to the door of the Emergency Room. A trauma team was there to meet us. The gurney was unloaded and whisked away. I suddenly stood alone on the sidewalk. My phone vibrated and I saw a text message from my wife:

Got the call. On my way to the hospital.

At first I wasn't sure who had called her. Then I remembered she was on-call for the clinic. She was coming to operate on either the commissioner or my uncle.

Now there was nothing for me to do but settle into the waiting room and trust the medical team to do their best. And hope God wasn't ready to face Uncle Wayne.

Ten minutes later, Commissioner Graham James was brought by a second ambulance. Mayor Whitlock waddled alongside the gurney, moaning like he was the one who had been shot. A security guard stopped him as James continued down a corridor. Whitlock looked bewildered, uncertain what to do next. He didn't see me, but looked back through the sliding glass doors of the Emergency Room entrance. He grabbed the lapels of his seersucker suit and tried to pull the coat flat across the curve of his torso. He stepped forward, wringing his hands in a great show of consternation.

Melissa Bigham hurried up to him. I watched their animated conversation and was tempted to join them, but I couldn't endure the mayor's histrionics. After a few minutes, Melissa turned away and went to the admissions desk. The mayor took a deep breath and left.

Melissa asked the woman at the desk a few questions. The woman pointed at me, evidently telling her I'd arrived with the EMTs. Melissa spun around, gave a slow shake of her head, and walked over to me. I stood. She kept walking, opening her arms to give me a comforting hug.

"I'm so sorry, Barry. Any update?"

"Not so far. He wasn't shot. It's a head injury from falling." I gestured for her to sit and then took the chair beside her. "But I don't know what happened, other than somebody named Toby McKay attacked the commissioner."

Melissa eyed the waiting room. The only other occupants were a Hispanic family consisting of a young mother, an older woman I assumed was the grandmother, and a toddler cradled in the mother's lap. The child looked like he was running a fever.

Melissa leaned closer and spoke in a whisper. "I interviewed several people who were right there when it happened. McKay jumped from the curb about twenty yards in front of the commissioner's convertible. He shouted as he ran. Most people heard, 'You ruint me, you son of a bitch. You ruint me.' Then he fired a shot. While everyone else stood paralyzed with fear, your uncle ran out and intercepted him. During the struggle, the gun went off and your uncle fell backwards. Both men lay in the street and neither moved. Tommy Lee was only one car ahead and was the first authority on the scene. He called it in immediately."

"What do you know about Toby McKay?"

"Not much," she said. "He has a small apple orchard east of town. He lost most of his crop last year from the codling moth outbreak. He'd tried to save money by cutting back on pesticides and it backfired."

"Why would he blame Commissioner James for that?"

Melissa shrugged. "I don't know. Yet." She stood. "As soon as I write what happened, I'll focus on why. I hope you hear good news on your uncle. It sounds like he was a real hero." She paused and her eyes moistened. "And that's the way I'll tell it."

She'd been gone only a few minutes when Archie and Mom arrived. Mom started crying when she saw me. Archie looked scared, all of his usual confidence and cockiness submerged by genuine concern.

Mom and I hugged and I tucked her cheek against my shoulder. "He wasn't shot. He fell and hit his head. The medic said his pulse was strong." In three sentences, I'd shared all that I knew.

"Can we see him?"

"Not yet. They don't know the extent of his injuries. Susan's on her way."

I felt Mom relax at the assurance that her daughter-in-law would be here.

"What can I do?" Archie asked.

Mom broke away. "Thank you, Archie. I appreciate your bringing me. I'll be fine now."

Archie looked at me. "Barry. Anything? Should I stand guard at the funeral home?"

I had to smile at the offer, as if our business was vulnerable like an unlocked bank vault. Then I thought again. There had been instances of funeral home thefts of embalming fluid that kids used to soak cigarettes or marijuana and create a cheap drug with a high like PCP. And then there was the matter of Toby McKay's body. Most likely it would go to the hospital for autopsy, but at some point we might become involved. How awkward was that? Taking care of the funeral for the man my uncle killed. Somehow, I didn't think that would fly for either party.

"Mom, did you lock up?"

"Yes. And turned on the answering service."

The service would forward calls to my cell phone.

"Then, we should be covered, Archie."

He spread his hands. "So, I should just turn myself in at the jail?"

For a second, I didn't understand his question. Then I remembered the float, the Boys and Girls Clubs, and the fundraiser Archie had worked so hard to put together.

"If you want, but I'm sure there will be no problem if you want to wait a day or two before being locked up."

"No. I said I'd go to jail after the parade. I'm going to keep my word. I don't want to disappoint the kids on the float. They've already had one disappointment today."

Archie took my mother's hand. "And your brother's going to be all right, Mrs. Clayton. I just know it."

As he disappeared through the sliding doors, Mom whispered, "He's always been an odd one, hasn't he?"

"He's always been Archie."

We had just sat down when Susan came from the inner corridor, wearing scrubs with the surgical mask dangling from her neck. Her face was grave. So grave that a chill ran through me. I didn't want to hear what she was about to say.

"We're moving him to Mission," she said.

Mission was the hospital in Asheville, a much larger facility with many more resources.

"You're not going to operate on him?" Mom asked.

"Connie, we need to keep him in an induced coma. He has a severe concussion and the most imminent danger is swelling of the brain. Mission has the latest equipment and a medical team that handles this kind of situation more frequently. Fortunately, skull damage is minor, but we've got to get through the next twenty-four hours."

"Will you go with him?" Mom asked.

"No. I'm about to go into the O.R. with the commissioner. But Wayne will be in good hands. You and Barry should go on to Asheville."

Mom nodded. I realized we had a problem.

"My car's at the high school and Archie brought Mom."

"You've got the key to mine on your ring. Take it. I'll get a lift to yours and then come to Mission. Keep me posted. I'll check my phone when I can." She gave Mom a hug, held it, and then broke away to hurry to her patient.

Mom sniffled and blinked back tears. She managed a wan smile. "Barry, you married over your head."

When we arrived at Mission, Uncle Wayne had already been admitted into the Intensive Care Unit. Since the procedure involved keeping him in an induced coma, visiting was discouraged. A nurse suggested I leave a contact number so we could be reached in case there was any change. She said they were monitoring cranial pressure, and although the readings were high, the measurements didn't seem to be increasing. She expected the doctor would keep him in that state till at least early evening. We would have plenty of time to return before he regained consciousness.

Mom thanked the nurse and turned to me. "Since we're here, why don't we sit a few minutes? I feel better knowing he's just down the hall."

The special family area for the ICU wasn't crowded. On the Saturday of Labor Day weekend, most activity occurred at the regular ER. That parade of admittees represented barbecues gone awry, hotdogs lodged in throats, and broken arms and ankles resulting from roughhousing in the backyard or climbing a treacherous mountain rockface. The holiday fracas, as Susan called it, was the reason both she and her colleague, Dr. O'Malley, had been on-call at our local hospital. But most of these injuries didn't rise to the level of intensive care, and so Mom and I sat in a corner of an empty room where we could talk undisturbed.

"I don't like him being in a coma." Mom wrung her hands in her lap.

"It's the best approach if there's brain swelling. Susan wouldn't have said otherwise."

"But your uncle's old. What if the coma does something to his cognitive abilities? I've heard general anesthesia is to be avoided for that reason. It can trigger dementia."

I didn't know to what extent such a cause and effect had been proven, but I knew perfectly well what drove her fear. My father had developed early-onset Alzheimer's, and Mom, Uncle Wayne, and I had watched a vibrant, intelligent, and young man lose his personality right before our eyes and finally die unable to recognize any of us. His illness had brought me home from a career in law enforcement and tied me to the town I'd been determined to leave.

But that tragedy had created relationships that I now cherished. My marriage, my partnership in the funeral home with Fletcher Shaw, and the opportunity to fulfill part of my dream by being Tommy Lee's part-time deputy and frequent lead investigator. Good things could grow from tragedy. But at that moment, my uncle's recovery was all that mattered.

My cell rang. I recognized the number of Tommy Lee's mobile.

"Mom, I'm going to step out in the hall and take this."

I walked toward an exit sign for a stairwell. "This is Barry."

"How's your uncle?" Tommy Lee asked.

"Mom and I are with him at Mission. They're keeping him in a coma and monitoring his cranial pressure. The doctors are cautiously optimistic. Thanks for checking."

"Call me if there's any news. Wayne's one of a kind. We need to hold onto him as long as we can."

"I will. Anything more about why Toby McKay did what he did? Melissa Bigham said it might relate to last year's crop failure."

"That's tied in but we believe what drove him over the edge was this year's."

"His crop failed again?"

"It grew too well. Toby used old batches of lead arsenate, a pesticide that's been banned for years. He sprayed so frequently the chemicals infused through the skin and into the apple itself. The USDA and NC Department of Agriculture ordered the entire crop destroyed."

"What about crop insurance?"

"I doubt if he had any. Probably couldn't afford it. He and his family were on food stamps. And no insurance is going to pay a claim that was caused by illegal activity."

The words Melissa said that Toby shouted, "You ruint me," became clear in their context. "So, Commissioner James symbolized the forces against him."

"Yep. That's probably part of it."

He let the sentence hang out there.

"Part of what?" I asked.

"You didn't ask me how I knew he was on food stamps."

"I assumed someone saw him using them."

"Actually, they don't use stamps any more. I found his EBT card."

"What's that?"

"Electronic Benefit Transfer. The state government issues it and money is deposited each month for approved food items. The merchant is paid by swiping the card. At least that's the way it's supposed to work."

I could tell by the tone in Tommy Lee's voice that the card was more than an indication of Toby McKay's poverty.

"Where'd you find it?"

"In Rufus Taylor's wallet."

"Rufus who owns the convenience store out on 64?"

"Yep. Taylor's Short Stop. Some kids found his body behind the counter about forty-five minutes after your uncle saved Commissioner James."

"You out there now?"

"Yep. When your uncle's out of danger, I could use your help, Barry. The SBI will be all over the commissioner's shooting, but Rufus was one of our own and I'm not going to let the state boys run over us. It's our case and I want you on it."

Chapter Five

I tried to get Mom to go home or at least spend the night with Susan and me. She was adamant about remaining.

"What if he wakes up and we aren't here?" That question met every proposal I suggested and it was all I could do to get her to the restroom by agreeing to enter if something happened.

Fortunately, I was discharged from that responsibility when Susan arrived around six that evening.

She reported Commissioner James had sailed through his shoulder surgery and would be released in a few days. He'd asked about the man who had stopped his assailant, and when a recovery room nurse informed him that his surgeon was the man's niece-in-law, James had insisted upon speaking to Susan.

She delivered his gratitude to Mom with the promise that the commissioner would come to see Wayne before returning to Raleigh.

The three of us spent a restless night in uncomfortable chairs only to greet the dawn with no change in my uncle's condition.

Mom awoke with a start when a ray of sunshine pierced through the blinds and struck her eyes. She blinked and looked around the room. "What about Democrat?" In all the craziness of the day before, she'd forgotten about our dog.

"Fletcher heard what happened," I said. "He went up to the house and gave him food and water. Freddy's on alert if we need him."

Freddy Mott worked part-time when the workload grew too heavy.

Susan stretched in her chair. "Would anyone like coffee? I'll be happy to make a run to the cafeteria."

Mom shook her head, but I stood. "Yes, but I'll get it. I need to stretch my legs."

Before Susan could object, I ducked into the hall. I wondered if there had been any overnight developments in the Rufus Taylor murder, and I was anxious to talk to Tommy Lee. But, it was only six-thirty, and yesterday had to be as exhausting for him as it was for me. I decided I'd wait another hour before trying to reach him.

At six-thirty on Sunday morning, the hospital corridors were practically deserted. The only patrons in the cafeteria were staff who were coming on or off a shift change. I got two cups of black coffee and headed back to the intensive care floor. My phone vibrated on my belt, signaling a text message, but with each hand wrapped around a hot cup, I could only quicken my step. I assumed the message was from Susan and there had been a development.

When I entered the waiting room, I knew what the text had said. Tommy Lee sat on the other side of Mom with his broad, rough hand atop hers. He looked like he'd spent the night in the room with us. A dark crescent hung beneath his good eye and a matching portion appeared from underneath his patch. Gray stubble coated his unshaven cheeks. His wrinkled uniform spoke to hours on-duty and perhaps a few winks of sleep in his office.

"Good morning, Barry." His gravelly voice rumbled hoarser than usual.

"Thanks for coming." I nodded, handed Susan a coffee and offered the second one to him.

He waved it away. "No, I'm caffeined to the gills. Another cup and I'll be bouncing off the walls. I just came by to say Patsy and I are very upset about what happened and praying for your uncle's recovery. And to tell you the department has been flooded with calls of concern from hundreds of people. Wayne's action was so selfless and brave, and it was witnessed by so many that he's become a hometown hero." A smile crept through the serious cast of his lips. "P.J. said Wayne will never have to pay for another haircut."

Pete Peterson, Junior, aka P.J., owned Mr. P's barbershop, the business started by his father and, for over seventy-five years, the gathering place for men's gossip on Main Street. My uncle would treasure free haircuts more than a Congressional Medal of Honor.

"That's very sweet," my mother said. "And I know you must be exhausted. Why don't you go home, Tommy Lee? Barry will let you know if there's any change."

The sheriff took a deep breath and nodded slowly. "I think that's a good idea." He stood. "If there's anything you need, Connie, don't hesitate to ask."

"We won't. Give Patsy my love."

Tommy Lee looked at me. "Walk to the elevator?"

"Sure." I followed him into the hall.

Instead of heading for the elevators, the sheriff turned toward the stairwell where I had taken his call the day before. He moved through the door and onto the landing. Then he listened for footsteps.

His voice dropped to a whisper. "We arrested Sonny last night."

"Who?"

"Sonny McKay. Toby's twenty-five-year-old son."

"I never knew either one of them."

"Well, they kept to themselves out in the county."

"Did Sonny kill Rufus Taylor?"

"Maybe. But we arrested him at the hospital where he showed up drunk and belligerent. He demanded to see Commissioner James. He said he needed to tell him why his father did what he did."

"What was the reason?"

"He said he'd only talk to James. Wakefield and Hutchins brought him in and booked him on a drunk-and-disorderly charge. We're letting him sober up in a cell, and then maybe he'll be more cooperative."

"Any forensics on Rufus?"

A door squealed open on the landing above us. Tommy Lee held up a finger and said nothing. The footsteps went up.

"We're running prints and ballistics," Tommy Lee said. "We might find it's the same gun Toby used."

"Could Rufus have been undiscovered that long?"

"Depends on how busy the store was. The kids who found the body rode their bikes and saw only Rufus' pickup. They went straight to the candy section. It took them a while to decide what they wanted. Then they started searching for Rufus so they could pay. They thought he was in the bathroom. One of them peered behind the counter and had the presence of mind to use the store phone to dial 911. Given a slow day with most of Rufus' local customers in town for the parade, he might not have had any business for a while."

"Enough time for Toby McKay to shoot him and be in position on the curb of Main Street?"

"I'd say unlikely, except for that EBT card."

"Maybe Toby left it last time he was in. It was a coincidence." I quickly added, "But never trust a coincidence."

Tommy Lee chuckled. "Maybe you'll make a decent investigator yet." He clapped me on the shoulder. "I don't mean to burden you with a case. Not while we're all worried about your uncle. I just thought you'd be interested."

He left down the stairwell.

When I returned to the waiting room, I found Mom and Susan speaking with a man in a white coat whom I assumed to be a doctor. Susan introduced me to Charles DeMint, the physician in charge of Uncle Wayne's treatment.

"I was just telling your wife and mother that Wayne's cranial pressure is decreasing. We feel we can safely bring him out of the coma. Once he's out, we'll run a battery of tests, and we'll especially want to make sure there's no subdural hematoma."

The smile on Mom's face faded at the sound of the ominous words.

"Can you explain that?" I asked.

"It's not bleeding in the brain, but bleeding outside within the tissues protecting the brain's surface. The fall could have torn blood vessels there. At first, minor bleeding might not be noticeable or cause any symptoms, but as the blood collects it puts pressure on the brain. Was Wayne on blood thinners?"

"No," Mom said. "He prided himself on not being on any medication."

Dr. DeMint nodded. "When he regains consciousness, we'll run our tests, including another CT scan." He left us with the assurance that in a few minutes a nurse would allow us to visit.

And she did. We entered a glass-walled room and found my uncle lying on his back with so many tubes and wires attached that he looked like a collapsed marionette. His breathing was more regular than when he'd been sprawled on Main Street.

Mom hurried to the bedside and rested her hand on his shoulder. "Oh, Wayne," she whispered. "Don't you leave me."

We stood in silence for a few minutes, silence except for the staccato beeps of monitoring equipment.

Then Mom looked back at me. "I'll be fine, Barry. It's clear to me that Tommy Lee needs you."

Susan gave my hand a squeeze. "I'll stay with her. We'll keep you posted."

I was torn. At the moment, all we were doing was staring at an unconscious man in a hospital bed. But, we were doing it as a family.

"Your uncle acted to save a man's life," Mom said. "Don't you think he would want you to do the same?"

I wondered if Mom had somehow learned of Rufus Taylor's death, or was it simply her intuition, which never ceased to amaze me? She must have picked up some visual cue between Tommy Lee and me.

Whatever the impetus, her words rang true. Uncle Wayne wouldn't want me standing over him while a potential killer could still be at large. At this point, there was only circumstantial evidence linking Toby McKay to Rufus' death. And the timeline for driving from the small convenience store in the county to the parade on Main Street was very tight. How feasible was it that Toby could have made that trip in time? I was also curious about what Toby's son, Sonny, knew about his father's rampage. I wanted first crack at interrogating him once he sobered up.

Tommy Lee brought Sonny McKay into an interview room. A rank, sour odor preceded him. His head was down and the front of his tee-shirt was stained with vomit. He wore dirty cargo pants cuffed over heavy black work boots. His sandy hair lay askew and when he finally looked up, his dark eyes were bleary and bloodshot. His right cheek sported a blue bruise he must have suffered during his intoxicated melee.

Sonny was a good head taller than me, with a build the mountaineers would call high-pocket scrawny. I noticed Tommy Lee hadn't cuffed him, but I saw Deputy Reece Hutchins positioned just outside the interview room door. Tommy Lee pulled it closed behind him. Sonny and I didn't say hello or shake hands. It wasn't that kind of encounter.

Tommy Lee gestured for him to sit on the far side of the table and then he and I took chairs opposite. The sheriff set a Tascam digital audio recorder on the table, started it, and gave the date, time, and names of persons present.

"Sonny, do you know why you're here?" Tommy Lee asked.

The man nodded.

"You'll need to speak up," the sheriff instructed.

"Cause I got drunk and disorderly." He spoke the words like a penitent five-year-old.

"Yes. And you were trying to force your way in to see Commissioner James."

"I wanted to tell him my daddy didn't know what he was doing. That I was sorry."

"Why did your daddy try to shoot James?"

Sonny gnawed on his lower lip for a few seconds. "Because he said our apples weren't no good. We couldn't even sell them for juice."

"And you didn't feel that way about the commissioner?"

"I was upset, but I'd told daddy we shouldn't use them old chemicals. He should have used his money to buy the legal stuff."

"Why didn't he?"

Sonny shrugged. "He said he couldn't borrow any more money."

"He borrowed money? Where was he getting it?"

Sonny shifted uncomfortably in the metal chair.

"Where was he getting his money?" Tommy Lee persisted. "I know he was on food stamps and last year's crop failed as well."

Sonny dropped his gaze to the recorder. "I don't know. He wouldn't tell me."

"He was getting money from Rufus Taylor, wasn't he?"

The man's head snapped up and his eyes widened. "No. Not from Rufus." He emphasized the word *from*, which sounded odd to my ear.

"Who then?" Tommy Lee demanded.

"I tell you, I don't know."

"If it wasn't Rufus, then why did your daddy kill him? Why did Rufus have your daddy's food stamp card in his wallet?"

Sonny froze, and what had been exasperation transformed into fear.

"You found it in his wallet?" he whispered.

"Yes. Why was it there?"

The man squeezed his lips together like a vice.

"Why was it there, Sonny?"

He refused to say a word. Tommy Lee looked at me. My turn.

"Sonny, when did you last see your daddy yesterday?"

"About nine. Saturday mornings I always drop by and Momma fixes pancakes."

"So, you don't live with your parents?"

"No. I've got a trailer on the other side of the orchard."

"And is that your full-time job? Working in the orchard?"

"No. I work at Harold Carson's Auto Repair. I like fixing motorcycles the best."

"Did you have any idea your daddy was planning to attack Commissioner James?"

"No. First it came up was when Momma mentioned the parade and that James would be in it."

"And what did your daddy say?"

"Nothing. He just slammed down his fork and got up from the table. He left and we heard his truck start. He never said where he was going."

"Did you try to go after him?"

"After him where? Like I said, I didn't know where he was going."

"Did you have any reason to believe he might have gone to Rufus Taylor's store?"

"No."

I leaned forward across the table and gave him a hard stare. "Then how do you think your daddy's EBT card wound up in Rufus Taylor's wallet?"

Again, fear registered across Sonny's face. "I don't know. Rufus must have stoled it."

"When did you leave your momma?"

"About an hour later. I ate up the pancakes and then hung

around expecting Daddy to return. Momma said he was just upset about everything and was probably driving around to cool off."

"Where did you go after that?"

"I walked back to my place. I worked on my Triumph and then Momma came with the news."

"That's a motorcycle, not a car?" I asked.

"That's right. I had parts spread all over the driveway. We took off for the hospital in my truck." He faltered, his voice choking. "I had to identify Daddy's body. I didn't want Momma to have to do that."

"How did your mother learn what happened?"

"My Aunt Nelda called her. Nelda Overton. That's Momma's sister. She met us at the hospital."

"And then you left them," I stated.

He nodded. "I went to Shuman's Road House. Had a couple of beers and a few shots to calm my nerves."

"Then you came back for your mother?"

He nodded again.

"Speak up," Tommy Lee said.

"Yes. I reckon so. I don't remember too much."

"And you also tried to see Commissioner James," I said.

Sonny looked at the sheriff. "I wanted him to know it wasn't Daddy's fault."

"Whose fault was it?"

He said nothing.

"Was it Rufus Taylor's?" I pressed.

Sonny dropped his chin to his vomit-stained shirt and refused to look at us. A knock sounded on the door.

"Come in," Tommy Lee said gruffly.

Reece entered carrying a few sheets of paper. "Preliminary forensics on Rufus." He turned to me. "Archie's asking to see you."

Tommy Lee flipped quickly through the pages. "Reece, take Sonny back to his cell."

When Reece and his prisoner had left, Tommy Lee handed me one of the sheets. Rufus had been shot once in the chest and once in the head. The recovered slugs were twenty-two caliber.

"But Toby McKay used a thirty-eight," I said.

"That's right. Time for me to get a search warrant from Judge Wood. We'll need to go through the houses of both Toby and Sonny. Might have been a squirrel rifle, might have been a pistol. And I want you to visit the crime scene with me. Are you good with that?"

"Unless something changes with Uncle Wayne."

Tommy Lee nodded. "Of course. Now, while I ring the judge, you talk to Archie. Then we'll take separate cars in case you have to peel off."

Archie was sitting on the cot in his cell. His laptop was open beside him. On the floor was a takeout bag from the Cardinal Café. The door was unlocked. For a prisoner, he seemed to have plenty of comforts. From his worried look, I knew something was bothering him.

"How are the donations going?"

He closed the laptop and stood. "Not so good," he whispered. "I think the shooting yesterday overshadowed the publicity. So, I'm writing all my clients, reminding them where I am. Sort of a blog. I call it *Letters from a Gainesboro Jail.*"

I couldn't stifle a laugh. "Archie, you're not Martin Luther King, Junior."

He held a finger to his lips. "Not so loud. I know. But I'm imprisoned for my cause."

"Is that why you wanted to see me?"

He stepped closer and jerked his head toward the near wall. "No," he whispered. "It's the man in the next cell. The deputies call him Sonny."

"Yeah. What about him?"

"Well, he kept me up last night with his moaning. And then he got sick. I heard him puking so I asked if he was all right."

"What did he say?"

"That he was a dead man. They killed Rufus and he would be next."

I felt a tingle in my neck at the possibility that Archie could have learned something significant.

"Did he say who they were?"

"No. He said he didn't know. But Rufus had known. He was part of them. And now with what his daddy had done, they'd be coming after him. I figured the daddy had to be Toby McKay."

"What did you say?"

"I told him I could help him. That I knew people."

"What people?"

"Well, you. But I didn't use your name. I didn't even say they were police. Just that I had influence and could provide protection."

"Archie, you're an insurance salesman. You're not Eliot Ness."

Again, Archie's finger went to his lips. "He'll hear you. I didn't give him my real name."

"What name did you give him?"

Archie reddened. "The first one that popped into my mind. Brad Pitt."

"And he bought that?"

"I told him I wasn't the movie star."

"You actually think he needed clarification?"

"He didn't see me. At least not till Reece came and took him out a little while ago."

"He say anything?"

"No. He just smiled and mouthed, 'Hi, Brad.'"

"And you've never seen him before?"

"Nope. Not before last night. He wasn't exactly a prospect." Archie grinned. "Want me to pump him for information? I told him I was in for robbery. I think he was impressed."

I wanted to scream, "You're not Brad Pitt, you're Archie Donovan, Junior," loud enough for Sonny to hear and end this ridiculous charade. But, at least Sonny had talked to him, whereas Tommy Lee and I had gotten the silent treatment.

"Don't engage him anymore," I said. "At least until I talk to Tommy Lee. Sonny will probably be cut loose pretty soon anyway."

"Okay. One question."

"What?"

"Can I still be Brad Pitt?"

Chapter Six

"Brad Pitt? He told Sonny he was Brad Pitt?" Tommy Lee stared at me with incredulity.

We were waiting in his office for the search warrants to be delivered.

"Not *the* Brad Pitt. And Sonny told him more than he told us."

"Only because he was drunk." The sheriff got up from his desk and walked to his Mr. Coffee machine to refill yet another cup.

"Sonny said he was a marked man," I said. "That they would get him like they did Rufus. Archie offered him protection."

Tommy Lee choked in mid-swallow. "Jesus, have we ever seen any sign that Archie has a brain?"

"No. And yet his whole concocted story is so ludicrous it could pass for the truth. I mean what undercover agent would call himself Brad Pitt?"

"And Sonny bought it?"

"Archie says Sonny said, 'Hi, Brad' as Reece escorted him to our interview."

Tommy Lee paced behind his desk for a few seconds before collapsing into his chair. "This goes against my better judgment, but if Archie can find something out, then I guess we'd better back him up. How did you leave it?"

"I told him not to engage in any more conversations, but he could keep his Brad Pitt name."

Tommy Lee swiveled his chair and stared out the window behind his desk. "Just when I think this job can't get any weirder." He sighed and spun back around. He pressed the intercom button on his phone. "Marge, what deputies are here?"

"Just Reece and Steve."

"Tell them I need to see them in my office. You might as well join them."

In only a few minutes, Deputies Reece Hutchins and Steve Wakefield came in. Reece eyed me suspiciously, as if I were somehow aligning myself with the sheriff against him. Wakefield, the older of the two, seemed unperturbed by being called to the office. He'd been summoned thousands of times. Marge Colbert slid in between the two men, her expression one of curiosity. She'd picked up that something was astir by the tone of Tommy Lee's voice.

Tommy Lee and I stood.

"What I'm about to tell you is going to sound crazy," Tommy Lee began. "I'll get the craziest part out of the way first. As long as Sonny McKay is here, we're to call Archie Brad Pitt."

The three couldn't have looked more bewildered than if Tommy Lee had announced he was from Jupiter. Wakefield was the first to recover. "Is it a breach of procedure to ask for his autograph?"

"Yes. He's not that Brad Pitt." Tommy Lee filled them in on Archie's overnight conversation and the potential to gather more information.

Marge shifted uncomfortably. "How long are you planning to hold Sonny?" she asked. "He's an only son and his father just died. His mother must need emotional support."

Marge's concern squelched our brief levity. We had no evidence to hold Sonny on a murder charge, and now that he'd sobered up, he should be allowed bail. Archie, on the other hand, could be looking at a life sentence if he didn't start getting some donations.

"A fair point," Tommy Lee said. "Thank you, Marge. We'll keep him till mid-afternoon. We'll charge him with a misdemeanor and release him on his own recognizance. In the meantime, we'll stay clear of the cells other than normal rounds. Be sure and let dispatch know, as well as any other officers who might come in, that Archie is now Brad Pitt."

"Sonny doesn't know me," Wakefield said. "Can I be George Clooney?"

"No. And none of this is funny. Remember Barry's uncle is lying in a coma as a result of yesterday's confrontation and Rufus Taylor's dead."

"Sorry," Wakefield muttered.

"You can bring Archie to Interview Room 2. Call him Brad. Say the sheriff wants to question him. Marge, you and Reece should be ready to intercept anyone coming in and give a heads-up."

A few minutes later, Tommy Lee and I entered the interview room to find Archie grinning with a smile so broad that the Cheshire Cat would have been envious. The sheriff dismissed Deputy Wakefield and motioned for Archie to sit at the table. Tommy Lee and I took chairs opposite him.

"So, I understand you have an alias, Archie," Tommy Lee said.

"It was spur of the moment. To be honest, I didn't want a violent man knowing my name."

"But he did say Rufus was killed by some unnamed group."

"Yes, a group that he was part of."

"That Sonny was part of?"

Archie shook his head. "That Rufus was part of. Sonny didn't make any claim except that they would be after him next."

"Did you ask him who these people were?"

"Yes. He wouldn't say."

Tommy Lee turned to me. "What do you think?"

"I think Sonny's scared. He certainly came across that way when we interviewed him."

"You offered him protection?" Tommy Lee asked Archie.

The insurance-agent-turned-jailhouse-snitch squirmed. "I was just trying to calm him down. I was worried. I heard him throwing up. Anyway, he didn't take it."

"I want you to ask him again," Tommy Lee said.

"Why would he take it now?"

"He was drunk as a skunk when we brought him in. Was he still drunk when you talked to him in the middle of the night?"

"I couldn't see him, but he was slurring his words."

"Good. Then I want you to play it this way. Tell him I pressed you to give up anything he might have told you. That I offered to recommend leniency to the D.A. on your robbery charge. A murder conviction is a much bigger fish than a robbery."

"But he didn't tell me anything," Archie said.

The sheriff held up a finger. "Point one, he doesn't know that or can't be sure. His memory of last night is fuzzy at best." He raised a second finger. "Point two, you don't have to give him any information. Say you know he didn't kill Rufus but he told you about his father's involvement in the food stamp scam and the people running it. You're willing to give him an insurance policy."

Archie's mouth opened. "You want me to sell him an insurance policy?"

"In a manner of speaking. Say you can get the names to your lawyer who will keep the information confidential unless something happens to him or you. Then they'll be released to the police. Assure him these people wouldn't dare touch him then."

Archie looked at me and then back to Tommy Lee. "What food stamp scam?"

I didn't know what the sheriff was talking about either.

Tommy Lee's one eye narrowed as he studied Archie. "Can you keep a secret?"

Archie looked indignant. "Of course I can."

"No, don't give me such a flip answer. Can you keep a secret that could have deadly consequences?"

Archie paled. "What kind of consequences?"

"Well, for starters, Rufus is dead. It wasn't a hold-up and he was shot with a twenty-two. That smacks of a professional with a suppressed semi-automatic. Sonny could very well be in danger. He won't cooperate with me but he might latch onto you."

Archie licked his dry lips. "I can't protect him against an assassin."

"I'm not asking you to. We'll handle that. You just tell him that he talked about the food stamp fraud. Then you get the names and you're out of it. Your conversation with Sonny is not to be shared unless we're in court. The secret is we found Toby McKay's Electronic Benefit Transfer card in Rufus' wallet. It replaced physical food stamps and it's used like a credit card. My guess is Rufus had loaned Toby money and demanded the card as collateral. Each month when the account was replenished, he processed fake purchases through his store. And if he used Toby's card that way, he could have been running the fraud with others and splitting the cash."

"And Toby didn't kill him?"

Tommy Lee shrugged. "Maybe. Maybe Toby went for Commissioner James and Sonny went for Rufus. But unless we find that one of them owned a twenty-two with a ballistics match, then my money's on something wider and more sinister. So, we'll keep your identity a secret and you keep the secret that you ever spoke with Sonny."

Archie's hands started shaking. "Can I have protection too?"

Tommy Lee shot me a glance telling me he wasn't going to like where this conversation was going. "Why?" he asked.

"Because I kind of posted on Facebook that my cellmate was the son of the man who shot Commissioner James."

"And Brad Pitt?"

Archie shook his head emphatically. "No. I didn't say anything about that."

"Then when you get back to your cell, you post an admittance that Sonny wasn't actually your cellmate but rather was at the other end of the corridor. Can you do that?"

"Yes, sir."

"And then let Reece take the computer and mobile phone out of your cell. Sonny will probably be released before you and he'll pass your cell door. Did he see that stuff when he was out earlier?"

"No. Everything was under my cot."

"All right. Then you can leave them there." Tommy Lee stood. "Are we clear on what you're supposed to do?"

Archie and I both rose.

"Yes, sir," Archie said. "Tell him he talked last night and offer him protection."

"Good. We're going to cut him loose mid-afternoon. Then you go back to your Facebook posting like none of this happened. Do me and you both a favor. Raise the money and get the hell out of my jail."

Armed with our search warrants, Tommy Lee and I first caravanned to Toby McKay's house. Sonny had said his mother Pauline McKay had been with her sister Nelda Overton, but we didn't know whether Mrs. McKay had stayed at her sister's or returned to her own home.

The orchard bordered Highway 64 and the farmhouse was on the backside. A dirt road long in need of fresh gravel looped around the apple trees. I followed Tommy Lee in my jeep, staying back far enough to avoid the dust cloud stirred by his patrol car.

The road ended at a patch of sparse grass and weeds that passed for the front yard of a small farmhouse. The siding was clapboard with peeling, faded white paint. A wooden porch tilted toward concrete steps without a banister. But my attention focused on two dark blue sedans parked on either side of the steps. The whiff of government suddenly filled the air.

Tommy Lee pulled in back of the first and signaled for me to park behind the second. We effectively pinned both cars against the porch. I got out and waited as the sheriff came over to me.

"Well, we don't have to worry about getting in," he said.

"Who do you think is here?"

Tommy Lee walked between the two sedans. "State boys. Probably Sid Ferguson, the special agent in charge of this region. Since Graham James is an elected official, the SBI's got to pee its scent on the case. Ferguson's putting in his face time so he can issue a firsthand report."

"Do we have a jurisdictional problem?"

Tommy Lee grinned. "Let's see whether or not Ferguson greets us with open arms."

As we stepped up on the porch, a white man in a dark suit came out the front door. His gray hair and lined face pegged him somewhere north of fifty. He opened his arms wide, but raised them palm out as double stop signs.

"Whoa, Sheriff. Mrs. McKay isn't here. You'll have to wait outside while we execute our search warrant."

"Good to see you, too, Sid." Tommy Lee retrieved his folded warrants from his chest pocket and held the one for Toby McKay's home in front of the other man. "I'm not here to see Mrs. McKay. I'm here with my own warrant."

Ferguson shook his head. "We've got this one. You can go back to DUIs and escorting funerals."

Tommy Lee kept his cool and I could see the SBI agent had expected a different reaction to his barb.

"And what one would that be?" Tommy Lee asked.

Ferguson looked at me as if to say *Is this guy kidding?* "McKay's attack on the commissioner."

"Different case. But you can play nice and I won't go back to Judge Wood to report that you impeded a murder investigation. Last I heard Commissioner James was alive and recovering nicely while the perpetrator was dead in the morgue."

The SBI agent's eyes widened. "Murder? That convenience store shooting? It's tied to this?"

"Circumstantially. That's why my deputy and I are coming inside. Unless you'd prefer you and I arrest each other."

Ferguson scowled, but said nothing. He withdrew into the house and we followed.

The living room was sparsely furnished with an old floral sofa, two rockers, and a small flat-screen TV and over-the-air antenna sitting on what looked like a bedside nightstand. Two agents wearing latex gloves were pulling the cushions off the sofa and running their hands into the crevice between the base and back. They both looked up, clearly annoyed by our presence.

Ferguson cleared his throat. "Our esteemed colleagues from the Laurel County Sheriff's Department are working a potentially overlapping case. They have a proper search warrant." He turned to Tommy Lee. "But, Sheriff, I suggest instead of our stepping over each other, you and your deputy monitor our search and then you're free to conduct your own."

"All right," Tommy Lee said.

"What are you specifically looking for?" one of the agents asked.

"Evidence that Toby didn't operate alone."

"That's our task too," the agent replied. "Anything that might show a conspiracy."

"And firearms," Tommy Lee added. "A twenty-two would be nice, preferably semi-automatic."

"Really?" Ferguson asked. "That's an odd caliber for a mountaineer unless it's a rifle."

"Our victim took two shots, close range. One to the body, one to the head. Nothing was stolen."

The three agents looked at each other, all drawing the same conclusion.

"You think it's a hit?" Ferguson asked.

"The possibility's crossed my mind. But I don't think the trigger man was Toby."

"Then what ties Toby to the crime?"

"I'll have to get back to you on that. We're just starting and I'm trying to work the case in between the DUIs and funeral escorts."

Ferguson's jaw tightened. "If the convenience store was a hit and you can tie it to the man who tried to assassinate James, then I'm very interested."

"Well, then why don't we share some information and avoid a pissing contest? You first."

Ferguson took a deep breath. He didn't like being mocked in front of his agents. "All right. What do you want to know?"

"Have you run financials on Toby yet?"

"No. We will, but it's Sunday and because of Labor Day, we don't have access till Tuesday."

"Okay. Can I have your word I'll see them when you see them?"

"Yes. Now what's the link?"

"The victim, Rufus Taylor, had Toby McKay's EBT card in his wallet. I need to find out if there's an innocent explanation or if Rufus was cashing it out. The financials could help explain that."

"You talked to FNS?" Ferguson asked.

I knew FNS stood for the USDA's Food and Nutrition Services. They had their own set of investigators charged with rooting out fraud in the food stamp program, whose official name, SNAP, stood for Supplemental Nutrition Assistance Program.

"Like you said, it's Sunday," Tommy Lee answered. "And I'm not ready for another level of law enforcement to complicate life. Are you ready to have them in your lap as well?"

Ferguson shook his head. "I've got a full plate." He smiled with what appeared to be genuine amusement. "And I don't have to do funerals." He turned to his agents. "Back to it, gentlemen. Find the sheriff his weapon and we'll close two cases in one day."

My cell signaled an incoming text. I snatched the phone from my belt.

Uncle Wayne regained consciousness

wrote Susan.

Has no memory of the shooting.

I handed the cell to Tommy Lee.

He read the message. "Go," he said.

"What's up?" Ferguson asked me.

"My uncle was in a coma. He's come out."

"I'm happy for your family," he said, with all the enthusiasm of anticipating a trip to the dentist.

Tommy Lee put his hand on my shoulder. "His uncle is the man who stopped Toby McKay and the reason you're not dealing with a murder case."

Ferguson reddened. "Then I'm really happy. He was a brave man and the entire state owes him a debt of gratitude."

I smiled to show no hard feelings. "He's been promised free haircuts for life."

The agents laughed.

"I'd take a bullet for that," Ferguson said. "Tell him the SBI sends wishes for a speedy recovery." He shifted his gaze to Tommy Lee. "And we'll have total cooperation on the investigation from our end."

"Same here," Tommy Lee replied. "I need to cover a few things with Barry. I'll walk him to his car."

I stepped out on the porch with the sheriff behind me.

"Let's take a quick look around back," he said.

He took the lead. We passed a rusted oil tank that fueled the furnace and a water hose stretched from a faucet to a chicken coop.

"What are we looking for?"

"We're not looking, we're foraging. I want to assess the McKays' food supply."

An outbuilding sheltered an old tractor hooked to a trailer loaded with ladders. More than a hundred empty bushel baskets stood stacked against the back interior wall of the shed. Between that building and the orchard lay a vegetable garden that had yet to exhaust its produce for the season. Late corn, beans, and tomatoes were closest to us. The furrowed patch must have been at least half an acre.

Tommy Lee took makeshift concrete-block steps up to a back porch door. He found it unlocked and we entered. The porch was fitted with a large work sink, wooden counters, and pegboards holding large cooking instruments. The space stretched across the back of the house. Part of the wall was covered with shelves of empty mason jars and cardboard shoeboxes. The only interior door went directly to the kitchen.

Tommy Lee opened one of the boxes and found it filled with jar lids. "This is where Mrs. McKay does her canning. Let's check the other side."

We continued our loop around the house and saw double doors closed over a slanted concrete wall on the far side. Tommy Lee lifted one of the doors to reveal steps descending under the house to the cellar.

He raised the second door and let it drop on the dirt. "Let's check it out."

The air temperature dropped ten to fifteen degrees. The cellar floor was packed earth. The house floor above was no more than six feet over us, and Tommy Lee had to stoop. He found a bare light bulb hanging from a cord and pulled the chain switch. The first thing we noticed was an oil furnace tucked up against the wall closest to the outside tank. The other walls were actually shelves rising from the floor to overhead crossbeams. They, too, held mason jars but these were sealed and filled with vegetables. Other shelves held cans of store-bought items like Vienna sausages and Spam.

"Good little food stock," Tommy Lee said. "Productive garden, chickens for eggs and meat, venison in and probably out of season, and maybe mountain trout if he's got a stream on his acreage."

"What's he need with food stamps?"

"The one green he can't grow in his garden—cash. He's got the low income to qualify, especially with two crop failures, but food's not the problem. I believe he used the card fraudulently to get cash. Without cash, how's he pay his taxes, vehicle insurance, heating oil? All those things that even a rudimentary lifestyle requires in the modern world."

"And Rufus was his money supply?"

"What's the old phrase? Follow the money? Go check on your uncle, and then be ready to start down that trail."

Chapter Seven

I found Mom and Susan standing on either side of Uncle Wayne's bed. Mom held a cup and straw as my uncle took a few sips of water.

He motioned for Mom to move the drink away from his face and gave me a weak smile. "Throat's raw," he whispered.

Monitors and IVs were still hooked to him and a white bandage encircled his head like a fallen halo.

"Then don't talk," I replied.

"Need to. Alone." He looked first at Susan and then my mother.

"Connie, why don't we run down to the cafeteria?" Susan said. "We need to eat something."

Mom nodded at Susan's suggestion and handed me the water. "Don't let him talk too much."

When they'd left, I pulled a chair bedside. "Now, don't push yourself. Whatever you have to say can be said slowly. Okay?"

"Hmm," he grunted. "Two words. What happened?"

"Do you remember anything?"

"Just waiting at P.J.'s for the parade to start. I remember seeing the sheriff's car."

Uncle Wayne had probably been hanging out with some of his barbershop buddies.

"And Susan and Mom didn't tell you anything?"

"That I stopped some man trying to shoot the commissioner." He paused for a couple of breaths. "And he died. But they sugar-coated everything."

Mom wouldn't have wanted to go into details about Toby McKay, and Susan was probably reluctant to upset either of them.

"I want to know," Uncle Wayne insisted.

So, I gave a summary of what I saw and what I knew, including the murder of Rufus Taylor, but omitting the discovery of Toby McKay's EBT card.

A few tears trickled from the corners of my uncle's eyes. "You're telling me I killed a man?"

"No. A gun went off. McKay's more likely to have pulled the trigger than you. He'd already wounded the commissioner and a second shot at closer range could have been fatal. Witnesses say you definitely saved a life. That's what you need to focus on."

"I can't remember any of it."

"That's normal. You've suffered a head trauma. You very well might not remember this conversation, and we might have to have it again. But, both the commissioner and the State Bureau of Investigation have expressed their gratitude. I'm proud of you."

He bit his lower lip and raised an arm to brush away more tears. Wires and IV tubes blocked his motion. I found a box of tissues and wiped his cheeks.

He took a deep breath and eyed the cup of water. I held the straw to his lips and he sipped a few swallows.

"What about McKay?"

"He died at the scene. There was nothing anybody could do."

"I mean about his body. Did we get the business?"

He asked the question without any trace of irony. Like we were serving any other client.

"I think the body's still in the morgue. And the family might want to go elsewhere, given the circumstances."

"But we're the best in western North Carolina. I won't be there. Fletcher and Freddy can handle it without you or me going near the family. I won't have the man I killed getting second-rate service somewhere else."

I smiled. His logic was vintage Uncle Wayne, and I felt a great relief that his unique brain seemed to be undamaged.

Shortly after Mom and Susan returned, Dr. DeMint entered. My uncle had fallen asleep and the doctor gave a brief report that they would keep him another night in ICU and if all went well, move him to a regular room tomorrow. But he cautioned us that Uncle Wayne's age might mean a slower recovery and he wanted to make sure his balance, walking, and other functions of normal daily living were thoroughly evaluated by physical therapists. In short, he recommended my uncle remain at Mission for at least four or five days to be on the safe side.

When DeMint left, Susan said, "Don't worry, Connie. Barry and I will work out how to get you here and back each day."

"No. You've got your patients and Barry needs to help Tommy Lee. I'm going to call Hilda Atwood. She's an old friend, a widow like me, and she's always asking me to stay with her. Her house is less than two miles away. I'm sure she'll be glad to help."

Susan and I agreed that Mom's plan made sense, and Susan volunteered to take her back to the funeral home to pack. I said I'd stay with Uncle Wayne, but Mom insisted that if there was anything I could be doing to help Tommy Lee, then I should make that my priority.

I phoned Tommy Lee as I drove away from the hospital. A little over two hours had elapsed since I'd left him with Sid Ferguson and his agents, and I wondered if I could catch up with him at Sonny's trailer.

"How's your uncle?" were his first words.

"The doctors are encouraged. My uncle's upset that McKay's dead and he's trying to come to grips with actions he can't remember. But, there's nothing more for me to do, so I'm headed back. Where are you?"

"Just leaving Sonny's."

"Any luck?"

"Toby had a twelve-gauge, an old thirty-aught-six, and a twenty-two bolt action—the standard mountaineer arsenal of a rabbit and bird gun, a deer rifle, and a squirrel and varmint rifle. Sonny had a sixteen-gauge shotgun and a pump twenty-two. Ferguson took both twenty-twos and I'm sending him the slugs from Rufus' body."

"He took them or you gave them to him?"

"I gave them. He can run the ballistics faster than I can. And we found motorcycle engine parts spread out where Sonny said he'd been working on a bike."

"What's your gut tell you?"

"That there'll be no match from ballistics. Rufus wasn't killed by the McKays, but he might have been killed because of them."

"Is Sonny still in jail?"

"Yes, but I'm going to release him."

"Would you hold off till I get there?"

There was a pause. "Why? You want to re-interview him?"

"Just have a little conversation."

"One on one?"

"If you're okay with it?"

"Knock yourself out. We'll be waiting."

This time I retrieved Sonny myself, being sure to pause at Archie's cell on the way.

"Pitt, I'll be back for you later. Think about what we told you."

Archie gave me the okay sign and slid his laptop under the bunk. "Go to hell," he said in the gruffest voice he could muster.

I moved on to Sonny. He sat on his bed, his head in his hands. "Come along, McKay. Just a few more questions."

He didn't bother to look up. "I ain't got nothin' to say."

"Then you can listen to me. Let's go. The sooner we start, the sooner we're done."

Sonny got to his feet. I unlocked the cell and escorted him to the same interview room. He took his seat at the table.

"Where's the sheriff?"

"He's deciding what to do with you." I slid into the chair opposite him. "We want to cut you a break."

"How's that?"

"Tell us what you know about your daddy's EBT card. Why did Rufus Taylor have it? Who's been using it for cash?"

Sonny pushed back his chair. "Look, I don't know nothin' about that. If I did, I'd tell you. My daddy must have left it on the counter or something."

"And that's the truth?"

"Yep. Maybe Rufus was stealing cards. Maybe that's why he got shot."

"Okay. We'll leave it there for now."

Sonny visibly relaxed. "So, when can I get out? I need to check on Momma. And we have a burial to tend to."

"What can you tell me about Pitt?"

"Who?"

"The movie star next to you. Brad Pitt."

"He ain't that Brad Pitt."

"So, you've been talking to him?"

Sonny shook his head. "Nothin', man. He was worried about me when I got sick last night. More concern than I got from anybody here."

"He talk about why he was in?"

Sonny looked wary. "Don't you know?"

"I want to know what he told you."

"Some kind of robbery. I didn't ask and he didn't say any more."

"Nothing about the others in his gang?"

"He has a gang?"

"Oh, yeah. Brad's quite the wheeler-dealer, and he's got a slick lawyer. He'll be out soon. My advice is stay clear of him."

Sonny spread his hands. "Hey, he asked if I was okay. That's it."

I stood. "All right. One last thing. Your father's body should be ready for release tomorrow. You and your mother need to notify the morgue who's taking receipt."

"You mean like a funeral home?"

"Yeah. Clayton and Clayton's the only one in this county, but there are others nearby."

He looked embarrassed. "They all cost about the same?"

"The local one will be least expensive."

"Your name's Clayton?"

I smiled. "That's right. But ask for Fletcher Shaw. He'll take good care of you."

I walked Sonny back to his cell and then found Tommy Lee in his office. He looked up from a series of color photographs on his desk. "How'd it go?"

I shrugged. "He's still denying any ties between his father and Rufus. So I tried to reinforce Archie's persona as a tough guy, but that's a hard sell."

Tommy Lee sighed. "Well, bring him back to Interview Two. I'll take one more crack and then cut him loose."

"Will you have someone on him? He seems genuinely scared."

"I don't have the manpower for 24/7. Not and devote attention to Rufus' murder." He lifted one of the photographs. "These are from the crime scene. Nothing to go on. Not even signs of a struggle."

"Maybe he knew his attacker."

"Can't rule it out. Too bad Rufus had no CCTV footage."

I thought about our one piece of connecting evidence. "Can we get a list of all the EBT cards Rufus ran in the last month? If it's a scam like you theorize, we ought to find a pattern."

"Already made the request through Ferguson. But don't expect any response till after Labor Day." He rose from his desk. "Pull Archie into Interview One before I get Sonny. Keep him in there till Sonny leaves."

I didn't move.

"What?" Tommy Lee snapped.

"I don't like Sonny going out uncovered."

"I didn't say he'd be uncovered. I just can't have surveillance around the clock. I've got a GPS tracker on his pickup and plan two-shift coverage. Once he beds down for the night, we'll pull back. That's the best I can do."

I found Archie so engrossed in his laptop screen that he didn't hear me approach his cell.

"Okay, Pitt. We're going to go through it all again and then again until you loosen those tight lips." I knew my dialogue sounded straight out of a Grade B movie, but Sonny wasn't exactly a sophisticated film critic.

Archie jumped and snapped the laptop shut. "You're wasting your breath. I've got nothing to say."

At least he didn't address me as "copper." I unlocked the door and he slid the computer under his bunk.

As soon as we were in the interview room. Archie clapped his hands and actually jumped in the air.

"I did it! I raised the bail." He sat on the edge of the table and dangled his feet in the air. "A certified check is coming Tuesday as soon as the banks open."

"A single check?"

"Yep. The whole ten thousand."

"That's great. Congratulations. So, how much is the total, counting the original five hundred and whatever else you raised?"

"Oh, that five hundred was seed money. I said that to get the ball rolling. Now I don't need to give it."

I started to argue that a pledge was a pledge, but realized it was Archie. As he'd said in the cell, I'd be wasting my breath.

"Who made the contribution?"

He gave me a sly wink. "One of my loyal clients who wishes to remain anonymous. The person said my *Letters from a Gainesboro Jail* were very moving. So, I'm free to go as soon as we wrap this business with Sonny."

"Did he tell you anything?"

"No, but he wants to."

I suspected Archie's fantasy of a secret undertaking with Sonny was leading him to an exaggerated assessment of their relationship. "How do you know that?"

Archie hopped off the table. "Because he asked me to come see him when I made bail. He gave me directions. A trailer on the north side of their orchard."

"Why wouldn't he talk now?"

"He said the walls have ears. He thinks our cells are bugged."

Archie's explanation sounded plausible, but the prospect of an outside meeting changed the whole dynamics of his ruse.

"I don't want you to take it any further."

"Ah, come on, Barry," he whined. "He's ready to talk. Isn't that what you wanted?"

"Yes, within the safety of our jail, not in a trailer on the side of a mountain where I can't give you protection."

Archie threw up his hands. "But aren't you giving him protection?"

"That's different. And it's not as complete as I'd like because we don't want him to know he's being monitored."

Archie stepped closer. "I can do this, Barry. You put a wire on me, I go in, I get the names, and I'm out. Why are you against that?"

"Because you're not law enforcement, you're a private citizen. You're not talking through a cell wall, you're face-to-face with someone who might think he's told you more than he did. I mean you pushed him into that belief. He might not see you as protection. He could see you as a loose end."

That possibility gave Archie pause, and I pushed on. "Remember, we haven't totally ruled him out as a suspect in Rufus Taylor's murder. He only has his mother for an alibi."

"Then why is he scared of these other people? He brought them up, I didn't. He was drunk and unlikely to be lying. He has names and I can get them for you. At least ask Tommy Lee."

I couldn't refuse that request, although I wasn't certain what the sheriff's answer would be.

"Why are you so hell-bent on doing this, Archie?"

"Because I like your uncle. And I think he's in the hospital because of something Sonny McKay knows. And I want someone to pay. Don't you?"

We met fifteen minutes later in Tommy Lee's office. Sonny had left for the hospital to get his pickup, the one Tommy Lee had gotten a court order to tag with a GPS tracker he'd borrowed from the SBI.

The sheriff listened stone-faced to Archie's pitch. I argued the points about Sonny still being a suspect and the lack of protection we could provide a private citizen who was basically acting as an extension of the Sheriff's Department.

When we'd both made our case, Tommy Lee leaned back in his desk chair accompanied by the squeal of its worn springs. "Archie, I share Barry's concerns for your safety, and for enlisting the aid of someone who is not a trained officer of the law. I would feel much better if we could completely rule out Sonny as Rufus Taylor's killer. But, we don't have to make a yes or no decision today."

"What do you mean?" I asked.

"Sonny is going to be tied up with his father's funeral arrangements. At least for the next day or two. He thinks his jail friend Brad Pitt has to make bail, so a delay in Pitt's visit to his trailer is perfectly logical. In the meantime, we need to determine with more certainty that Sonny isn't a killer. Then, I think we'll give Archie his shot."

"All right," I conceded.

Tommy Lee snapped his chair forward and gave Archie a hard stare. "But till then you stay out of sight and away from that section of the county. Sonny's going to be coming in and out of town and I don't want him running into you in the Cardinal Café."

Archie grinned. "Home and office, sir. Just my home and office."

Chapter Eight

I spent most of Labor Day Monday at the hospital where Uncle Wayne continued to improve. He mostly slept, but by evening his appetite returned and we spent dinner watching a rerun of the old *Andy Griffith Show*.

Fletcher called during *Wheel of Fortune* to say the Gainesboro hospital was releasing Toby McKay's body the next morning and that Sonny and his mother were coming to the funeral home at ten.

"Handle it however you want," I said. "I'll stay clear. Just be warned that we're probably going to be paid in vegetables."

"I'll see if I can negotiate for a pie."

"Make sure it isn't made with their apples."

"Oh, right," he said. "And if payment's a problem, I'll avoid as many hard costs as I can. I'll keep you posted." He paused, and I was ready to hang up. "Oh, one more thing. We're also getting Rufus Taylor's body. We'll have some logistical juggling to do."

"I can help with Rufus," I said. "Have you heard from his next of kin?"

"A son came in from Winston-Salem. I met him this afternoon. I understand Rufus was divorced and the ex is out west somewhere. The son wants a short service in our chapel on Wednesday morning. Burial's up at Twin Creeks Baptist Church. That's also where McKay will be buried."

"Okay. Try to push any service for McKay till Thursday. Do you know where the son's staying?"

"He said he's at his father's house. It's about a quarter mile from the store. His name's Roger Taylor. Nice guy. About thirty. He's pretty shaken by the murder."

After we hung up, I wondered if anyone had interviewed Roger Taylor about his father. That could be an important piece of our investigation. And I thought about another potential hole in our case. I'd neglected to ask Tommy Lee if he'd interviewed Sonny's mother. Between dealing with Uncle Wayne's injuries and Archie's self-initiated undercover work, I hadn't inquired about the status of Mrs. McKay. If the family had a need for food stamps, she should be as aware of the existence of the EBT card as anyone. I left Mom and my uncle to step into the hospital stairwell to phone Tommy Lee in relative privacy.

"Can you talk?" I asked.

"Yep. It's just Patsy and me grilling burgers and trying to cram the holiday weekend into two hours. Everything all right?"

"Yes. I'm with Mom and Uncle Wayne. He's making good progress."

"Give them both my best."

"Thanks. Listen, I spoke to Fletcher who said we're receiving Toby McKay's body tomorrow. Sonny and his mother are coming for a consultation at ten."

"Well, since you'll want to stay clear, you can work with me. I want to talk to Sonny's boss, Harold Carson, at the auto repair garage. And I'm pushing Agent Ferguson to get the ballistics on those twenty-two rifles our search turned up. The sooner we clear Sonny, the sooner Archie can make his play."

"Have you interviewed Mrs. McKay?"

"Not yet. Ferguson spoke with her this morning regarding the attack on Commissioner James. He sent me his notes. She claims to be completely unaware of any sign that Toby was about to go off the deep end. I was holding back talking to her until we learn more about how the EBT card was being used. I want a little more background, in case the tone of the interview shifts to an interrogation."

Tommy Lee believed in being prepared and it was always good to have the subject of an interview think you don't know as much as you do.

"Fletcher tells me Rufus Taylor's son is in town," I said. "They'll have a service on Wednesday."

"Yes. He's coming to the department tomorrow morning at nine."

"Then I'll be there. Enjoy your burgers."

He laughed. "I'll try. Although Patsy's limiting me to a single beer. One more thing. Have you talked to Archie?"

My stomach tightened at the thought that Archie could have already created some problem with our plan. "No. Is something wrong?"

"You could say that. As far as I know, he hasn't done anything stupid in the last twenty-four hours. Are you keeping close tabs on him?"

"No."

"Maybe you should check in with him. Let him know when Sonny and his mother are coming."

"All right. I'll be glad when he's out of the mix."

"Well, I'm counting on you to keep him corralled until then."

I knew he wasn't joking. "Thanks. You really know how to ruin a holiday."

I phoned Archie's cell. It rang about five times before he picked up.

"Hi, Barry," he whispered. "I'm with some clients. Can I call you back?"

"No need. Just wanted you to know Sonny will be coming to the funeral home in the morning."

"Okay. I'll keep to the office." His voice seemed strained.

"Everything okay?" I asked.

"Yes. We'll talk later." He hung up.

The night of Labor Day and Archie's with clients, not friends? I wondered what could be so urgent.

On Tuesday morning, Roger Taylor arrived at the Sheriff's Department twenty minutes early. Tommy Lee and I were meeting in his office and had the crime scene photos of Roger's murdered father spread across the desk.

Tommy Lee instructed his administrative assistant, Marge, to escort Mr. Taylor to one of the interview rooms, bring him a cup of coffee, and assure him that Tommy Lee and I would join him in a few minutes.

Tommy Lee gathered up the photos. "So, you can see there's nothing out of the ordinary in these pictures. No items knocked askew, no jimmying of the cash register. Rufus just seems to have fallen backwards behind the counter from the impact of the slugs, although a twenty-two wouldn't pack the wallop of a larger caliber."

"Do you know when the last purchase was rung up on the register?"

"Ten twenty-five. About twenty minutes before the boys found the body."

"And Toby McKay was shot around ten," I said. "So someone could have learned of Toby's shooting and had approximately forty-five minutes to get to the convenience store."

"That's assuming there's a connection between the two deaths."

"I thought the EBT card was that connection."

"As an item, it connects to Toby, but what's its relationship to Rufus? That's what I mean by connection. And how do the card and the murder connect? That's what I hope we can learn or at least uncover from Roger Taylor." He gestured toward the door. "Go ahead. Take the lead."

Roger Taylor was sipping coffee when we entered the room and introduced ourselves. As a break from procedure, Tommy Lee sat at the table beside him and I took the chair opposite.

Taylor had a long face with pocked acne scars, sallow skin, and thin, straw-colored hair. If he was thirty, it was a hard thirty.

"Thank you for coming in," I said.

Before I could utter another syllable, he said, "I was working Saturday morning. You can check with my boss man. Stokes Equipment Rental. I took a backhoe to a jobsite near the Virginia line." His voice carried a smoker's rasp.

"Okay. But you aren't a suspect, sir."

He laughed. "Like hell, I ain't. I know you boys always go for the family first. And my father and I weren't always on the best of terms. Not since my mama split from him."

"How long ago was that?"

"About fifteen years. When I was fifteen. That's how I wound up in Winston. Her people were from there."

"When was the last time you saw your father?" I asked.

"July Fourth. Brought my girlfriend up and we stayed at the Motel 6. She went shopping and I ran by the store to say hello. We'd gotten along a little better since I've been out on my own. He gave me a six-pack of Colt 45."

"Do you know why anyone would want to kill him?"

"Robbery, I guess. Ain't that what happened?"

"We don't believe so. Nothing was taken."

Roger Taylor looked stunned. "Somebody just shot him?"

"No," I said. "Somebody shot him for a reason. So, let me repeat the question. Who would want to kill your father?"

"I don't know. He kept to himself. The store was earning enough to live on. His partner was happy."

I looked at Tommy Lee. He arched an eyebrow.

"Partner?" I asked.

"Yes. He had a partner. He told me about a year ago someone was interested in buying in."

"Who was the partner?"

"He didn't say. Just that he'd now get his stock for a lower cost. Like the partner had better contacts or could buy in bigger volume."

"Did this partner work at the store?"

Roger Taylor shook his head. "Nah. He was behind the scenes."

"What's going to happen to the store now?" I asked.

"What do you mean?"

"Did your father have a will? Is his share of the store going to the partner for some agreed price?"

Taylor rubbed his palm across his thin lips. I could see the question threw him.

"I hadn't thought that far. Everything should come to me, shouldn't it? Then I'll work out some kind of deal because I ain't coming back here to spend my days sitting behind the counter of Taylor's Short Stop. And I sure as hell ain't gonna sit there and get shot."

I nodded to Tommy Lee to take the lead.

"No, we wouldn't want that to happen," Tommy Lee insisted. "Maybe you should figure out who's your father's lawyer. Did he have one for the divorce?"

Taylor shrugged. "I guess so. My mother would know. Would he be the one to help me?"

"I'd start there," Tommy Lee advised. "He might have drawn up a will for your father. Or the business arrangement for the business partnership. We'd like to know the name of the partner so we can talk to him. Maybe they had a common enemy."

"Okay. I'll try to find out today. I've got to get this wrapped up pretty quickly and get back to my job."

Tommy Lee patted Roger Taylor's shoulder. "We'll help any way we can. Maybe we can track down some of that information for you."

"Thanks."

Tommy Lee stood and asked another question before Taylor could rise.

"Did your father ever mention how much business he got through food stamps?"

"Food stamps?"

"Yeah, although he might have called them EBTs or Electronic Benefit Transfer cards."

"No. He just said more people were coming into the store. Do you think a poor person killed him? Took food rather than cash?"

"Not at all," Tommy Lee said. "It's just like with credit card receipts, we'd have an idea of who was shopping at the store. Somebody might have seen something. Poor people have eyes. There's no reason to think they'd have it in for your father."

Taylor nodded. "He'd let people run up a bill. That's why he and my mother often argued over money. That and he was bad to drink. You know what I mean?"

"We do," Tommy Lee said. "And he deserves justice. So, as you learn where things stand with his affairs, let us know. No piece of information is too trivial. Understand?"

Taylor stood and shook the sheriff's hand. "Yes, sir. Thank you." He turned to me. "You own the funeral home, right? Will you also be handling my father's burial?"

"Fletcher will. The man you spoke with. I'm spending as much time on this investigation as I can."

He started to say something, but his eyes teared. He nodded and left the room.

"What do you think?" I asked Tommy Lee.

"I think we need the name of Rufus' partner. That's our lead."

Harold Carson's Auto Repair was one-tenth garage and nine-tenths junkyard. Old cars and pieces of cars lay strewn on a hillside behind a three-bay metal building. An invasion of kudzu had launched an assault from the upper edge of the field, its vines and broad green leaves swallowing up everything in its path.

The current workload of pickups, SUVs, and sedans sat on an apron of scraggy lawn between the blue gravel lot and coarse pasture grass. Two men were bent over a fender and under the hood of a black El Camino pickup with flame decals burning down the side. All we could see of the mechanics were their rear ends.

"The big butt on the left is Harold," Tommy Lee said, as he swung his patrol car in a wide arc across the lot.

"Why have I been spending all my time on facial recognition techniques?"

He parked and opened his door. "Come on, smart ass. You can show off your interviewing skills."

The two men had turned from the engine at the sound of crunching gravel. Harold stood a roly-poly five-six and his colleague must have been a lean six-five.

Harold wiped his hands on a greasy rag as he walked toward us. The second man remained by the pickup as if we were there to repossess it.

"Howdy, Sheriff. What brings you boys out here?" He shook our hands. "Car trouble?"

"No. We're looking for Sonny. Just a few routine questions after what happened Saturday."

Harold shook his neckless head slowly and somberly. "Terrible thing. Don't know what got ahold of poor Toby's thinking. I heard he was distraught about his crop and the pesticide poisoning, but to do what he did. Guess you never know what will cause a man to break."

"Who told you he was distraught?" Tommy Lee asked.

"Sonny was worried. He asked me for some advance on his wages to help the family out. Said his dad had some unexpected bills."

"Did you give him the money?"

Harold snorted and his belly jiggled behind his bib overhauls. "Look at this place. I ain't exactly rolling in cash. To fix cars these days you need a damn computer. Don't know how much longer I can keep it together myself. It's just down to Charlie," he jerked his head toward the man by the truck, "Sonny, and me. But to answer your question, Sonny ain't here. I gave him a couple days off to take care of family business."

Harold didn't mention Sonny's stint over the weekend in our jail. It was a good bet the man hadn't been following Archie's Facebook page.

"You might check on him at home," Harold suggested.

"We were up there," I said, letting him think it was today. "We saw motorcycle parts out on the drive but not Sonny."

Harold's eyes went wide. "His Triumph Rocket?"

"Yes."

The mechanic turned to the other man. "Charlie, you ever known Sonny to leave parts to his bike outside?"

"Nah. Not Sonny. If he could marry that thing, he would."

The statement reinforced Sonny's claim that he'd left with his mother as soon as she brought him the news of his father's death.

I looked at one and then the other. "And neither of you know if Sonny was able to get money to help his father?"

"Nah. I would've helped him if I could," Harold said. "But times is tough all over."

I studied the renovated El Camino. "Looks like you got one good client, unless you've fixed that up on spec."

Again, Harold shook his head. "Would you believe that job's for Rufus Taylor? Fixing it up for his son as a surprise."

"Are you now stuck for a lot of money?"

"Nope. Rufus had been wanting to restore it for about five years, and finally saved up the cash money to do it. We were just doing some fine-tuning. All he owed was a few bucks for points and plugs. Hell, might just give the boy the damn thing. Kind of sad to have it on the lot now. If you see him, tell the boy to come pick it up as soon as he can. I ain't superstitious or nothing, but first Toby and then Rufus. They say troubles come in threes."

"When did Rufus give you the go ahead?" I asked.

"About three months ago. He said business was picking up at the store." Harold smiled. "Everybody knows there's no better place to put your money than a truck."

I doubted there were many financial advisors who adhered to that investment philosophy, but I wasn't about to argue with a man armed with wrenches. "I'll remember that. Thanks."

As we pulled out of the lot, Tommy Lee said, "That came with a bonus. The info on Rufus Taylor's prosperity."

"Yes. We got validation of Sonny's alibi and Roger Taylor's comments that his father's business was helped by a new partner. Where to now?"

"Let's go back to the office. I want to see if we've received a ballistics report and make sure the request for EBT card transactions is being expedited."

We'd driven about a mile when my cell phone buzzed. The call was from Fletcher.

"Barry. You haven't heard anything from Sonny McKay, have you?"

"No. I thought he had a meeting with you at ten."

"He did. Mrs. McKay is here with her sister and she was expecting to meet Sonny. He was going to take her home after our consultation. She's been calling his cell but he doesn't answer."

I felt my stomach knot and checked the phone for the time. Ten forty-five. "I'm with Tommy Lee. Maybe he knows something. I'll call you right back."

"What's up?" the sheriff asked.

"Sonny didn't show at the funeral home. He was supposed to meet his mother there."

Tommy Lee's face darkened. "Let's stay off the two-way. You got Reece's number on your phone? He's supposed to be watching Sonny's trailer."

"Yes." I scrolled to the number. Reece answered immediately. "Is this Barry?"

"Yes. Where are you?"

"On a side road where I can watch Sonny's driveway. He hasn't left yet."

I relayed the info to Tommy Lee and put the phone on speaker.

"Go to the trailer and check on him," Tommy Lee ordered. "Don't say you've been watching him, but that his mother had called us looking for him."

"Got it. Then what?"

"If he's okay, ask him to call his mom and then you return to your surveillance position. Give me a report back by Barry's phone as soon as you can."

The sheriff turned onto a secondary road that took us away from town and in the direction of Sonny's trailer. "I got a bad feeling," was all he said.

Less than ten minutes later, my cell rang. I connected to Reece, leaving the phone on speaker.

"Barry?" The tremor in his voice was audible.

"We're here."

"He's dead, Barry. Dead in his bed. Looks like someone shot him in the head while he slept. His head...his head's still on the pillow."

Chapter Nine

Sheriff Tommy Lee Wadkins' expression couldn't have been harder than if his face were chiseled in granite. His lone eye swept the sparse furnishings of Sonny McKay's bedroom in the rear of the single-wide trailer. The space contained a beat-up dresser, a TV tray converted to a nightstand, and a bed with Sonny's body lying prone atop wrinkled sheets.

His head rested on the pillow and faced the far wall. He wore a dingy white tee-shirt and light blue boxers. Aside from the entry wound in his temple, he could have been asleep. What little blood had flowed had been mostly absorbed by the pillow. I guessed he'd died instantly.

"Any sign of a gun?" the sheriff asked.

"No," Reece Hutchins said. "And I've never heard of anyone shooting themselves while lying belly-down."

"Then I'm going to request a mobile crime lab from Buncombe County. I want every bit of DNA, even if it's from a damn cockroach." Tommy Lee shook his head in disgust. "And I want a toxicology workup on his blood."

I understood he reacted to more than just the murder scene. His two-shift surveillance of Sonny had left the man exposed overnight, and he now second-guessed how seriously he should have taken Sonny's fears.

"Nothing more we can do here till the forensics team arrives." He signaled us to leave.

We passed a small eating area adjacent to the kitchen. An empty bottle of Rebel Yell whiskey sat on the table. A plastic drinking glass lay overturned beside it.

"Was the trailer door open?" I asked Reece.

"Well, the door was closed but it wasn't locked. Looks like someone popped it with a screwdriver."

The three of us stepped outside and examined the doorframe where something had been wedged to bend the metal enough to pry free the short bolt. Fresh scratches showed the damage was recent.

"What time did you get in position?" Tommy Lee asked Reece.

"Six o'clock. Wakefield left at midnight."

"So, a six-hour window. You didn't see any cars come out after you arrived?"

"No," Reece insisted. "And I stayed awake. There's an empty coffee thermos in the car to prove it."

"There's certainly no sign Sonny put up a fight," I said. "If the blood work confirms it, then Sonny must have been in a near stupor, flopped on his bed, and didn't hear his killer break in."

"How would they know Sonny wasn't standing guard?" Reece asked. "Sonny could have been ready to shoot them at first entry."

"Good question." I looked to Tommy Lee for his ideas.

"They could have known his habits," the sheriff said. "They were desperate enough to get to him that they took a chance. They might have been watching the house and saw Wakefield leave."

"It's possible," I said. "But easier to drop him with a rifle shot when he came out of the trailer this morning."

"What's your idea?" Tommy Lee asked. "Because my guess is the M.E. is going to put the murder shortly after midnight, based on body temp. Of course that's just my opinion, based on a skin touch."

"I'm not saying they didn't know his habits or that they weren't desperate to silence him. But, if Sonny knew them or they clearly appeared to pose no threat, then they could have approached the trailer with confidence. But Sonny was passed out and unable to open the door. When they got no response, they improvised."

"And just happened to bring a screwdriver," Reece said skeptically.

I shrugged. "I'm just floating ideas."

Tommy Lee looked at Sonny's pickup truck. Reece and I followed him over to the bed. A tool chest stood open against the back of the cab.

"Seem odd to you a mechanic would leave his tools exposed all night?" Tommy Lee asked.

"Want me to print them?" Reece asked.

"Yes. Though if whatever they used to force the door is in the tool kit, we'll know it because it'll be the only one wiped clean of fingerprints. Reece, I want you to take charge of the scene."

Reece's chest expanded, threatening to launch a few buttons into the air. "Yes, sir."

Tommy Lee looked back at the trailer. "So, I'll call in the mobile lab, M.E., and cover Ferguson and the SBI, although I guarantee they'll want to stay clear till we've got a parade lined up tying this murder to the commissioner's shooting. Then they'll jump in front to lead it. If they do come here, tell them everything has to run through me."

"You got it," Reece said.

When we were in the patrol car, Tommy Lee pulled out his cell. "I still want to keep this off the scanners." He called Carol, the dispatcher, and ran down the checklist of everything he wanted at Sonny's trailer. He also asked her to have his assistant Marge prepare a request for a search warrant for Rufus Taylor's house.

When he'd finished, I asked, "Where are we going?"

Instead of answering, he gave me an order. "Find out if Mrs. McKay is still with Fletcher. If so, tell him to keep her there till we arrive."

"Are you going to interview her?"

He gave me a sharp look. "I'm going to tell her that her son's been murdered. Then I'm going to do what I should have done right after Toby died—press her for answers, answers that might have saved her son's life if I hadn't been giving her grieving room. That mistake's on me, and I won't make it again."

"And Rufus Taylor's search warrant?"

"I want it in my hip pocket in case Rufus' son turns out not to be as cooperative as he appeared. We'll see him after Mrs. McKay."

I caught Fletcher just as he was preparing to walk Mrs. McKay and her sister to their car. Tommy Lee turned on the flashers and siren and we sped back to town.

Fletcher met us in the kitchen. "I've got Mrs. McKay and her sister in the parlor," he whispered. "They're confused as to why they have to see you, and I couldn't give them much of an explanation."

"Sonny McKay's been murdered," Tommy Lee said. "I have to break the news. Then Barry and I need to ask Mrs. McKay a few questions. I'd like to do that without involving her sister."

Fletcher's face paled. "Murdered? Where? When?"

I ignored his questions. "Is my mother here?"

"She's upstairs."

"Tell her what's happened and ask her to come down. She'll brew fresh coffee and can talk to the sister in the kitchen."

"What do you want me to do?"

"Whatever my mother asks you. Otherwise, hang close to the kitchen and be on standby."

"Let's do this," Tommy Lee said. "We'll give Mrs. McKay a few minutes with her sister before we split them up."

Fletcher went up the back stairs and I led Tommy Lee to the front parlor. Mrs. McKay sat on the sofa and her sister was on the edge of the wingback chair beside her. Mrs. McKay wore a shapeless black dress. Her sister's dress was rust brown and obviously more expensive.

Mrs. McKay rose, her face shifting to a scowl when she saw

Tommy Lee enter behind me. "What's so important? Don't you know we've got things to do?"

I stepped aside and let Tommy Lee take the lead.

"Mrs. McKay," he said softly, "please sit down. I'm afraid I've got bad news."

The woman's indignation evaporated and she looked at her sister. The other woman took her by the forearm and guided her to her seat.

Mrs. McKay started shaking her head back and forth. "I don't want to hear it. I don't want to hear it."

Tommy Lee let her continue this mantra until she stopped and looked up at us with frightened eyes.

Rather than tower over her, Tommy Lee crouched in front of her. "I'm very sorry to tell you that your son has been shot and killed. We found him in his bed and the door of his trailer had been forced open."

Her thin shoulders hunched, and then shook with silent sobs. Her sister moved from the chair and joined her on the sofa. Mrs. McKay turned her tear-streaked face away from all of us.

"I told him no good would come of it. I told him, but he wouldn't listen."

"You told who?" Tommy Lee gently prodded.

She turned back to the sheriff. "Did he suffer? Did they make him suffer?"

"No, ma'am. As best I can tell, he died in his sleep."

She leaned forward. "I've got to see him. I've got to see my boy."

She attempted to rise, but the sheriff was too close.

"You will," Tommy Lee said, "but right now we're trying to find his murderer. Sonny's trailer is a crime scene and we're required to perform an autopsy. Mrs. McKay, I'm being very honest with you. I know something is wrong in my county. Three men have died, two of them your loved ones. I also know Sonny was frightened of someone. He wouldn't talk to me, but he did share information with a fellow prisoner the night he was in our jail and he promised to provide more. And if they came after Sonny for what he knew, they may come after you."

"Sonny wasn't to blame," she whispered. "It was all Toby's idea."

Tommy Lee looked at Mrs. McKay's sister. "Mrs. Overton?"

"Yes?"

"I need you to wait in the kitchen with Barry's partner. It's important that I have a talk with your sister, and some of the information might need to remain confidential."

"Does she need a lawyer?"

"Not if she wants to move this whole process along so we can release Sonny to the funeral home as soon as possible."

"You go, Nelda," Mrs. McKay said. "I'll be all right."

I stepped over to help Nelda Overton from the sofa. The woman reached in her small clutch purse and handed her sister a lace handkerchief. "Take as long as you need, Pauline. Today, my time is your time."

I led the woman back to the kitchen where both Mom and Fletcher waited with a fresh pot of coffee. When I returned to the parlor, Tommy Lee sat on the sofa beside Pauline McKay. She dabbed at her eyes with the handkerchief, but seemed to be more composed.

Tommy Lee gave me a nod indicating I should take the rocking chair a little farther from the sofa than the nearer chairs. Evidently, he didn't want Mrs. McKay to feel hemmed in. She gave me a quick glance and then focused on the sheriff.

"I don't know who they are," she softly said. "I swear I'd tell you. I want them to pay."

Tommy Lee studied the woman for a few seconds. I didn't break the silence, knowing my role for the moment was to listen.

"I'm not saying you know who they are," Tommy Lee said. "However, I know you knew Rufus Taylor and I believe you know why he had your husband's EBT card."

Pauline McKay took a deep breath and her frail body trembled with an involuntary shiver. "Rufus demanded it. He didn't want us taking it to the other stores."

"Why would you do what he demands?"

"We've been hard up for cash money, Sheriff. That's no secret since we lost our crop last year. It hurt Toby's pride to have to borrow money, and he couldn't get none from any banks. My husband had been an apple grower all his life. I tended the vegetable garden and the preserving and canning. We bothered no one and no one bothered us. Then when the crop failed, we had bills to pay. Toby started buying stuff we needed through Rufus on credit."

"Credit's different than cash in hand," Tommy Lee said. "When did the arrangement change?"

Pauline McKay's eyes sharpened as she realized the sheriff was putting pieces together before she presented them. "When Rufus said he couldn't give any more credit without a plan to pay it back, Toby said he'd be good for every nickel when this year's crop came in. He already had the old pesticide and he'd only need some money to pay the migrants when picking season came. Then we had a surprise inspection by one of the wholesale buyers and they told the state Toby'd used the stuff with lead in it. We didn't think it would hurt nobody."

Tommy Lee nodded. "So, Rufus Taylor offered you a way out of your financial jam?"

The handkerchief went back to her eyes and she sniffled. "Rufus told Toby we could apply for food stamps. He had friends who would take care of the rest. Otherwise, his only choice was to put a lien on our land. Take us to court and force us to sell off property and equipment to pay our debts."

"Sounds like Toby's anger would have been toward Rufus and not Commissioner James."

Pauline tensed. She looked over at me. "Toby weren't scared of Commissioner James."

I didn't understand. "He was scared of Rufus Taylor?"

She shook her head. "Rufus weren't nothing but a yes man. He admitted as much to Toby. The EBT was a cash machine. There were convenience stores we were supposed to use. Like Rufus, they'd run up charges each month for food we didn't get and food they didn't sell. Couple a hundred dollars' worth. Rufus said it was reducing our debt, a debt that had been passed along to the people in cahoots with him."

Suddenly, Sonny's emphasis on the word "from" in his denial that his father was getting money from Rufus made sense. His father was getting money *through* Rufus.

Pauline McKay continued. "Rufus said someday, when we were paid up, they'd split the cash with us. Rufus told my husband he'd better go along because the people behind him wouldn't take no for an answer. Otherwise they'd come after him. Rufus said they'd hurt people. Even me. Even Sonny."

She stopped. The room fell silent, each of us thinking about how the warning had come to pass.

"That doesn't explain why Rufus had Toby's card," Tommy Lee said.

"Because a month ago Rufus decided he would be the one to control how and where the card was used. I guess he wanted more money running through his store. Maybe he was taking something off the top."

"All for a couple hundred dollars a month? That's seems like a small amount of money to be threatening people."

"We weren't the only ones falling on hard times. There's a lot of folks on food stamps who have money problems. You get ten families, and you might have two or three thousand dollars a month. You times that across other stores and other mountain counties, then what kind of money are you talking about, Sheriff?"

"Maybe enough to kill a man."

"Enough to kill my Sonny." She gave a humorless laugh.

"Rufus told Toby the debt would be paid off faster if Sonny got his own EBT card. But Sonny made too much money at the auto repair shop. Rufus said Sonny should ask to be paid for some of his hours in unreported cash so he could qualify. It would also save Harold Carson from paying as much for worker's comp and Social Security. When Rufus suggested it, Sonny said he weren't no welfare cheat. That really hurt Toby. Cut me, too, 'cause he was so much as calling us welfare cheats."

"When did you have this conversation?" Tommy Lee asked.

"Two, maybe three weeks ago. Then it come up again Saturday morning."

Tommy Lee looked at me. Sonny McKay had made no mention of it during any of our interviews.

"That's when he came over for pancakes?" Tommy Lee asked.

"Yes. I mentioned the parade and that the agriculture commissioner was in it. Sonny said the commissioner's the one who should be on food stamps and not us. Sonny said it was a disgrace. That's when Toby shoved the table against Sonny's chest, got up, and yelled, 'goddammit, I'm not taking any more shit off you. You'll see I ain't afraid for me. Not for me. You'll see.'"

"What did you think he meant at the time?" Tommy Lee asked.

Pauline McKay wiped the handkerchief across her wrinkled cheek. "That he was going to confront Rufus. But I was wrong. He went for the commissioner. I guess he wasn't afraid there'd be any danger to me or Sonny. But he was wrong."

Tommy Lee shifted on the sofa and for the first time flipped open his notepad. "Did Rufus ever tell Toby the names of the people he was working with?"

"If so, he didn't tell me."

"Could Toby have told Sonny?"

"I don't know. I think he tried to explain the bind we were in and that Rufus was only a small part of the problem."

"So, Sonny understood that there were people who posed a threat to you and your husband?"

"Probably. Toby wanted him to understand why we'd been forced into doing what we'd done."

Tommy Lee looked at me. Her statement fit with the fear Sonny had exhibited. And Sonny must have had additional information his mother didn't know, if he'd been willing to talk to Archie, aka Brad Pitt, about getting protection. The murder of Rufus Taylor would have confirmed for Sonny what his father had said about dangerous people. Maybe his drunken efforts to see Commissioner of Agriculture Graham James had been an attempt to tell James what Sonny later thought better of after he sobered up. Given the events, I understood how Archie's proposal for protection sounded enticing. Had Sonny's information died with him, or had he prepared some document for when Archie came to see him? Sonny's trailer deserved another search.

"Mrs. McKay," I said, "we appreciate your help at this most difficult time. Your husband and your son both deserve justice for what happened to them. We believe Sonny wanted to share information that he either got from his father or from Rufus. Do you know if Sonny had a spot where he put special papers or documents? Sort of a hiding place?"

"What kind of papers?"

"Oh, maybe a car title, warranty documents, or any special keepsakes?"

"No. The trailer's in Toby's name. Sonny's got the truck, so there's a title to that somewhere. Of course, his Triumph motorcycle. There'd be a title and registration for it as well. But I have no idea where they'd be."

"If you think of something, no matter how trivial, please let us know." I didn't have any other questions.

Tommy Lee closed his notepad without having scribbled so much as a letter. "Mrs. McKay, you've been staying with your sister, right?"

"That's right. But I'm fixing to go home today."

"I advise against that, ma'am. The person or the people who

did this to your son are running scared. Whether Sonny knew anything or not, they didn't take any chances. They very well could believe you pose a threat to them. Do you think it's possible to stay with your sister a few days longer?"

"But she lives over in Canton. She can't be carrying me back and forth. Somebody's got to feed the chickens and check on the house."

"We'll do that," Tommy Lee assured her. "It's clear to me your husband was worried about your safety. He took a desperate and foolish action, but despite his mental state at the time, he knew Rufus was involved with ruthless people. If he were here, what would he want you to do?"

Pauline sniffled and took a hard swallow. "Go with Nelda. But I've got a funeral..." she faltered a second…"two funerals to tend to." She turned to me. "Both my men. Gone in a weekend. Leaving me with two funerals." She kneaded the lace handkerchief into a ball. "I know this sounds bad, but is there a discount?"

Chapter Ten

Tommy Lee and I stood in the funeral home's parking lot and watched Pauline McKay and her sister leave for Canton. The sheriff had promised that a deputy would check her house, feed the chickens daily, and if she needed to return for clothes or personal items before the funerals, he would provide an armed escort. Given the horrific circumstances that had turned her life upside down, Fletcher and I agreed to delay any service for the father and son until the following week.

When the car had disappeared down Main Street, Tommy Lee asked, "What do you think?"

"I think she told us what she knows. Toby got caught up in some criminal enterprise that he couldn't control. The loss of this year's crop was only going to push him deeper into their clutches. He was afraid to take them on and lashed out at Commissioner James."

"My hound dog could have come to that conclusion, Sherlock. But why was Toby afraid? Because Rufus told him his debt had been taken over by some bad people? Like a resold mortgage?"

"Well, something must have spooked him. And then there's Rufus taking possession of Toby's EBT card. Was that Rufus' initiative or the people behind him?" I thought about the few times I'd crossed paths with the store owner. "Frankly, I don't think Rufus had the brains to organize the kind of operation Pauline McKay described."

"And he might not have had the brains to leave well enough alone."

"You mean if he was skimming?"

"Or too loose with his new-found income. The restoration of the El Camino advertised that Rufus had suddenly been flush to pay for the work in cash."

"Do you think Rufus pushing for Sonny to get an EBT card was part of a plan to branch out on his own?"

Tommy Lee scowled at me. "Now how am I supposed to know that? The man's dead and not talking." He gestured to the funeral home. "How many dead people in there have told you their plans?"

"It's just that I'm continually amazed at your deductive abilities."

The sheriff laughed. "Sorry. I forget how impressive I can be to those less skilled. So, maybe Rufus was skimming or setting up his own thing. But I don't believe that's the motive for his murder. It had to be tied to Toby's actions at the parade. Otherwise, it's an incredible coincidence." Tommy Lee started for his patrol car. "Let's get the search warrant for Rufus' house. Maybe we'll find he has something to say, after all."

It was a little after two in the afternoon when we turned into Rufus Taylor's driveway. The house appeared to have been a small cottage that over the years had been built out haphazardly with additional rooms. The structure held the architectural integrity of a preschooler's Lego creation.

A van with a Winston-Salem Motors bumper decal indicated Roger Taylor was here. Tommy Lee gave a sharp rap on a warped screen door. Its torn mesh allowed easy entrance for any insect smaller than a robin. The pine inner door displayed a network of knots and cracks rivaling the most intricate spider web. Tommy Lee opened the screen door and knocked harder on the wooden one.

"I ain't in there." The voice preceded Roger Taylor's appearance around the far corner of the house. He wore a stretched tee-shirt with the faded words "Coon Dog Day 2017" stamped across the chest. The event occurred annually in nearby Saluda. His brown cotton twill work pants were fastened at the waist by a large safety pin and the extra leg length was rolled up to his ankles. The wardrobe told me Roger had run through whatever he might have quickly packed in Winston-Salem and now was making do with what he could wear of his father's thinner, taller sizes.

He halted, surprise squelching his irritation. "Sheriff, I was just about to call you."

"About what?"

"My dad had an old Camino pickup out in the barn. Somebody's stolen it."

Tommy Lee let tired springs slam the screen door shut and walked closer to Roger. "It's at Carson's Auto Repair. Your father was fixing it up for you." The sheriff looked at me for corroboration.

"That's right. We saw it this morning. Harold's done a nice job."

Roger rubbed a hand across his mouth, trying and failing to conceal the tremor in his lips. "Is that why you're here?"

"Yes," Tommy Lee said. "It's all paid for. Harold said just settle up for new plugs and points. But we're also here to look through the house and property for any clues as to who might have killed your father."

Roger Taylor eyed us skeptically. "I've started going through his things. Nothing strange so far. I'll let you know if something turns up."

"This is a police matter," Tommy Lee said. "We need to conduct a search in a methodical way. We have a warrant, but I'd like to have your cooperation. That might serve you well later on."

"What do you mean?" Roger asked.

"If we find your father was engaged in some questionable activities, it will be clear to all that you knew nothing about them."

Roger Taylor looked away, clearly weighing the sheriff's words. Then he turned to face us. "I didn't know anything about the Camino, right? You believe that was news to me, don't you?"

"It appeared so," Tommy Lee agreed.

"And I know nothing about how my father was running his business. So, you can come in and look for whatever you want."

We followed Roger into the front room. On the left, mismatched chairs and a threadbare sofa were set in a semi-circle around a stone fireplace. On the right stood an oval table that at one time might have been the family dining area. Now the surface was covered in boxes of assorted crackers and cookies that Rufus must have brought from his store.

"Where do you want to start?" Roger asked.

"Your father's bedroom," Tommy Lee said.

The interior layout of the house reflected the mishmash construction visible on the outside. We walked through an old kitchen with cracked linoleum flooring and a stained porcelain sink. The refrigerator looked like it was only one generation removed from an icebox used by my great grandparents. The first room beyond the kitchen was a den with cheap paneling and a single overstuffed recliner facing a wide-screen TV. I suspected the room might originally have been a bedroom before the other rooms were added.

A bathroom stood to the right and on the left a door led to a bedroom. But Roger walked through that room to a second one beyond it. The odd floor plan required a pathway that meant walking through one bedroom to get to another. Both rooms had unmade beds, and I assumed Roger was sleeping in the first one rather than take over his father's.

"This is it," Roger said.

Tommy Lee stepped past him. "Fine. Wait in the doorway. You can watch but don't interfere."

Roger retreated to the first bedroom. Tommy Lee slipped on latex gloves and I did the same.

"Check the closet," Tommy Lee said. "I'll take the dresser drawers."

I pulled a string connected to a bare bulb light fixture in the closet's ceiling and started sorting through clothes and personal items. The articles consisted of two cheap suits, one lightweight tan for summer and a charcoal gray for winter, a few dress shirts with fraying collars, and assorted jeans and sweatshirts.

I turned all the pockets inside out but found nothing. Four pairs of shoes lay on the closet floor: one black dress pair with worn heels, one pair of hiking boots, a pair of ancient Reeboks, and a pair of green Wellingtons. I reached into the toe of each shoe and discovered with disgust where Rufus kept his dirty socks.

Ball caps and rain hats filled a few shelves. I lifted each and found nothing underneath. The top shelf was wider, extending out over the rod holding the hanging garments. I stepped back to get a better angle on what might be up there. Rufus' height would have made the shelf easily accessible. The corner of a gray metal box was just visible. I stood on tiptoes but the box was out of reach.

I turned and saw Tommy Lee on his hands and knees, peering under the double bed. "You're taller than me. See if you can reach whatever's on the upper shelf."

As he got to his feet, the sheriff's knees cracked like dry branches. I stepped aside and glanced back at Roger. He seemed curious as to what might be stored on the shelf. Tommy Lee's fingers crested the top edge of the box, enabling him to slide it toward him until it dropped into his other hand.

He set it on the foot of the unmade bed. "Have you seen this before?" he asked Roger.

"Yeah. Dad used to collect pennies in it. I'd forgotten about it."

The box looked like something a small business would use for petty cash. It was about a foot long and eight inches wide. There was a keyed latch on the side and a small wire handle attached to the top.

Tommy lifted it a few inches. "Too light to hold many pennies now."

He set it on the mattress and pushed the latch's button. The top opened on squeaky hinges.

"He never kept it locked," Roger said. "The key was lost years ago."

Tommy Lee pulled out a bound stack of twenty-dollar bills. Then he pulled a second and a third. "I'd say his pennies have increased in value."

Roger's mouth dropped open. "Jesus. Do you think he stashed that away from the store? You know, in case of a robbery?"

"Maybe," Tommy Lee said. "But my guess is we're looking at five or six thousand dollars. Pretty good cash register reserve."

Roger shook his head. "Am I going to have to sort this mess out? What bills need paying? What supplies need to be ordered? Where the hell is his partner? That's what I'd like to know."

"So would we," I said. "Have you found his lawyer yet?"

"I just got a name from my mother this morning. During the divorce, her lawyer dealt with Bert Graves, whoever the hell he is."

"We know him," Tommy Lee said. "Call his office this afternoon and tell him I advised you to see him as soon as possible."

Graves was a second-tier attorney who operated solo and was known for taking any case that walked through the door or rode by in an ambulance.

From the box, the sheriff lifted several pages that had been folded in half lengthwise. Some were from a newspaper; some appeared to be plain white paper. He spread them out flat. The longest newspaper article was from the *Charlotte Observer* and dated last October. The story was about fraud in the food stamp program and documented cases in Charlotte and the eastern part of the state where investigators from the Food and Nutrition Services and the SBI had cracked rings of convenience and small grocery stores who accepted EBT cards for the purchase of off-limits items like cigarettes and beer. The worst offenders simply rang up items that never left the store and split the cash paid from the benefit account with the cardholder. That scam had all the trappings of what Rufus Taylor and Toby McKay had been doing.

The white pages were Internet reprints of similar stories from news sources around the country. Big busts in Detroit, New York City, and Trenton. The scams ran into the millions of dollars and I began to understand we weren't dealing with some nickel-and-dime corner store operation.

A smaller article from the Asheville paper last April was the most disturbing. A fourth-grade girl in rural Buncombe County had gotten off the school bus to find the headless body of her cat stuffed in the family's mailbox. The bus driver was just pulling away when he heard the child screaming. He stopped the vehicle and ran to help her. Then he called the police. The girl's father, a Buddy Smith, owned a small grocery store. He said he'd caught some older boys shoplifting beer the night before. He didn't know them, but believed they might have targeted his family for revenge. Smith was quoted as saying, "There's some sick people out there." Rufus or someone had circled the one line in the news story identifying the store as "Wilmer's Convenience Corner."

"There weren't any shoplifters," I said.

Tommy Lee gathered up the papers. "No. And it wasn't revenge. It was a message."

Our search of the rest of the property turned up nothing. We watched Roger count the cash in the metal box, gave him a receipt for it and the news articles, and took them as potential evidence. Although we had no direct proof linking the money and the El Camino restoration to earnings from the food stamp fraud, the temporary confiscation gave us some control over Roger.

We instructed him not to say anything about what we had found. His role was to follow the legal path for settling his father's estate and discover this new partner in the process. In the grand scheme of the murder investigation, the money and a restored pickup weren't items we'd refuse to return if their connection to a crime remained murky. Our objective was to find who killed Rufus and Sonny, not convict a dead fraud suspect.

When Tommy Lee and I arrived at Sonny's trailer, activity was winding down. The mobile crime lab was packing up and the head technician reported they'd lifted prints from the front door, the tool chest, the whiskey bottle and glass, and numerous knobs and open surfaces where the UV light revealed good images.

As Tommy Lee had predicted, the M.E. estimated the time of death to be between midnight and three a.m. The body had been transported to the morgue for a full autopsy. There was no exit wound, and the working theory was a light-caliber bullet had ricocheted inside the skull and caused extensive brain damage.

The small trailer felt claustrophobic and Tommy Lee asked Reece to step outside away from the forensics team. We walked to a storage shed about ten yards away.

Tommy Lee leaned against a wall of rough plank boards. "I covered Ferguson with a quick phone call. Any state boys show up?"

"No," Reece said. "Only who you requested."

"Good. Did you find any papers?"

"A utility bill and a bank statement were in a kitchen drawer."

"Nothing else? He didn't have a place for his truck or motor-cycle titles?"

"No."

I looked around the driveway filled with police vehicles lined up behind Sonny's truck like they'd cornered it after a high-speed chase. "Where's the motorcycle? He must have finished working on it yesterday."

Reece pointed to the shed. "It's in there."

A sliding wooden door on overhead rollers covered an area large enough for a small tractor to drive through. Reece grabbed a wrought-iron handle and pulled the door to the left. A shiny black motorcycle with chrome pipes stood just inside.

"His bike's probably worth more than everything else he owned combined," Reece said.

I remembered the comment by Charlie the mechanic that Sonny would marry his motorcycle if he could. I walked around the sleek machine. A black helmet dangled from a chin strap looped around the handlebar. A black leather pouch sat on the rear fender just behind the seat. Double buckles sealed the flap closed.

"Did you check the saddlebag?" I asked Reece.

He flushed. "No. There was a lot going on."

I made no comment as I slipped on a pair of latex gloves. The metal buckles could yield a clean set of prints.

I found a pair of dark goggles, leather riding gloves, and a small weatherproof packet closed by a Velcro strip. Inside was the North Carolina Department of Motor Vehicles registration and the bike's title. There was also a folded piece of white paper. Scrawled in a mix of cursive and print handwriting was a list of names. They were not the names of people; they were the names of more than twenty stores. Two names jumped out at me: Taylor's Short Stop and Wilmer's Convenience Corner.

Chapter Eleven

When we returned to the Sheriff's Department, Tommy Lee immediately went to his office to call Ferguson and push for any information the SBI might have. The discovery of the list of stores, coupled with Pauline McKay's statements and Sonny's desire for protection, fueled the theory that Rufus and Sonny had been murdered, either under the orders of, or directly by, a person or persons running a network of food stamp fraud.

I, however, set the investigation aside and phoned Mom at the hospital for an update on Uncle Wayne.

"How is he?"

"Restless. Today wasn't a good day."

"Well, you knew he'd be anxious to get out."

Mom sighed. "He's running a fever and they've started him on a heavy dose of antibiotics."

My throat went dry. "Is there an infection in his brain?"

"No. A spot of pneumonia in his right lung. In addition to the antibiotics, they're coming in every two hours with breathing exercises and nebulizers to try to knock it out."

I felt a little better. Developing pneumonia in the hospital wasn't that uncommon. There's probably more bacteria and germs per square foot there than in a shopping mall at Christmas. But at Uncle Wayne's age, pneumonia was nothing to fool with. Susan said she and her medical colleagues often refer to it as the "old folks' friend" because it will take them when they're suffering from a prolonged terminal disease, sparing them pain and misery.

"I'm leaving the department now," I said. "Can I bring you anything?"

"I'm fine. You don't need to come." She spoke the words without real conviction. I knew she was worried about her brother.

"No. I want to see him. Tommy Lee and I are finished for the day. I can swing by the funeral home and be there in thirty minutes."

A pause. Another sigh. "Well, if it's no trouble, it would be nice to have Wayne's electric razor. I'd like to keep him looking as neat as possible."

"All right. Anything you need?"

"My knitting. It's in the canvas bag in the bedroom. I might as well be productive."

I parked behind the funeral home a little after five and saw Fletcher's Miata in the same spot it had been earlier. I felt a twinge of guilt that so much of the business of the funeral business was falling on him while my "part-time" deputy duties consumed ten and twelve hours a day.

I found him and his fiancée, Cindy Todd, sitting at the kitchen table. Cindy worked as a loan officer at the Bank of America branch a few blocks away. The petite, attractive woman was not just the perfect mate for Fletcher but gave him credibility with the locals. She'd grown up in Gainesboro and her mother ran the Cardinal Café, whereas Fletcher was a native of Detroit. Grieving families don't want to entrust their loved ones to strangers. Cindy's engagement meant Fletcher was now accepted as part of the town's family.

Seeing them at the kitchen table presented a believable image of what could come to be in the years ahead after my mother and uncle were gone.

"You okay, Barry?" Fletcher stood.

I realized I'd been staring at them.

"Yes, sorry. Thinking about something from the case."

Cindy rose and lifted Mom's knitting bag. "Your mother called and said you were coming by." She bent over and picked up a second bag. Mom's overnight valise. "I put your uncle's razor in here, as well as some clothes she wanted for herself."

"Thank you."

She handed them to me. "Fletcher told me about Sonny McKay. That's just terrible. I feel so bad for Mrs. McKay."

"I hope that was all right," Fletcher said. "I figured the word was out."

His comment reminded me that the murder hadn't generated media coverage. Tommy Lee had kept it off the scanners, but no one was denying what had happened. I remembered Melissa Bigham of the *Vista* was taking the two weeks after Labor Day off. Otherwise, she probably would have beaten the crime lab to the scene. "It's fine. We're just keeping it low-key. We're starting with forensic evidence. Afraid I can't say any more."

"Sure. We understand," Fletcher said. "And don't worry about anything here. Freddy's clear to work the next two weeks and Cindy's offered to help any way she can."

After eliciting a promise from Fletcher to let me know if things got crazy, I headed for Mission Hospital in Asheville. I phoned Susan and she insisted on meeting me after stopping at our house to feed Democrat.

I'd just disconnected when the cell rang again. The caller ID flashed "Archie." Tommy Lee was supposed to let him know when to initiate contact with Sonny. Had he heard about the murder or was he calling to put the now-defunct plan into action? Either way, I wasn't ready to deal with him. I let the call go to voicemail.

Uncle Wayne was asleep. The color I'd seen in his cheeks the previous day was gone. Instead, his pallid face looked tense and troubled. His fingers twitched and kneaded the bed sheet. His breathing rasped. A clear tube supplied a boost of oxygen to each nostril.

Mom was reading a book in the visitor's recliner. She set it aside and stood. "Here, let me take those."

She grabbed the valise and knitting bag from my hands and placed them on either side of her chair, building a nest with her possessions.

"How is he?" I asked.

"Fever's down to one hundred one. They're hopeful that the antibiotics are taking effect."

"Have they discussed putting him back in intensive care?"

"No. The treatment would be the same, and as long as he's breathing on his own, they'll keep him here."

"How about you? Are you getting any rest?"

"Enough. Hilda's waiting on me hand and foot." She smiled. "I actually find it easier being here rather than constantly having Hilda attempt to do things for me."

"Maybe I should stay at Hilda's."

Mom laughed and gestured to the recliner. "Why don't you sit? I know you've had a long day. Have Mrs. McKay and Sonny decided how to handle Mr. McKay's funeral?"

I realized Mom had been out of touch with the day's events.

"I'm fine, Mom. Why don't you sit? I have some things to tell you."

She gave a worried glance at Uncle Wayne and did as I requested. I told her about the murder, avoiding details. The tears came as she grieved for Pauline McKay—a woman who in less than a week lost both her husband and her son.

"Fletcher's being very consoling," I said. "He's helping her reschedule the funerals, and Freddy's available to assist as much as needed. So, I don't want you to worry."

She nodded. "I'll try. But it's hard not to. I sit here all day, looking at my brother and realizing neither he nor I will ever be any younger than we are right now. Time is moving into twilight for both of us."

"Mom, I'm sure he's going to make a full recovery. And you, you've got more energy than I do."

"Barry, I look at your uncle and I see an old man who I worry about going up and down stairs. I see myself facing a future with few options and a loss of control. Wayne will need rehab, possibly at home. I'll do what I can, but what I won't do is become a burden to you and Susan. You made one sacrifice coming back to help with your father. I'm not going to let you make another." She bit her lower lip and looked out the window. The sun sat low on the mountain ridges.

"Mom, you're not a burden. We'll get through this together."

"Yes. But I believe your uncle and I can make it work better for everyone if we move out of the funeral home."

A part of my mind heard her statement with relief. This was the logical, rational action I hoped she would take. But, a larger part, spanning from childhood, recoiled at the prospect, surprising me with its intensity. I'd not known Mom in any other context. To me, she was as much a part of the funeral home as the creaking floorboards or Formica kitchen table. Fletcher and Cindy were suddenly aliens invading a space I wanted to preserve.

"I made a call," she said. "To Alderway. I asked if they had any rule against a brother and a sister sharing a two-bedroom unit. They don't."

Alderway, a retirement community about five miles out of town, offered a continuum of options from independent living to critical care and dementia services. Several of Mom's friends were already there. As those places go, Alderway was safe, secure, and beautifully maintained. But my first thought was the nickname bestowed upon the complex. Black humor dubbed it, "Clayton's Waiting Room." In other words, Alderway was the last stop before our funeral home.

Three sharp taps sounded from the doorway. An elderly man brandishing a gnarled rhododendron walking stick entered.

"Reverend Pace!" Mom rose from the chair, thrilled to see the visitor.

"I'm so sorry, Connie. I would have come sooner but I was

out of town for the weekend." He opened his arms and engulfed Mom with a hug.

Reverend Lester Pace was a vanishing breed. Nearly eighty, he still roamed the hills serving a few isolated Methodist congregations as a circuit-riding preacher, although instead of a horse, he rode a Plymouth Duster. His worn jacket and string tie could have come from the Salvation Army and were probably as old as his car.

He'd preached at funerals my grandfather had conducted. A larger-than-life figure, he held himself above no man, woman, or child. With his weathered, lined face, white hair and piercing eyes, Lester Pace was a paradox of gentleness and ferocity. What he elicited from those who crossed his path was respect, which often grew into reverence. Far from the fire and brimstone image a first glance might create, Pace was a rugged shepherd tending a flock that lived on the margins. His very presence seemed to charge the air around him.

"Barry." Pace shook my hand and the calluses on his palm were like sandpaper. "You've got a full plate, don't you, son?"

"Yes, sir. It's all very tragic."

He nodded gravely, and then looked at Uncle Wayne. "What's his status?"

Mom repeated the latest on the pneumonia and treatment.

Pace leaned on his walking stick. "Connie, your brother's the strongest man I know. To stop Toby McKay with no regard for his own safety shows heart and courage. Those two things, plus the medical team, and God's power will serve him well. So, you have to have faith that whatever happens will be for the best."

The old preacher eased by us and went to the bedside. He laid his hand on Uncle Wayne's arm just above the IV and bowed his head in prayer. Mom and I stood in silence. I believed if anyone had a direct line to the Almighty, it was Lester Pace.

I heard footsteps behind us. Susan entered, and then stopped just inside the doorway. She held a bag from Lenny's Sub Shop.

Supper. I'd insist Reverend Pace join us. If Jesus could feed five thousand with five loaves and two fishes, we could stretch three sandwiches to feed the four of us.

It was during Pace's blessing of the subs that I thought about the people he served. These were the victims of opioid abuse, the proud but poor who needed Medicaid and food stamps to survive. These were the people who would turn to the Rufus Taylors of the region for credit. They were the ones susceptible to schemes for turning a food benefit into cash. Pace knew these people and would keep their confidence. But he also might offer guidance as to who could be behind what appeared to be a criminal enterprise. He would protect his flock from the wolves. Now was neither the time nor the place to broach the subject, but I decided a conversation with the good pastor could be valuable.

We left the hospital at eight-thirty. Uncle Wayne had awakened for a few minutes and seen all of us. He managed to croak out two sentences: "I ain't dyin'. Go on about your business." Those few words seemed to sap his strength and he went back to sleep.

Susan and I left when a medical team came in for the breathing treatment. Reverend Pace said he would take Mom to her friend Hilda's as soon as they were finished and Mom had told her brother good night.

Susan and I had driven separate cars, and I rode home accompanied only by my thoughts. The case retreated to the back of my brain as the impact of Mom's proposal to leave the funeral home launched a barrage of questions I should have been preparing for. How much would Mom and Uncle Wayne need to buy into a place like Alderway? What was the monthly fee? How could she access her equity in the property of the funeral home without hurting the resources and cash flow of our business? What would Uncle Wayne's share be and how much could he contribute? That question brought me to the sobering corollary—would Uncle Wayne even be here?

The case, Uncle Wayne's illness, and Mom's future were all swept from my mind when I drove up the driveway to our house and saw Archie Donovan's Lexus parked by the front porch. Susan pulled in behind me and I knew she was asking the same question: what was Archie doing here at nine o'clock at night?

The interior courtesy lights of the Lexus came on as Archie opened the door. Susan had turned on the porch lights when she'd swung by to feed Democrat, and Archie stepped up into their glow and waved like we were visiting him.

"Hi, Susan," he said with a nervous smile. "Barry, I left you a voice message but you must not have checked it."

"We've been at the hospital."

"Oh, of course." He stepped back to clear a path to the front door. "How's Wayne doing?"

"Not so well. He's contracted pneumonia."

"Gosh. I'm really sorry to hear that. Can I do something? Take care of the dog?"

"We're all right. What do you need?"

He glanced at Susan as if she might be a foreign spy.

"Would you like a glass of wine?" she asked him. "Or I could put on a fresh pot of coffee."

"No, thanks. I just need to talk to Barry a few minutes."

"Very well. But if you change your mind, I'll be up a little while longer." She unlocked the door and left it open behind her.

I appreciated her subtle reminder that it was late.

"You want to come in?" I asked Archie.

He walked to the front door and closed it. "Barry," he whispered, his voice quivering. "I heard about Sonny. Shot dead, right in his own bed."

"Yes. I meant to call you."

Archie's eyes were wide, reflecting the yellow cast of the porch lights. "If someone silenced Sonny, do you think they could be coming after me?"

"I don't see how. Sonny hadn't told you anything yet. No one knew you were planning to talk to him."

Archie looked away. His silence spoke a message that made my stomach turn.

"Archie. No one knew, right?"

"I didn't tell anyone about the food stamp scam."

"Who did you tell what?"

"I swore to keep it a secret."

"Then why the hell are you on my doorstep?"

Archie took in a staggered breath. "Because I'm afraid. I'm caught between professional standards of client confidentiality and what is probably coincidence."

"And you don't want to bet your life on a coincidence."

He nodded.

"Let's start with what you said."

"Well, this client had read my *Letters from a Gainesboro Jail* blog and asked me if I'd seen the man whose father attacked Commissioner James. Like you suggested, I said that Sonny wasn't in the next cell. Just that our paths had crossed."

"And?"

"I said I'd told him I was a robber because I didn't want someone like him knowing my identity. I said Sonny had been impressed and wanted to talk to me after his release. He had information that he wouldn't tell anyone else."

I could hear Archie telling his client those words, making himself seem important, the James Bond of Gainesboro.

"This was last night," I said. "When I called you and you couldn't talk."

"Yes." Archie paced back and forth on the porch. "But these people wouldn't have known Sonny or Toby. They were just curious."

"So, you tell them you're going to have a secret conversation with Sonny, and then during the night, Sonny's murdered. Did you say you were doing this on your own?"

He grimaced. "I said it was undercover work."

"For who?"

"I just said for the big boys."

"Jesus, Archie. The FBI? Why would you fabricate such an outrageous claim?"

"I never said FBI."

"Well, I don't think 'big boys' conjures up the image of the Laurel County Sheriff's Department. What guarantee do you have that your client didn't tell someone else?"

"Because I learned a secret from them."

"Them?"

"Yes. And their secret is more important than what I told them. That's why they wouldn't tell. At least I thought they wouldn't tell."

"Until you learned about Sonny."

"Like I said, I'm caught between client confidentiality and what's probably a coincidence."

"No. You're caught between client confidentiality and an obstruction of justice charge."

"Barry, I promised them. They asked me if our meeting was a privileged conversation like with a lawyer or a priest."

"You'd better find a lawyer and a priest," I snapped. Then the phrase triggered a memory—Janet Sinclair asking me the same question in our funeral home six weeks before.

I got up in Archie's face. "The Sinclairs. Your clients are the Sinclairs."

He jumped back like I'd jabbed him with a cattle prod. "How did you know?"

"Never mind that. Tell me this secret or I'm arresting you right now."

He looked over his shoulder at the front door as if Susan might be eavesdropping behind it. "Their identities," he whispered. "They're not who they say they are. They're in the Witness Protection Program."

Chapter Twelve

As soon as Archie told me the Witness Protection story, I called Tommy Lee. He insisted we meet immediately, and so at ten that night, Archie, Tommy Lee, and I sat in the great room of my log home and analyzed the veracity and implications of this unexpected development. Susan had retired to our bedroom, understanding the confidentiality of our conversation and knowing I would have done the same if one of her patients had dropped by for an urgent medical consultation.

I brewed a pot of coffee and set out a bowl of pretzels, giving Democrat a warning glare not to touch them. The dog whined and retreated to his cushion in front of the hearth.

Tommy Lee got right to the point. "Tell me how your stint in jail even came up with the Sinclairs?"

Archie rubbed his sweaty palms on his thighs. "The charity fundraiser. The Sinclairs made the ten thousand-dollar donation."

"You said you were going to get a certified bank check today. Why did they need to see you last night?"

"Mr. Sinclair called me yesterday afternoon and asked to meet. He apologized for calling on Labor Day, but said his wife had made the donation without considering their cash flow needs. They had every intention of honoring the commitment to the kids and that perhaps I could help."

"How?"

"He wouldn't say over the phone. He said it would be better if we could meet in my office."

"Were they a long-standing client?" Tommy Lee asked.

"No. I'd never met them before. Mrs. Sinclair had called for an appointment a month or so ago. It didn't get on my schedule and so I missed it. I apologized, but she never rescheduled."

"The Monday after the Fourth of July," I interjected. "The morning you met me about the float idea."

Both Tommy Lee and Archie looked at me with surprise.

"How come you remember that?" Tommy Lee asked.

"Because Janet Sinclair came to the funeral home to inquire about pre-planning for her and her husband. She showed up early claiming her insurance agent didn't keep a meeting."

"It wasn't my fault," Archie said defensively. "She requested the meeting the night before by leaving a message on our answering machine. I didn't get it till after you and I met, Barry."

"When did she make the funeral home appointment?" Tommy Lee asked me.

"That morning," I said. "My mother took the call before I arrived. I really didn't know anything before sitting down with her." I explained her strange request not to involve a New Jersey funeral home and to deal directly with the cemetery. I also said the cemetery had no record of plots owned by a Sinclair family.

Tommy Lee leaned forward in his chair and snagged a pretzel. "That's consistent with WITSEC." He used the short word commonly used for the program. "A new name severs all ties and they'll probably have to offer the cemetery some proof of their former identities."

"She said the surviving spouse would give instructions, or an attorney would provide the information in the case of simultaneous deaths."

Tommy Lee chewed the pretzel and chased it with a sip of black coffee. "If they were in WITSEC, the burial instructions probably give their real names, and your contact with the cemetery would create a lower profile than your dealing with a local funeral home. That would protect the surviving spouse." He turned to Archie. "But I don't understand why they confided in you."

"Like you said, new identities shut the door on the old. They told me the U.S. Marshals helped them get some assets moved into the new names, specifically bank accounts. Mr. Sinclair stressed they weren't criminals, but that he was an innocent accountant who discovered anomalies in a client's books who turned out to be laundering money for the mob. His testimony put some chieftains away but at the cost of being on a hit list."

"Okay," Tommy Lee said, "but what does that have to do with you?"

"Some assets didn't get transferred. Specifically, three insurance policies. A policy on the husband, another on the wife, and a second-to-die policy on both of them."

"Better explain that last one."

"It insures two lives but doesn't pay out till the second person dies. You get more insurance for less money because odds are one spouse might significantly outlive the other, and it mitigates what could be some health concerns if one of the two is a higher risk. They told me the beneficiary of that policy was the ASPCA. They're very charity-minded."

"Why don't they just apply for new policies under their new names?"

Archie looked at us like we couldn't understand that two plus two equals four. "Money. There's a lot of cash trapped in those policies. Each was a single premium and they dumped three hundred thousand in each. That means they paid enough so that no additional premiums are needed. The cash in the policy will grow tax-sheltered and unreported. The death benefit will be paid tax-free, and I don't know the face values but they might be two or three times the premium. But now they have no control over them. How do you make a claim when a strange name is on the death certificate? How do you borrow against the value or surrender the policy if your name no longer matches that of the owner?"

"Have you seen these policies?"

"No. They described them exactly the way I described them to you."

"So, you don't know the Sinclairs' original names?"

"No."

Tommy Lee looked at me and shook his head. "Somehow that just doesn't sound right."

"Well, it is," Archie exclaimed. "It's a great financial planning tool, if you remember not to piss off the mob."

I didn't doubt Archie's assessment. It sounded better than mechanic Harold Carson's advice to invest your money in a pickup truck. But I was getting the same vibes as Tommy Lee. "That seems like a lot of money for an accountant to earn."

"Evidently, his wife had a sizable inheritance," Archie said.

"What's his job now?" Tommy Lee asked.

"He's a manufacturer's rep for a line of sportswear. He said the marshals helped him get the job and he covers North and South Carolina and Georgia. Mrs. Sinclair helps him with his paperwork. The new life's going fine, but they'd like the financial security of owning those policies again. That's where they'll pull the ten thousand for the Girls and Boys Clubs."

"What could you do to help them?" Tommy Lee asked.

Archie grinned. "I came up with an option. I mean the policies are theirs. They should be able to get them back."

"You care to explain?"

His smile faltered. "I mean I outlined a possibility. I didn't tell them they should do it."

Tommy Lee grunted. "Sounds like this option has legality issues."

Archie shook his head. "No. Not since all the names are the same people. Look, you can't transfer ownership to another person without triggering a tax event. The insurance companies would report it. It needs to be an exchange involving the same individuals, like rolling over an IRA. But the Sinclairs can't do that because of their name change. So, I said they could form a corporation and list the owners or officers as themselves—and their old identities—four people. You can transfer a policy into a corporation as long as the original owners are corporate officers."

Archie stared at us like we should now see the obvious. Tommy Lee and I just stared back.

"So," Archie continued, "the Sinclairs set up a corporation. They can do that easily through an online service that will even file it with the North Carolina Secretary of State. They add their old identities as two officers and then file an ownership transfer to the corporation. The names match, the insurance company is satisfied it was a permitted transfer, and the Sinclairs are one step closer. Then they document that the old identities leave the corporation, but ownership stays with the corporation owned solely by the Sinclairs. They now have control in their new names." Archie raised his hands, palms up. "Problem solved."

I looked at Tommy Lee. I didn't know insurance regulations, but it sounded plausible.

Tommy Lee let out a long breath. "Impressive. But, Archie, you know what you've done?"

"Sure. Freed up ten thousand dollars for our kids."

"Maybe. You also explained how to launder hundreds of thousands of dollars."

Archie paled. "No. It was their money."

"But you don't know the source. You're trusting their word. These are the people you told you'd be talking to Sonny. If they murdered him, do you think they'd hesitate to lie about their finances?"

Archie ran the tip of his tongue over his dry lips. "Well, check with the marshals. They can tell you if they're innocent people."

"I'll tell you what the marshals will say. 'We can neither confirm nor deny.' Marshals have one responsibility—to protect their witnesses. They won't tell you who's in the program and they won't even tell you if someone left the program. WITSEC participants sever all ties with their old world. To do otherwise voids their protection. Just by telling you, the Sinclairs violated the agreement. If I check with the marshals, they'll stonewall me. And I'm a fellow officer of the law. Then they'll go straight to the Sinclairs. Who do you think that loops back to?"

Archie swallowed. "Me."

"That's the way I see it."

Archie's gaze shot back and forth between Tommy Lee and me like he was watching a high-speed tennis match. "Well, what are you going to do about it?"

Tommy Lee shrugged. "Not my problem. You're the one who couldn't keep a secret. You're the one who bragged you were going to talk to Sonny. What are you going to do about it?"

"Send Gloria and the girls to her mother's in Weaverville. Demand round-the-clock police protection for me till you arrest these people."

"On what charge? Talking to an insurance agent?"

For a few seconds, Archie could only sputter unintelligible syllables, then managed to plead, "You've got to help me."

"Then here's what you're going to do: Nothing."

"Nothing?"

Tommy Lee leaned forward and set his coffee cup on the table. "You can send your family away, but keep it low-key. You go about your business as if Sonny's murder had nothing to do with you. How did you leave it with the Sinclairs?"

"They said they'd think about it and get back to me."

"What would your role be?"

"Get the paperwork from the insurance companies, help them fill out the forms, and then send it in."

Tommy Lee nodded. "So, you'll do exactly what they want. Your goal is to learn their real names. No less, no more. Can you do that?"

"Yes, sir."

"Good." Tommy Lee stood. "Keep us posted through Barry. If you need to meet, do it at the funeral home and stay clear of the Sheriff's Department. My guess is if they're going to take your suggestion, they'll do so within the next few days. If not, place a follow-up phone call. That would be natural and also you're expecting that ten-thousand-dollar donation."

Archie and I rose from our chairs.

"And if they renege on that?" Archie asked.

"Then let it go. You'll have done all you can."

"And you think I'll be safe?"

Tommy Lee stepped close and gently grasped Archie by his arm. "You will be, if you do as I say. And remember, the Sinclairs might have nothing to do with Sonny. The decision to kill Sonny could have been made earlier and have nothing to do with you. It sounds like their concerns go back to July before any of this happened."

"That's right," Archie said. "They wanted to talk about this back then." He looked at me, relief flooding his face. "Just like the funeral planning."

"Yes," I agreed. My mind jumped back to the day of my conversation with Janet Sinclair, Uncle Wayne's phone call from Forest Glen Cemetery, and Susan's setting of Robert Sinclair's broken leg. A possible connection flashed and I saw a new investigative path open. One that for the time being, I'd keep to myself.

Tommy Lee and I stood on the front porch and watched Archie's taillights wink out as he drove around the bend in my driveway.

"You going to check with the U.S. Marshals?" I asked.

"Not yet. Like I said, they'll neither confirm nor deny. They wouldn't tell me if they placed a mob informant next door to my house. I need to draw a few more cards before I play my hand."

"Like what?"

"Like the real identities of the Sinclairs. If Archie gets them to reveal their names on the forms for the transfer of the policies, I go in with the leverage to embarrass the marshals."

"Embarrass them?"

"Yes. They may have placed active criminals in my county. A big scandal broke last year in Arizona when a mob killer used his new identity to commit fraud across the country. He was an alleged real estate developer who took millions of upfront money, and then drove the projects into bankruptcy after pocketing the funds. It was a sixty-five-million-dollar debacle. The investors had no clue who they were dealing with because our own government fabricated a squeaky clean new identity and history for him."

"And the man was a killer?"

"Self-confessed. But his testimony brought down some mob kingpins, which made the prosecutors happy. Then the marshals protected him for being a witness, but who protects the public from him? Local law enforcement's never told that a career criminal has just settled in their community."

"And Robert Sinclair could be like this guy in Arizona?"

"Why not? I don't believe the Sinclairs simply ran out of time to change their policies before disappearing into the program. I think they were hiding money. Probably from the marshals themselves. Relocation support includes a financial stipend until the protected witness gains employment. They would want to qualify for as much as they could."

"But exposure could endanger them. I assume there's still a mafia bounty on Robert Sinclair's head."

Tommy Lee poked me in the chest with a forefinger. "That's the damn point. The marshals won't let that happen, so I'm hoping they'll tell me what I need to know. If it turns into a murder conviction, they'll drop the protection. Then if the mob bumps off Robert Sinclair, it's not on their watch. They can still tout they've never lost a witness while in their program."

Tommy Lee stepped off the porch and headed for his patrol car.

"You made a good point that Sonny could have already been a marked man," I said.

Tommy Lee turned. "I know. Robert Sinclair could be a wild goose chase. That's why our main areas for pursuit are the ballistics we've got, Rufus and Toby's financial records, and the trail of EBT card-use."

"And finding out who Rufus took as a new partner in the store," I reminded him.

"Yes. Roger needs to see the attorney as soon as possible. But enough for tonight. We'll start first thing in the morning."

"I need to be at the hospital."

"Oh, sorry." Tommy Lee walked back to me. "I should have asked how Wayne was doing."

I gave him a summary of my uncle's condition.

"You take care of your family first," Tommy Lee said. "In the morning, I'll just be pushing Ferguson and the SBI to expedite their findings."

I found Susan in bed reading *Southern Living* magazine. Democrat had flopped out on my side. He grudgingly hopped off when he saw me pull my pajamas from a dresser drawer.

"Everything all right?" Susan asked.

"Things have taken a strange turn. Tell me whatever you can about Robert Sinclair."

Chapter Thirteen

At seven the next morning, a uniformed state trooper stood outside the door to Uncle Wayne's hospital room. He held a paper cup of coffee in one hand and a pastry in the other. As he saw me approach down the corridor, he set the coffee on the plastic chair beside him.

I, too, was in uniform, and I trusted he freed his hand to shake mine rather than draw his service weapon.

"I'm Deputy Barry Clayton. My uncle is the patient. Is there some problem?"

He returned the greeting with a handshake and a smile. "Commissioner James insisted on seeing your uncle. He was released last night but is flying out from Asheville to Raleigh. A four-hour car trip would be too taxing, given his wound."

"Are you here because of further threats?"

"No. I'm here because the governor wants James to have an escort, at least till he's home."

"Am I free to enter?"

The officer glanced at his wristwatch. "Yeah. Please do. You might help hurry the commissioner along or we're going to miss the plane."

I knocked as I opened the door and found James standing at the head of the bed. Uncle Wayne was awake and either James or a nurse had inclined the mattress to a more comfortable sitting position. My uncle's color looked better and he smiled when he saw me.

"Here he is. The man I was telling you about. My nephew."

From the effusiveness of his words, one would think I'd discovered a cure for cancer.

The commissioner had his right arm in a sling and the bulge beneath his shirt indicated protective bandaging on his shoulder. Graham James was around sixty, a big-boned, square-jawed man who looked like he'd be as comfortable in bib overalls as he would in a tailored suit.

He extended his left hand. "Pleased to meet you. Your uncle says you're the Sherlock Holmes of Gainesboro."

"Obviously, he's delirious," I said.

"He'll get to the bottom of what happened, Graham. You wait and see."

Graham, I thought. Uncle Wayne and his new best friend were certainly chummy.

"I don't doubt it," James said. "Not if he takes after his uncle. Anything you can share with me, Barry? The SBI reports that the man Wayne stopped just flipped out."

I hesitated to answer. Ferguson had given the commissioner the story as far as his investigation had gone. And the SBI was being extremely cooperative so I didn't want to throw Ferguson under the bus. But it dawned on me that the Commissioner of Agriculture could be both an asset and an ally as our own case followed a trail into the world of food stamps and state-administered benefits. The USDA and James' agriculture department had to have a close working relationship.

"That's correct, as far as what we know regarding your attack. But there are some other elements that we are tracking that could reveal additional pressures that created Toby McKay's mental state. This isn't for public consumption, so I need both of you to keep the information confidential."

A politician loves nothing more than to get confidential

information. I didn't trust him not to leak it, or Uncle Wayne to remember it was confidential, so I restricted my comments to indications that Toby McKay might have been involved in a food stamp scam which further squeezed him financially. When he lost the second crop, he took it out on the commissioner as the symbol of his troubles.

"We're pursuing the food stamp fraud in connection to McKay and others. In fact, we might need your department's assistance as we dig further."

"Absolutely." With his free arm, James fumbled in his pocket for his wallet and awkwardly fished out a business card. "Have you got a pen?"

I pulled a ballpoint from my shirt pocket.

"You write. My left-handed chicken scratch will be illegible." He handed me the card. "I'm giving you my personal cell number. Day or night, you call if we can assist. I know many of the FNS investigators, if this thing moves into federal territory." He gave me the ten-digit number and I repeated it back.

Commissioner James turned to my uncle and patted him on the shoulder. "You're going to lick that pneumonia, Wayne, and then you're coming to Raleigh. That's an invitation from me and the governor. Bring the whole family. I don't care about your political persuasion. We'll have a good meal and a good time."

As he left the room, he whispered to me, "I want you to keep me informed on his progress. If we need to get him to a bigger hospital, just say the word."

I thanked him and promised to stay in touch.

"That man's a talker," Uncle Wayne said, as I returned to the bedside.

"What time did he get here?"

"I don't know for sure. The nurse had just been in, and she said it was six-thirty."

"I hope he didn't tire you out."

"No. It was good to see him." My uncle took a deep breath.

"It let me know I didn't simply kill a man. I saved a life. I can rest easier having seen that life in the flesh."

"And how are you feeling?"

"Weak as a newborn kitten. But the nurse said the fever broke during the night. Looks like I won't be family business quite yet."

I had to laugh. He sounded like he was apologizing for not being a customer of Clayton and Clayton.

Mom arrived a few minutes later and was ecstatic at her brother's progress. Dr. DeMint came by on his rounds and agreed that it looked like the worst was behind us. But, he said Wayne would need another day or two in the hospital and then a few more days in on-site rehab. DeMint wanted no chance for a relapse.

I had breakfast with Mom in the hospital cafeteria and then said goodbye. Rufus Taylor's service was at eleven and I decided I should cover the funeral home while Fletcher and Freddy Mott were up at Twin Creeks Baptist Church for the burial. I also had a call to place and I wanted to have the Sinclair file in front of me.

"Forest Glen. How may we serve you?"

The woman's voice sounded familiar but it had been almost two months since I'd made the original call.

"This is Barry Clayton. Clayton and Clayton Funeral Directors in Gainesboro, North Carolina."

"Yes, Mr. Clayton. We've spoken before, haven't we?"

"That's right. I had a question about the cost for opening a grave. But you said things were crazy and you called back later and spoke with my uncle."

A few seconds of silence followed. I could visualize her trying to reconstruct the phone calls.

"Yes, the day we had the excitement at the graveside service. I'm sorry I had to be so abrupt. Do you need that grave prepared?"

"No. I was just reviewing the file and thought I'd better double-check the information." I repeated the figure Uncle Wayne had entered in the estimate.

"That's correct," she confirmed. "And I remember now that I couldn't find the family's plots listed in the registry."

"Confusion on our end. Don't worry about it. I'm curious, since we both deal with a lot of funerals, what was so crazy that day?"

She laughed. "Have you ever had someone fall out of a tree?"

"No. That would be a first."

"Well, one of the mourners climbed a tree about forty yards away. Rumor was there was some kind of family rift and he didn't want to be seen. One of our gardeners spotted him. In his hurry to climb down, he fell. He gave a yell loud enough to be heard by those at the graveside. Then he ran, or rather hobbled, through the monuments to his car on the other side of the hill. Some of the men sitting under the funeral canopy got up and started chasing him, which caused even more confusion."

"They catch him?"

"No. He managed to get away. We don't know how long he'd been up there. The interment was at ten. One of those gravesides before the church service at eleven. When you called, we were dealing with the police."

"The police were there for a man in a tree?"

"The police were monitoring the attendees. The deceased was Bobby Santona, alleged head of the Santona crime family. He died in prison. Police speculated the man in the tree could have been taking pictures for some rival."

"Did he have a camera?"

"Not that anyone saw. And as far as I know, he was never identified. Our gardener was asked to look at mug shots. Either he didn't recognize the man or he was too scared to say he did."

"Are there a lot of Santona plots?"

"Oh, yes. They've got a big section with who goes where all

recorded. When a gang war breaks out, we can have multiple burials on the same day. I guess things must be calmer in North Carolina."

"Not really. I was once shot at a graveside service. I've got father and son gunshot victims to be buried next week. Some guy falling out of a tree would be a welcomed relief."

When I hung up, I looked at the notepad where I'd written "Bobby Santona." Was a jailed crime boss in Paterson, New Jersey, connected to our killings? Bobby Santona—Robert Sinclair. They couldn't be the same person, but they could be in the same family. I did an Internet search on Bobby Santona. He'd been convicted four years earlier on racketeering charges. One of the frauds involved tire disposal where his crew would pick up worn tires from trucking firms and then have an inside man process them through a New Jersey state-run facility without charging the firms the required fee. Instead, Santona would collect a fee lower than the state's. The trucking firms had lower expenses and Santona kept the money. New Jersey couldn't understand why tire disposal expenses were out of ratio with collected revenue. Then one of the family members was flipped by the FBI—not only on the tire scheme but other illegal operations as well. He was said to be close to the mobster's books and his identity was withheld from the press.

Robert Sinclair, on the day of Bobby Santona's funeral, needed treatment in Gainesboro for a broken leg. I logged onto Google maps and checked the travel time from New Jersey. Just under eleven hours. Susan got the call from the hospital twelve hours after the tree escapade. The trip was doable, although he must have been in a hell of a lot of pain. How much pain could you endure if you had a mob hit team pursuing you?

Another thought struck me. Was Janet Sinclair's sudden need to meet with Archie and me that July day fueled by her husband's return to New Jersey? Had he insisted on attending a funeral service despite her objections? Was that urgency rekindled by Toby

McKay's attack on Commissioner James? The connections were tenuous at best. I feared so tenuous that if we moved too quickly and telegraphed our suspicions, evidence would be destroyed and the Sinclairs could disappear. Following that trail had to be done quietly and secretly.

I printed out the information from the computer and took it to Tommy Lee.

His assistant Marge stopped me as I passed her desk.

"The sheriff's in with Special Agent Ferguson of the SBI. He said you should join them."

I looked at the closed door and then the pages in my hand. I didn't want to disclose the Santona possibility beyond Tommy Lee. "Marge, can I leave these with you? I'll discuss them with the sheriff after Ferguson leaves."

"You got it." She slid the papers into her top drawer.

"How long has Ferguson been in there?"

"Maybe fifteen minutes. No longer."

"Thanks." I knocked on the door and waited until I heard the familiar gruff, "Come in."

Tommy Lee and Ferguson were both seated, the sheriff behind his desk and the SBI agent in one of the two visitors' chairs. As I took a seat, I noticed a stack of computer printouts under Tommy Lee's right hand.

He patted them with his palm. "Sid was kind enough to bring these by in person. It's the ballistics report on the slugs from both murders. Rufus and Sonny were killed by the same gun. A twenty-two. No match to either man's rifle. Gas and powder burns on Sonny's entry wound prove the muzzle was placed directly against the skull, an awkward angle to use if the gun was a rifle."

"A revolver or semi-automatic?" I asked.

"We don't know for sure," Ferguson said. "There was no brass at either scene, but if the shooter fired a semi-automatic and then picked up the casings, it would look the same as if the shells stayed in the revolver's cylinder. If I had to guess based on the assumption that this was a professional hit, I'd say a semi-automatic. Burns on Sonny McKay suggest a suppressor, and that's not going to be used with a revolver."

"You run the ballistics through a database?" I asked.

"Yeah. No hits, either state or federal."

Tommy Lee leaned forward across the desk. "So, we've confirmed the same murder weapon which suggests a common motive for the two killings. That's no surprise. I've given Sid a copy of the list of stores we found in Sonny's saddlebag."

"I'll share them with the FNS investigative office in Raleigh," Ferguson said. "See what they know. It's a faster approach than asking to run the EBT transaction records for every store. None of us likes to feel we're on a fishing expedition for some conspiracy theory wild goose chase."

I wondered if Tommy Lee had shared Archie's revelations that the Sinclairs claimed to be in Witness Protection. I doubted he had, since they had no connection to Ferguson's line of inquiry.

"Thanks for your help, Sid," Tommy Lee said. "Whatever you can do to push this through the interdepartmental bureaucracy will be appreciated."

Ferguson slid back his chair and stood. "Well, we've got to stick together against the bureaucrats." He shook Tommy Lee's hand and then held onto it. "There is one possibility that I want you to watch out for."

"What's that?"

"What if Toby McKay attacked Commissioner James because he was ordered to? If he was in debt and threatened, he might have been coerced."

Tommy Lee smiled. "Who's offering conspiracy theories now?"

Ferguson dropped the sheriff's hand and shook mine. "I know it's unlikely, but even a blind pig finds an acorn once in a while."

"Or a one-eyed sheriff," Tommy Lee said.

We walked Special Agent Ferguson out of the department.

After goodbyes, I told Tommy Lee I had some new information. I picked up my Internet research from Marge and returned to his office. I repeated my conversation with the Forest Glen representative, the coincidence of Robert Sinclair's broken leg, and the death in prison of a New Jersey mobster named Bobby Santona. I gave him the copies of the newspaper articles of Santona's conviction and that someone close to him had betrayed him.

He read everything twice. "Do you know when the Sinclairs moved to Gainesboro?"

"No. I guess we find out when they bought their house. If it's more than four years ago, then we can rule them out."

"I'll send Marge to the courthouse to check the register of deeds. Even if it's within the last four years, I'd like to hold off and see whether Archie learns their names through his insurance scheme. That will be extra ammunition when I confront the marshals."

"What do you want me to do?"

Tommy Lee glanced at his watch. "It's one-thirty now. When was Rufus' funeral?"

"Eleven."

"See if you can track down his son. I want to know when he's seeing the attorney. Rufus' new business partner is still our most significant person of interest."

There was a knock at the door.

"Yeah?" Tommy Lee barked.

Marge stuck her head in. "Roger Taylor's here. He'd like to see you or Barry."

Tommy Lee looked at me. "So much for your tracking." He turned back to Marge. "Send him in. And then I want you to look up the residence of a Robert and Janet Sinclair. Find out from public records when they purchased it."

Tommy Lee and I stood, ready to receive our timely guest.

Roger Taylor came in wearing an ill-fitting charcoal gray suit that had to be from his father's closet. I realized he'd had no other option to wear at the funeral.

Without a word of greeting, he blurted out, "I just came from the attorney. He said my dad came in a few months ago and updated his will. He left everything to me, including the store. It's debt-free. There's no partner. No partner at all."

Chapter Fourteen

Roger Taylor was clearly happy with the news. His father had specifically named him as his heir and set up the business to cleanly transfer to him with no partner attached. Roger said the attorney, Bert Graves, was listing the restored Camino pickup and the discovered cash as part of the estate to be moved through probate as quickly as possible.

"I want to sell the store as fast as I can," Roger said. "Mr. Graves told me I need to get someone to keep the store open so it doesn't lose its value. I don't know nothing about running a store, so he's suggesting we find a possible buyer with a lease-to-purchase deal. You know, run the store for the estate until everything clears and I can sell it outright."

While Roger was talking, I was coming to grips with the no-partner setback. My theory that Rufus had been directed by some criminal element who had bought into his business had just evaporated. But if Rufus was doing the EBT card scam on his own, why had he told his son he had a partner? Was it to explain the cash influx, or was this partner silent, so silent that he didn't want his name appearing on any documents? If that was the case, Roger might soon find himself confronted by threats and intimidation.

Roger Taylor cleared his throat and looked uncomfortable. "Mr. Graves wanted to know why you had taken my father's cash. He called it liquidity that I'll need for legal fees and probate taxes. He wants to know what evidence you have that it's linked to any crime."

Tommy Lee nodded thoughtfully. "Well, Roger, we're in the middle of a murder investigation. The cash could have been the motive. Maybe somebody knew about it and tried to force your father to hand it over. Until I've had a reasonable amount of time to pursue our leads, that cash is staying locked in a safe in our evidence room. And if the store was as profitable as it appears, you might want to rethink your rush to sell it. Tell your employer you need a leave of absence. Show this community the Taylors don't turn tail and run."

Roger reddened. "Is that what you think I'm doing?"

"Well, you did say you didn't want to get shot. But I was thinking about all those friends and neighbors who shop at the store. What will they say? Someone murders your father and you don't stay around to push us to find the killer? You put some stranger in the business, assuming you can find someone, while you disappear?"

Roger ran his fingers through his hair. "But I've got a job. My boss man will fire me."

"Maybe. Or maybe he'll think differently if I tell him you're helping me with the investigation."

Roger's eyes narrowed. "What do you mean?"

"Your father told you he had a partner, right?"

"Yeah, but the partnership must not have worked out. My dad owned the store free and clear."

We were still standing. Roger's announcement about his meeting with the lawyer had catapulted us into the conversation without any of us sitting down.

Tommy Lee gestured to one of the guest chairs. "Have a seat, Roger. We need to talk."

We sat, Tommy Lee behind his desk and Roger and me side-by-side across from him.

The sheriff pointed a finger at the nervous young man. "Just because there's not a legal document doesn't mean someone else wasn't involved in your father's business."

"You mean like a silent partner?"

"More like an invisible partner," Tommy Lee said. "We don't know how silent he was when it came to dealing with your father. We don't know what kind of leverage might have been applied that doesn't show up in legal paperwork. Do you get my point?"

Roger shifted uncomfortably in his chair. "You're saying he might have crossed the wrong people."

"I'm saying he was gunned down by what looks like a professional hit. You don't know anything about that, do you?"

Roger threw up his hands. "Good God, no. I keep telling you my dad told me nothing about his business, other than he claimed he had a partner. And he only mentioned it once last year."

"Then your ignorance is your best protection. You run the store as the inheriting son and you might get contacted."

"By who?"

"That's the damn point. We want to know who. I'm sure any inquiry you get will be very low-key. You let us know. We take it from there. You're helping us find your father's killer, Roger. Isn't that important to you?"

His eyes teared. He nodded his head.

"Then I'll talk to your boss in Winston-Salem, and I'll speak to Bert Graves. But I don't want you to tell either of them what we're doing. I don't care that Bert is your lawyer, it's strictly between the three of us. I'll release the money and any claim on the Camino. And if there's anything I can do to waive estate restrictions, I will. You should start going through your father's records of accounts payable to find his suppliers. They'll be helpful because they want you to be successful so that you'll be a continuing client. Are we good?"

"What if whoever killed my father is watching me? What if they saw me come in here?"

"Anybody asks you, you came in because your lawyer told you to talk to us about the cash we found in your father's house. That's been resolved. From now on, you talk to Barry. You can do it through the funeral home. People will just think you're settling up your father's affairs." Tommy Lee looked at me. "Can you have Roger pay on some kind of installment plan so there's a record of an ongoing relationship?"

"Yes. That's no problem."

"And if I feel threatened?" Roger asked.

"We pull you out," Tommy Lee promised.

Roger was shaken, but he agreed to do it. Tommy Lee had him sign a receipt for the cash and then we ushered him out the back door.

"You think he's up to it?" I asked when we returned to Tommy Lee's office.

"Not if he gets severely threatened. Then I'll yank him immediately. But I think it will be a light approach, if anything. The smart move would be to leave him alone. That's why I don't think he's in any danger."

"Then why do it?"

"Because we're fishing. The more lines we have in the water, the better chance of a strike."

"What other lines have we got?"

Tommy Lee grinned. "I'm glad you asked that question. How would you feel about going on food stamps?"

I waited until Susan and I had finished supper and we were sitting on the back deck, enjoying the fresh air of a clear, mild evening. I was drinking Chardonnay. Susan, opting for Italian sparkling water, had poured herself a glass of Pellegrino.

I'd planned to talk to her about Mom's newly found resolve to move to a retirement community with Uncle Wayne, but that conversation could wait. Tommy Lee had created a new priority.

When I'd asked Susan the night before to tell me all she ethically could about Robert Sinclair, I'd shared our suspicions about her patient and how he could have broken his leg in Paterson, New Jersey. She confirmed that the injury might have happened as many as twelve hours earlier, but that it had set nicely and she'd released him from her care just last week.

"We've had no new information on the Sinclairs," I said, steering us into the topic I wanted.

"Nothing from Archie?"

"No. And it's not the kind of thing he can push. They'll either go for his idea or not. Or they might go for it but find some other insurance agent to handle it."

"I still don't understand how great an idea it is if one of them has to die to collect the money. I mean I understand why they have to get everything in their new names or else the policies are useless."

"The way Archie explains it, the ownership is the key, not the beneficiary. The owner can cancel the policy and take the cash value, which would create a tax event for anything earned above the initial premium, but then those taxes are settled and the money is clean and paid to the new name. But, the more likely scenario is the owner will borrow cash from the policy. That's not a taxable event. When the insured person dies, the death benefit simply pays off the loan and all taxes are avoided."

"Can Archie monitor the policies?"

"He might be able to if the Sinclairs make him the agent of record. But all this could be happening and still not tie into our investigation of the deaths of Rufus and Sonny. Right now we've got Janet and Robert Sinclair as persons of interest because Archie told them about his pending conversation with Sonny. We've got Roger Taylor running his father's store in the hopes that he might be approached by whomever is behind the EBT card scam. Tommy Lee now wants a third angle explored."

"What?"

"The list of convenience stores we found in the saddlebag of Sonny's motorcycle."

"Sounds like you'll need to go through a federal or state agency."

"That's one avenue, but do you think Tommy Lee is the kind of sheriff who outsources his investigation?"

Susan laughed. "Hardly."

"So, he's asked me to go undercover."

Her laughter abruptly ceased. "What?"

"He wants me to get an EBT card and use it at some of the stores in counties where I won't be recognized."

She set her glass on the deck beside her chair and turned to me. "I don't think that's a good idea at all. Two men were murdered."

"Which is why we've got to get to the bottom of this. Honey, that's my job."

Even in the evening shadows, I could see her jaw clench. I realized how both "Honey" and "that's my job" sounded so condescending. I changed tack. "I'll just be buying stuff. I won't be arresting or confronting anyone on my own. We're just looking for a way in. Tommy Lee hopes Archie, Roger Taylor, or I will catch a break and then he'll move with a full team. That could include the SBI, U.S. Marshals, and whoever else might have a jurisdictional claim. But first we've got to proceed with caution and discretion. At this point, Tommy Lee's fishing and we don't want to scare off the fish."

"At this point?" Susan repeated sarcastically. "Barry, that is the point. You're bait, and you don't know whether you're being dropped into a pool of guppies or sharks."

She picked up her glass of water and went into the house. Democrat padded after her. I guess even my dog was mad at me.

I took a healthy gulp of wine. Susan will cool off, I thought. It was my fault for not using the most tactful tone in sharing my new assignment. I would tiptoe around the eggshells our conversation had created and apologize for dismissing her concern.

I'd talk to Tommy Lee about any safeguards we might employ. The EBT card should be in my real name so I didn't have to remember an alias or worry someone might yell "Barry" in a store. I'd limit myself to counties the farthest away. And I'd have to improvise a subtle approach that didn't raise any suspicion I was an undercover cop.

I drained the wineglass and got up. I didn't want Susan and me going to bed with any anger smoldering between us. I'd bounce these ideas off her and ask for any additional suggestions. In fact, the argument actually made me feel good. It's hard to be angry when you know the other person's action was motivated by only one thing—love for you.

Chapter Fifteen

I met Tommy Lee in his office the next morning at seven. The Mr. Coffee pot was already half gone, letting me know he'd been working for at least an hour. He greeted me with a hot mug and a single photocopy of a list in his handwriting.

"We're accumulating moving parts," he said. "This isn't the big whiteboard like they have on the TV cop shows, but it's good enough for you and me."

I studied the page. At the top he'd written:

> Archie Donovan?

The whole list read...

> Archie Donovan?
> Sinclairs—surveillance, Barry
> Barry and EBT card
> Roger Taylor?
> EBT card records for stores and Toby McKay
> Toby, Sonny, and Rufus financials
> Santona crime family

I read the list a second time. "Why the question mark beside Archie and Roger?"

"Because there isn't much we can do about them. We can only react."

"What about setting up a check-in schedule? Not make it their decision when to report."

He nodded. "All right. Work out what's best for you. I guess the funeral home is still the logical choice."

"You've got me down for surveillance on the Sinclairs. Is that a solo gig?"

"I thought we'd get double mileage out of your undercover role. Archie says Robert Sinclair's a manufacturer's rep. If he travels, you can pick a couple of days at random to see if that's what he really does. And you can make EBT purchases if those travels take you near any of the suspected stores."

I set the list on his desk. "I want to talk about that. There are certain conditions I'd like to discuss."

Tommy Lee pursed his lips and gave me a penetrating one-eyed stare. "Conditions? What? You want combat pay?"

I wasn't going to throw Susan under the bus for worrying about me or even mention the discussion she and I had the night before. "No. Call them safeguards. I want to approach stores that aren't in adjacent counties. It reduces the risk of running into someone I know. And we should get the card in my name, just in case I do cross paths with someone who knows me. With our luck, it will be as I'm checking out."

"All right. We still have to work out the best way to get a card. You can't go applying through our local social services."

"I might have a way around that." I told him about Commissioner James' offer to help.

"Get on it right away," Tommy Lee ordered. "Stress that the fewer people who know about it, the better. What else?"

"Money. We need some way to fund the account."

Tommy Lee rubbed his palm across his unshaven chin. "Right. It's federal money administered by the state. See if James will kick in funds, if he has some discretionary pool that's part of the Department of Agriculture's own budget. I can add a little money. I'd prefer to fund the balance without actually drawing on federal SNAP money. God, a forest would be decimated just to create paper for the government forms we'd have to complete.

Much better if you have a card that links to an account outside the real system."

"Okay. I'll talk it through with James. Once I'm going to these stores, I'll want to let you know when and where I'm entering, in case I don't come out."

He shook his head. "No. Not me. I might be tied up. Make those calls to Marge, and if she's not in, Carol or whoever's on dispatch. Check back no later than thirty minutes after the call."

"That might be a little tight for a productive conversation."

"Forty-five, then. If we're taking safeguards, then make them effective."

"Which brings me to the trickiest part—how to make an overture to break the law." I picked up my mug of coffee, signaling the sheriff I was through talking and wanted his suggestions.

He smiled. "Far be it from me, a lowly county sheriff, to tell a big-city-trained officer how to run his infiltration."

Tommy Lee was teasing me about my experience as a Charlotte police officer before my father's illness brought me back.

"Then what you're telling me is you haven't got a clue?"

"Here's my advice, smart ass. Go into a store with the mindset to get cash or restricted items. You know you're breaking the law, so you'll appear a little nervous. That will make the play seem natural. A two-pronged approach might work. Mix in an item or two forbidden for purchase—a pack of cigarettes or six-pack of beer. See what happens. If he refuses, you can always say you forgot or meant to buy them with cash. If the purchase goes through, then a second approach could be to try to return one of the items for a refund. You could offer to accept less money if the return can be paid in cash rather than credited to your EBT account. Now he's making money and you're making money. Get several documented exchanges like that and then I'll come in and we'll try to flip him. Pressure him to give us someone higher up the food chain."

I stared at Tommy Lee for a few seconds. "For a lowly county sheriff, you're not as dumb as you look."

"I know. People tell me I couldn't be."

"I've got the store I'd like to target with those techniques."

Tommy Lee sat back and thought a second. "Man, I feel sorry for the guy, but you're right, he's probably the most vulnerable."

I knew Tommy Lee had zeroed in on the same target—Wilmer's Convenience Corner and the man whose little girl's cat had been ruthlessly slaughtered.

"He might be afraid not to work out a cash-split," Tommy Lee said. "You could be testing him, making sure he's complying with whatever ultimatum a dead cat represented."

"If he turns, we'll need to protect him."

Tommy Lee's face darkened. "I'm not going to have another Sonny McKay on my hands. I swear to God, I won't."

I said nothing and picked up the list.

The sheriff glanced at his wristwatch. "If you don't have anything else, I suggest you track down Commissioner James as soon as you can so we can get the EBT account rolling."

I did have one more request, the one Susan had insisted upon. "I want a gun. Not my service pistol but a small concealed weapon. Can you make that happen?"

"You'll have it this afternoon. Now go to work."

I went to my cubicle. Seven-thirty. No one else was in the bullpen. Activity would pick up in half an hour. I took the commissioner's card from my wallet. He said to call any time. He probably hadn't thought it would be early the next morning.

I used my cell phone rather than go through the department's switchboard. At this hour, voicemail was my likely destination, and I wanted James' return call to get to me as soon as possible.

To my surprise, a hoarse voice answered, "James here. Good morning."

"Good morning. This is Deputy Barry Clayton. Wayne Thompson's nephew. Sorry to call so early."

"No problem. I've been at my desk since six-thirty. You know how things pile up when you're away. How's your uncle?"

"Much better, thank you. Your visit perked him up."

"Say nothing of it. He's the reason I'm back at my desk. So, how can I help you?"

I briefly highlighted our plan for my undercover role and used Tommy Lee's line about decimating a forest to satisfy the federal paperwork if we ran my EBT card through the official Supplemental Nutrition Assistance Program.

The commissioner understood immediately. "Yes, coordinating that through SNAP would be a bureaucratic nightmare. Our I.T. people should be able to work that out. We'll stripe an EBT card with a routing number and account in my department. I'll authorize a thousand dollars. Keep me posted."

"Thank you, sir. Obviously, we're keeping this close to our chest. At this point we don't know who might be involved. What kind of turnaround do you need?"

"I'd say two days. I'll FedEx the card. You should have it Saturday or Monday. What name should I use?"

"Barry Clayton. I'm trying to keep this simple."

He laughed. "My philosophy, as well. KISS. Keep It Simple Stupid. Every successful politician's mantra. Good luck."

I thanked him for his help and he asked me to give my uncle his best regards. We rang off and I looked at Tommy Lee's list. My undercover work couldn't begin until I had the EBT card. There was only one item I could begin immediately. Surveillance on Robert Sinclair. I realized I hadn't heard Marge's report on the Sinclair house, either an address or date of purchase. I buzzed Tommy Lee.

"What is it now?"

"Commissioner James is already at work. Card will come with a thousand-dollar balance either Saturday or Monday."

"Great." His voice perked up with enthusiasm.

"Meanwhile, I thought I'd see if I can do a little shadowing of Robert Sinclair. Did Marge get the information for the house?"

"Damn. I've got a mind like a steel sieve. Yes, I forgot to share it. The Sinclairs bought the home three and a half years ago. That fits within the timeframe of the Santona conviction. It could take the marshals several months to get the Sinclairs permanent residency. During the grand jury hearing and trial, they would have been shuttled between safe houses."

"What's the address?"

I heard him rustle through some papers.

"2235 Dogwood Circle. That's in Arbor Ridge Estates, off Hendersonville Highway. There's no mortgage lien on the property, so they must own it free and clear."

"What would you think about tagging his car with a GPS tracker? We could use the one we had on Sonny."

"No. Not yet. We don't have enough for probable cause. I don't want to go to a judge till we've got a more compelling argument. Do the best you can by sight. At this stage, I'd rather you lose him than get too close. We'll ramp things up when Ferguson gets me the financials on Toby, Sonny, and Rufus, or if Roger or Archie come through."

"Okay."

"Remember, Barry, when you're fishing there's a time for action and a time for waiting. We're in the part I hate. The waiting."

Waiting. Two hours of sitting in my jeep at a side road about fifty yards from the entrance to Arbor Ridge Estates, waiting for either Janet or Robert Sinclair to appear.

I'd changed from my uniform into jeans and a polo shirt, driven by the Sinclair ranch-style house, and recognized the silver Mercedes Janet had parked at the funeral home back in July. The sedan was in a double carport with a space vacant for a second vehicle. That was at nine o'clock and Robert must have already gone to work.

Now it was eleven and Janet hadn't left and Robert hadn't returned. I'd phoned Marge and asked her to run the Mercedes' plate and see if that information led to the second vehicle. She discovered an Infiniti QX80 SUV registered to the same address. Both were leased by a company called Sinclairity Sales. I assumed Robert must have been a clothing rep who was basically self-employed and had set up a company structure for tax advantages. It might mean Archie's plan could be easily implemented if a corporation already existed that could add the names of their former identities as officers.

For surveillance, Arbor Ridge Estates provided ideal conditions. It wasn't a gated community and it had only one entrance. Unless I fell asleep, the Sinclairs couldn't elude my tracking expertise.

At eleven-fifteen, the silver Mercedes turned onto Hendersonville Highway and headed for Gainesboro. I pulled out and quickly accelerated to the speed limit. Between the curves and rising and falling hills, the car was visible for only short periods. I trusted that as we neared town and traffic increased, I could move closer with less chance of being observed.

At the first stoplight, she made it through the yellow, while I got trapped by the red. Then a unibody truck turned on the road obscuring all sight of her. When the signal cycled to green, I could only cruise slowly and search for the Mercedes among the on-street parking and off-street lots. No sign of the woman. For all I knew she could have driven through town and gone to Asheville. I gave up and swung through the Bank of America branch parking lot, taking the shortest route to the funeral home. On the backside of the building, out of view from the street, I saw her getting into her car. She'd been in the bank. In her right hand she held a manila envelope that was fairly thick and could have contained documents, cash, or both. In those few seconds, I took close notice of her wardrobe—lightweight khaki slacks and a pink blouse. And I made a decision to drop the tail and let her go on about her business. My best move now lay inside the bank.

Across from the row of teller stations, three glass-enclosed offices offered private spaces for financial consultations. Two were occupied by bankers with customers. Cindy Todd, Fletcher's fiancée, was in the third and alone.

She got up as she saw me approach and smiled broadly. "Barry, good to see you. Can I loan you some money?"

"You know we can always use money."

Actually, that wasn't true. The funeral home was marginally profitable, and I had my part-time deputy income and Fletcher had the backing of his family's large funeral home corporation, a corporation that held a minority stake in our ownership and allowed us to get a significant discount on our supplies.

"What can I do for you?"

I shut the door behind me.

The young woman's brow furrowed as she picked up the signal that this wasn't merely a social call.

"Right now I'm not your future husband's business partner. I'm a deputy sheriff and I'd like some information on whatever you might be able to tell me about one of your customers."

She gave a furtive glance out the glass wall, then moved to her chair behind the desk and sat. She indicated I should take one of the two guest chairs. "We have pretty strict rules of confidentiality. I'm not sure how much I can help you."

"This is a police matter, but I don't want you telling me anything that would get you in trouble with your supervisor. Just a few basic questions and you can decline to answer whatever you feel you can't say."

She nodded. "Okay, I'll tell you what I can."

I smiled, trying to put her at ease. "There was a woman who was just in here. She wore a pink blouse and khaki slacks."

"Mrs. Sinclair," Cindy volunteered.

"Yes, is she a regular customer?"

"She's in several times a week."

"Really? Is that kind of frequency unusual? I mean with all the online banking these days?"

"Not for a business with currency deposits."

"Of course," I said, as if I should have known that. "That's for her Sinclairity Sales company."

"I think that's the name. I've only helped her occasionally."

"For a loan?"

Cindy laughed. "I wish. Sometimes when we're not busy, we help the tellers. We schedule them according to customer flow patterns, but a normally less busy time can suddenly be swamped."

I looked over my shoulder at the counter across the lobby. Two tellers were on-duty, and each served a customer. "I guess that's why your walls are glass."

"Yes. We're trained to be aware of what's going on at the windows. In fact, when Mrs. Sinclair was here, I could see she was antsy. So, I helped her."

"Just a few minutes ago?"

"Yes."

"Deposits?"

"Not today. She has a safe deposit box. One of us needs to go in the vault with her. Just to sign her in. We don't observe what she's doing."

"Does that happen often?"

Cindy shrugged. "I really couldn't say. I've assisted her a few times, but I don't think it's as regular an occurrence as her deposits."

"What about a personal checking account?"

Cindy looked uncomfortable at revealing personal customer information. "Maybe. But I'd better not go into her records without clearance."

"Sure. I understand."

"We aren't her only bank," Cindy said, anxious to be helpful. "My girlfriend Tina Logan works at the Wells Fargo branch on the other end of Main Street. She said Mrs. Sinclair has an account there."

"How did that come up?"

"We were at lunch one day and ran into Mrs. Sinclair. We both said hello, and Tina told me afterwards that she was in her branch a few times a week."

"Really?"

"Yes. But that's not unusual. Business owners not only have separate accounts but often use separate banks to keep personal and company funds apart, especially if there are business partners involved."

"Do you know who any of her business partners might be?"

"No."

"Do you know Mr. Sinclair?"

"No. But that doesn't mean he's not on an account with her. Many customers just use the ATM for simple check deposits and withdrawals and rarely come in."

I wanted to ask Cindy who might be on the signature cards for any of their accounts, but knew that would take this conversation into an area beyond a casual chat.

"Thank you." I said. "Let's consider this just between us."

"Has Mrs. Sinclair done anything wrong?"

"Oh, no." I flashed my most innocent grin. "The truth is Mrs. Sinclair promised a ten-thousand-dollar donation to the Boys and Girls Clubs, but we haven't received it yet." That part was true. "I was hoping maybe she'd come in to make those arrangements. I saw her get in her car with a large envelope, and, you know, it's kind of awkward to put pressure on someone for a charity donation."

Cindy seemed relieved by the lie. "She seems nice enough. Maybe that's why she needed to get into the safe deposit box. You know, sell off some bonds or stocks."

"You're probably right. So, again, I wouldn't want her to think I was checking up on her. It's just that the Sheriff's Department was a co-sponsor of the fund drive."

Cindy zipped her lips. "Mum's the word."

As I drove away, I thought how nothing about Janet Sinclair's business at the bank was suspicious in and of itself. But why would a sales rep's company generate cash revenue to be deposited? I assumed Robert Sinclair would be paid a commission by check or wire. And what was in the envelope? That was at least a promising development because my guess and hope were Janet Sinclair had gone to the safe deposit box to retrieve insurance policies. Policies that she would be handing over to Archie Donovan.

Chapter Sixteen

After leaving the bank, I spent a few hours at the funeral home going through paperwork and catching up with Fletcher. I didn't tell him about my conversation with Cindy and would treat it as no big deal if she happened to mention it to him.

Fletcher told me the double funerals for Toby and Sonny McKay were going to be held at Twin Creeks Baptist Church on Monday. There would be only a brief graveside service and the turnout was expected to be small. Fletcher assured me that he and Freddy Mott would be able to handle it.

We were wrapping up our business talk at the kitchen table when he abruptly changed the subject.

"Have you ever priced an elevator or chairlift for the funeral home?"

The question was so off-the-wall I could only stare at him.

"I mean for your mom and Wayne. We all hope your uncle makes a full recovery, but if his balance is a little shaky, Cindy and I worry about him on the stairs."

I hadn't thought about one of those wall-mounted chairlifts, but it was a potential option. An elevator would be pretty expensive and require a good deal of construction.

"No, I haven't priced them." I decided to share Mom's declaration about possibly moving to the Alderway Retirement Community.

"That could be a good thing," Fletcher said. "Especially while they both have their health and can establish some social connections. We had a tough time convincing my grandmother to move to a retirement center. After three weeks, she was mad at my mother for not making her move earlier."

"Well, we'd need to work out the financing. The business leases the property from Mom, and I know she'll need to get her equity out."

Fletcher nodded. "That could be worked out. Why don't you get three independent appraisals? That way a fair offer can be made."

"But we have to decide if either you or I buy it, or we split it, or the business purchases it. What are the housing plans for you and Cindy?"

He laughed. "No offense but I'm pretty sure she doesn't want to live in a funeral home. Initially, we'll be in my rental house. When we buy, I'd like something like you have. Out of town and relatively secluded."

My house was a cabin built from materials salvaged from four historic log homes scattered throughout the Blue Ridge. I didn't build it. A psychiatrist from Charleston purchased five acres of mountain property, assembled the logs into a new structure whose interior contained all the modern conveniences, and then fell ill and had to sell his mountain dream. My place was unique and Fletcher was unlikely to find something similar unless he created it himself.

"But that doesn't mean we couldn't share ownership of this property," Fletcher said. "We'll see how things play out."

"All right," I agreed. "And I'll check on the lift. As a kid, I slid down that bannister. Might be fun riding up."

I left Fletcher and returned to the Sheriff's Department around three. Tommy Lee was in his office scanning through a document.

"Close the door and take a chair," he ordered. "Ferguson gave me the last six months of bank statements for Toby, Sonny, and Rufus."

"Anything stand out?"

"I've just given it a cursory read, but Toby's activity was minimal. An occasional cash deposit and a monthly utility check that often brought the balance close to zero. If he was getting any money from his EBT card, Rufus was paying him in cash. On the other hand, Sonny had regular deposits into his account every two weeks. The auto repair shop paid him by check and the amounts varied slightly. I guess because Sonny worked by the hour."

"Any indication that Harold Carson was paying him additional money under the table?"

"No. And looking at the six-month totals, Sonny earned more than would qualify him for food stamps. He was telling the truth when he said he told his father he didn't want any part of the scam."

"But he knew about it."

"The list we found proves that. And it's believable that he wouldn't turn in his father, especially if hard times forced Toby into his situation."

"What about Rufus?"

Tommy Lee flipped through some pages. "That's more interesting. He had two checking accounts, a business one for the store and a second for his personal finances. The business had a mix of deposits from the major credit cards, EBT card transfers, a few personal checks, and cash. Rufus paid himself a modest salary by check with the proper withholdings. He had some part-time hourly cashiers who were paid by check. Now, we don't know if he was also slipping them cash from the register. I wouldn't be surprised if that were the case and he was avoiding employer payments to Social Security and Workers Comp. After all, that's what he suggested Sonny work out with Harold Carson."

"You think there was enough cash floating around to account for what we found in his closet?"

Tommy Lee set the papers aside. "I doubt it. Especially since he spent a lot of cash on the pickup restoration. So he had to be siphoning off the phony EBT card income somehow. I think that's where the accounts payable come in. Lots of payments to grocery suppliers and vendors. We need to see if they are all legitimate. I'd asked for Ferguson to run the financials on all the stores on Sonny's list, but he claimed that was overreach and he couldn't get the approval to pry into so many private businesses for a fishing expedition."

"It is a fishing expedition."

Tommy Lee threw up his hands. "Of course it's a fishing expedition. That's what I told Ferguson. I'm fishing in a pond with three dead bodies. He was sympathetic but claimed his hands were tied without more proof."

"What about tracking the EBT cards in those stores?"

"Ferguson made the request and was told the FNS would get back to him."

"He had to go through FNS?"

Tommy Lee shrugged. "Food and Nutrition Services is a federal program. They had to be covered. I don't know which will be worse—they say they can't help us or they say they can. Their help always comes with a price, a price that at the minimum means they'll want to meddle in our investigation."

The intercom on Tommy Lee's phone buzzed.

"What?" he asked, letting the line stay on speaker.

"There's a gentleman here to see you," Marge said.

From the tone of her voice we knew the gentleman had to be standing right in front of her.

"I'm tied up with Barry."

"He says to tell you he's an investigator with the Food and Nutrition Services. It's important he speak with you."

Tommy Lee snorted an involuntary laugh. "What did I tell you," he whispered to me. "I'm betting on those dreaded words, 'I'm from the government and I'm here to help you.'" He turned back to the intercom. "Put the gentleman in Interview One. Barry and I will be there in a few minutes."

The sheriff stood. "If this guy's a jerk, I might tell him thanks, but no thanks."

"If anybody can recognize a jerk, it's you."

"I know. So just wait until you see your next performance review."

Our visitor was seated in one of the chairs on the interviewers' side of the table. I didn't know whether he'd done that by chance or whether he was used to conducting interrogations and took it out of habit.

He stood and we shook hands. He introduced himself as Collier Crockett. He wore the standard issue dark blue suit and American flag lapel pin. I guess he didn't want us to forget his FNS credentials were federal. If he wore that wardrobe during an active investigation in the mountains, he'd stick out like a ballerina at a square dance.

Tommy Lee sat beside him and I was left with the suspect's chair. As the sheriff and I had quickly discussed in his office, we said nothing further. We didn't even ask what he wanted.

After about thirty seconds of awkward silence, Crockett said, "I understand you're working a case involving SNAP benefits."

Tommy Lee shrugged. "We're working a double homicide and the motive might be entangled with use of an EBT card."

"And you asked for records of benefit charges at Taylor's Short Stop?"

"Yes. The location of the first murder."

"And now you want benefit transactions for roughly twenty more stores?"

"Through the auspices of the State Bureau of Investigation. Our case overlaps with the attempted murder of Commissioner of Agriculture Graham James."

"But I understand Special Agent Ferguson wasn't able to obtain the necessary authorization for such a sweeping request."

"Then we'll proceed with our own petition."

Crockett's smile morphed toward a sneer. He folded his arms across his chest. "That's not going to happen."

Tommy Lee crossed his arms. "Really? Who made you king of our investigation?"

"Nobody. Pursue your leads but the EBT cards are out of bounds."

Tommy Lee dropped his arms and leaned closer to the FNS agent. "Let's cut the crap. You're running your own investigation and you're afraid we're going to come in like the Keystone Cops and blow up your case."

"Your words, not mine, Sheriff."

"Well, here are some more of my words, Mr. Crockett. You can stick your case where the Carolina moon don't shine, and if I have to haul each one of those store owners into this interview room and ask them to bring their EBT records, I will. Two of my citizens have been murdered and I don't give a rat's ass whether that screws your case or not. Now, I might not be able to force them to supply their records voluntarily, but they'll know they are on my radar and I'll inform them whatever they say will be shared with the SBI. That is unless you climb down off of your goddammed high horse and give me a good reason I shouldn't."

The slick agent went as red as a stoplight. "You're trying to blackmail me," he said with a voice so constricted it was more of a squeak.

"No." Tommy Lee bent in even closer. "Read my lips. I'm pursuing my murder cases down any and all avenues. And if you're blocking my way, I'll do whatever I can to run you over."

Crockett was not only pinned in his chair by Tommy Lee's invasion into his personal space, he was also caught by the sheriff's piercing one-eyed stare. In an instant, it became a battle of wills as to who would look away first. I began to think I might have time to go out for a hamburger.

Finally, Crockett chose a way to save face. He kept his gaze fixed on Tommy Lee's good eye and said, "Let me rewind and start this conversation over."

The sheriff leaned back in his chair. "Okay. We're listening."

"I came to North Carolina about four years ago. Before that I'd worked in New York, New Jersey, and Chicago investigating food stamp fraud. Not the guy who sneaks a bottle of Thunderbird on his card or splits a couple of bucks with a store owner. We were breaking up more sophisticated scams—a network that involved food suppliers, in addition to benefit-recipients and corrupt store owners."

"How'd it work?" Tommy Lee asked.

"Legal purchases would be made and the store owner would get the EBT card's deposit into his account. But the sold products would be restocked. Or sometimes trucked to another store. Keep reselling the same merchandise that you've only paid for once. All EBT receipts were for legally qualified purchases. It's just that the cardholder got cash instead, usually fifty cents on the dollar. And we come down to economy of scale. Too much for a single store owner to organize and finance, but not for a proven business enterprise."

"Like what?" Tommy Lee asked.

"Like the mob. They can redistribute the food, enforce the store agreements with the store owners, and intimidate any wayward customers who might decide to blow the whistle. But that rarely happens because everyone at every level is breaking the law. Once a food stamp user accepts a cash payment, they are part of the conspiracy."

"How do you break it?"

"Get the goods on someone and try to flip them."

"Is that what you're doing here?"

"Well, most of my work was in eastern North Carolina. Undercover. But we were making progress here."

I remembered the newspaper accounts of the busts in that part of the state. I looked at the slick Mr. Crockett and tried to envision him blending into the small tobacco towns that made up the bulk of eastern North Carolina's population.

"How long have you been in this area?" Tommy Lee asked.

"About six months. We've had our eye on Rufus Taylor. His death was a setback."

"Had you turned him?" I asked.

"We were close. I don't know if there was a leak or Toby McKay's rampage spooked someone higher up. We have other things working. That's why I don't want us stepping on each other. I mean I could make a case that your murders should be folded into our investigation, but I'm not going to push for that."

"Because it would be over my dead body," Tommy Lee said.

Crockett smiled. "I believe you've already made that abundantly clear. So, my proposal is you let me take care of the big picture. You look at individual grocery stores where you think there's a link, but not do a sweeping request for information that could swamp you in data analysis but be business as usual for us. I promise you when we nail them, and we will, your murder charge will trump and you can go after them tooth and nail. How's that sound?"

Tommy Lee scowled. "Like I'm putting all my eggs in your basket."

"Maybe. But they're still your eggs."

The sheriff thought for a moment. Crockett was right about our being inundated with EBT receipts that we didn't have the manpower to examine.

"Then who do you think killed Rufus and Sonny?" Tommy Lee asked.

"Outside muscle. Probably Chicago. We found ties between them and the rings we busted down east. You know how it is, Sheriff. It's like squeezing a balloon. Control a bulge in one place and it pops out in another. I might be wrong but I think that bulge might have appeared in your backyard."

"So, you don't know for sure that the mob is even here."

"No. But unless your homicides are some Hatfield and McCoy feud, I'm betting we turn something up. I just want to make sure we don't stumble over each other in the process."

Tommy Lee looked at me. "What do you think?"

I didn't know whether I was supposed to play good cop or bad cop. So, I gave an honest answer. "Give Mr. Crockett his run with the overall EBT conspiracy. I'll follow up on local connections we have to Sonny and Rufus."

"That's fine," Crockett quickly agreed. "And let's keep lines of communication open. If I find a connection to your murders, you'll be the first to know."

Tommy Lee stood. "All right. Let's hope each of us gets justice served."

"Good." Crockett rose and shook Tommy Lee's hand. "Sorry I came on a little strong. I'm passionate about my work, and I respect that you are too. I look forward to working with both of you."

Tommy Lee escorted Collier Crockett out of the department. I went straight to his office, knowing he'd want to debrief the meeting.

"What do you think?" I asked when he returned.

"I think that if Mr. Crockett sent his DNA to ancestry.com it would come back ten percent human and ninety percent horse shit. He's either just starting and wants to pump us for all we know, or he's well down the road and doesn't want us getting any credit for his bust. But, I'm willing to play along where the EBT records are concerned. We probably couldn't get them, and the analysis could be beyond our capabilities. We'll see how forthcoming he is. Meanwhile, Commissioner James has your card coming and we keep to our original plan. Nothing's changed there."

He walked behind his desk and slid open one of the side drawers. He pulled out a holster attached to a thin nylon belt. "Here's the gun you asked for. It's a Kimber Ultra RCP II. One of the smallest forty-fives you can carry. Seven shot magazine and weighs only twenty-five ounces. Three-inch barrel so you'll need close range but it has the punch to knock someone over if you hit any part of the body. Shoot at least fifty rounds at the range so you're comfortable with it. I figure you don't want a shoulder holster. This rig works under your shirt and around your waist to fit the small of your back. The holster straps are Velcro so you just yank the pistol free. I can get you an ankle holster if you prefer."

I took the gun and rested it in the palm of my hand. "What's RCP stand for?"

"Refined Carry Pistol. Just a marketing term. But you're refined, right?"

"As smooth as Collier Crockett."

Tommy Lee groaned. "Oh, please."

My cell rang. I pulled it from my belt. "It's Archie."

"Better take it."

"Hey, Archie. I'm with Tommy Lee. What's up?"

"They came in." Archie was so excited the three words came out as one."

"The Sinclairs?"

I saw Tommy Lee's eyebrows arch.

"Yes. They have a company. Sinclairity Sales. Only now they've added two additional corporate officers. Do the names Robert and Joan Santona mean anything?"

"Indeed, they do." I put Archie on speaker and repeated the names for Tommy Lee.

"Where are you now?" Tommy Lee asked.

"My office. Do you want to see these papers?"

"Yes. But don't bring them here. Barry and I will meet you at the funeral home at…" he glanced at his watch "…at five."

"Okay."

"Archie," Tommy Lee said.

"Yes?"

"Good work."

"Thank you, Sheriff."

I disconnected. "That's an interesting development."

"Yes. But not conclusive of anything. Remember, we're following this lead because Archie told them he would be speaking to Sonny McKay. But if this operation is being run out of Chicago, then the plan to hit Rufus was already in the works. And the Sinclairs wanted this insurance work done back in July. We know that's a fact because Archie missed the meeting."

"So, what are you saying? That Toby's attempt on James and Rufus' murder just happened to occur on the same day?"

"I have to recognize it's a possibility. I just don't want us getting ahead of ourselves."

"What do you suggest?"

Tommy Lee sighed. "Well, we already have the SBI and FNS involved. Hell, we might as well bring in the U.S. Marshals. Next it will be the FBI, the Park Rangers, and the security guards at Walmart."

"Those guys are good. Could be a career move if you ever lose an election."

"Nah. I've got my heart set on Costco."

Chapter Seventeen

Tommy Lee, Archie, and I sat in the parlor with three untouched glasses of Diet Coke on the coffee table in front of us. The sheriff and I were in chairs, and Archie had his briefcase open on the sofa cushion next to him.

"The three policies are from three different insurance companies." Archie passed them to Tommy Lee. "I have brokerage arrangements with each, so what forms I didn't have on file I was able to download."

Tommy Lee gave the policies a quick look, trusting Archie to understand the meaning of all the fine print.

"They are what the Sinclairs described," Archie explained. "Joan Santona owns a policy on Robert Santona's life and is the beneficiary. He owns one on Joan and is the beneficiary, and the second-to-die policy is owned by Joan with the ASPCA as the beneficiary."

"Why does the wife own that one?" Tommy Lee asked.

"No particular reason. Statistically, she should outlive her husband. And since much of the premium came from her inheritance, she probably wrote the checks."

"How much coverage do they have?" I asked.

"Because of the actuarial tables, Robert Santona's death benefit is about fifty thousand dollars less than Joan's, but all three policies are just shy of three million in total face value and close to a million in surrender cash value."

Tommy Lee passed me the policies. "And the corporate papers?"

Archie lifted a document from the briefcase and handed it to the sheriff. "They've made changes by adding their former identities, Joan and Robert Santona, to the list of corporate officers. They also designated the death benefits to go to the company, Sinclairity Sales. That works out great because the Sinclairs are actually the sole owners."

I followed Archie's narrative and while I thought I understood, a question popped into my mind. "But the name of the insured would have to stay the same, right?"

"Yes. Otherwise, a different person has different health conditions and is potentially a different age, so changing the insured couldn't happen under the same policy. They'd have two choices. The owner could surrender the policy and get the cash minus the taxes due, or the owner could obtain a false death certificate for the Santona name and claim that person had died. To collect the second-to-die, both Santonas would need death certificates. Collecting the benefits gives them a lot more money and it comes into the company tax-free. That's harder to pull off. The insurance companies want a death certificate with a raised seal, not a copy. Some also want an obituary from the newspaper."

"Did the Sinclairs ask you about that?" Tommy Lee asked.

"Yes. Robert said it as a joke, but I think he was serious. I wouldn't know where to get a false death certificate, but since fake passports and driver's licenses exist, they could probably find a source somewhere."

"Would the false claim have to come through you?" I asked.

"It could, or the owner could deal with the insurance company's service center directly. Usually the agent of record is sent a death claim kit to assist the beneficiary. There's an ulterior motive. The company wants to keep us close to the money so we can possibly put the funds into another of their products, like an annuity."

"What did you say when they asked about the fake death certificate?"

"I laughed and said I knew they were still alive, and then there was a little bit of awkward silence."

I bet there was, I thought. Robert Sinclair was clearly angling to collect the full death benefit on all the policies.

Tommy Lee handed the corporate document back to Archie. I returned the policies.

"Those ready to go?" Tommy Lee asked.

"Yes," Archie said. "I told them I'd FedEx them tonight."

The sheriff checked his watch. "Then you need to do that. When's last pickup?"

"Six. But I can drive to Asheville if I miss it. Final pickup there is eight."

"It's five-thirty now," Tommy Lee said. "We'd better let you go. Anything else?"

Archie nodded. "Yes. Before I came here, I ran a history on the policies. Each was an aggregate of smaller ones consolidated within the same company. That's permissible. Each was originally purchased as three one-hundred-thousand-dollar contracts. They were all taken out within the same year, which is unusual. That was five years ago."

"Why would they do that?" Tommy Lee asked.

"Lower profile. Not as big an initial policy that might create more scrutiny. Funds could have been drawn from different banks without writing a big check. At least that's my guess. I backtracked this history after the Sinclairs left. They don't know I did so."

"Will the policy changes come back to you?" I asked.

"Yes. I believe everything will be turned around by the middle of next week."

"Good," Tommy Lee said. "Then I'll want you to mail them that completed paperwork. Avoid seeing either of them if you can. At least until we clarify what role, if any, they played in the murders."

Tommy Lee's concern echoed my own. "Did you get Gloria and the girls to Weaverville?" I asked.

"Yes."

"As soon as you get those documents back, you join them."

"Barry's right," Tommy Lee emphasized. "You'll no longer be their insurance agent, you'll be their loose end."

I used the funeral home's Xerox machine to make copies of Archie's paperwork. Then we sent him on his way, urging him to work away from the office. I knew he got the message when he handwrote instructions that the executed documents were to be returned to his mother-in-law's address. His secret mission was over and he was taking no more chances.

Tommy Lee reached for his Coke; the ice had all but melted. He took a long swallow and wiped his lips with the back of his hand. "What do you think?"

"We still don't have any connection between the Sinclairs and our murder victims. The insurance angle appears more relevant to their past lives than the activities of Rufus and Sonny. If Robert Sinclair is actually a rep for sportswear, it's not the kind of product that would put him in contact with grocery and convenience store owners."

"No, but his sales territory could overlap. I think we've got enough for us to make an unannounced visit on Luther Brookshire tomorrow."

"Who's he?"

"A U.S. Marshal in the Western District of North Carolina. His office is in Asheville, but I have his home address. Six-thirty ought to be late enough so that we don't appear rude."

"You're going to pound on a U.S. Marshal's door at dawn?"

Tommy Lee grinned. "Only if there's no doorbell."

At six twenty-five, Tommy Lee pulled into the driveway of a brick ranch in the Beaver Lake area north of Asheville and parked behind a dew-coated green Ford Escape SUV. I was holding a file with all the information we'd been able to gather on the Sinclairs—from the purchase of their home to the transfer of the insurance policies. We also had what information we could collect on the Santona crime family.

I'd worked late at the department going through law enforcement data banks, New Jersey newspapers, and whatever Internet sources seemed credible. What was most intriguing was the speculation that Bobby Santona's son, Robert, might have been murdered just before the older Santona was arrested. Or he had gone into hiding to avoid similar charges. We now knew both those conjectures were wrong.

As I followed Tommy Lee up the front walk, I noticed a bumper sticker on the Escape that read, "Semper Fi."

"Brookshire was a Marine?"

"Yes," Tommy Lee said. "An MP. He went into police work before becoming a marshal."

"You sure you want to wake up a Marine? Maybe you ought to phone and give him a two-minute warning. No sense waking up the whole household."

"He is the whole household. Luther and his wife split about two years ago. Casualties of the job."

I knew the long, irregular hours of law enforcement took their toll on a married couple. I'd vowed to Susan that if we ever headed down that path, the deputy duties would go. I'd bury bodies, not our marriage.

Fortunately, for Brookshire's neighbors, there was a doorbell and Tommy Lee didn't need to announce our presence with a booming knock. He pressed the button several times and we heard a corresponding buzz echo through the house.

"Hold your horses! I'm coming." The raspy, shouted words sounded like the speaker's first ones of the morning.

Tommy Lee bent over and picked up the newspaper lying by the threshold.

Luther Brookshire threw open the front door and squinted against the light. He looked to be in his late forties and wore a pale blue terrycloth robe loosely tied around his waist. His brown hair was streaked with gray and retreating from his forehead.

"Tommy Lee. What the hell's going on?"

"Training a new deputy how to serve papers." The sheriff handed Brookshire the *Asheville Citizen-Times*.

The marshal laughed in spite of himself. "You son of a bitch. Come in and I'll make some coffee. Although I doubt I want to wake up and hear whatever troubles you've brought to my doorstep."

While the pot brewed, Brookshire put on clothes. Then we sat around the kitchen table, and, after Tommy Lee and our surprised host caught up on old times, Brookshire asked, "What do you need? I assume you're working something that's crossed my path."

"Not something, somebody."

"Oh? Who?"

"Your friend Robert Santona and his wife, Joan."

Brookshire's eyes flickered slightly as he tried to fake a quizzical expression. "Is this the guy supposedly killed in New Jersey? I think his father was convicted on racketeering charges."

"No. This is the guy parading around my county as Robert Sinclair. The one who might have whacked a key witness in my murder investigation Monday night."

Brookshire nearly choked on his coffee. "You know I can't confirm or deny something like that."

"I'm not asking you to. I have the proof." Tommy Lee nodded to me.

I set the file on the table, opened it, and then slid the contents to the marshal. "He told an informant he was in WITSEC. Here are some insurance policies that he evidently hid back from your people and is now trying to get at the cash values. My informant also happened to mention the name of our witness, the witness who was executed in his bed that night."

Brookshire rapidly scanned through the documents. "Interesting. Let's say, hypothetically, Robert Sinclair is who you say he is."

"Who *he* says he is," Tommy Lee corrected.

"All right. Who he says he is. What motive would he have? Was your witness a threat to anyone else? Did this informant leak to anyone else?"

Tommy Lee gave Brookshire a broad-stroke summary of the food stamp scam case. He shared the network of stores, the threats to store owners, and the potential cover Robert Santona's job offers in that he travels throughout the region.

Brookshire shook his head. "All circumstantial. I don't hear anything that ties him to any wrongdoing. And if he is Robert Santona and you expose him, then his blood will be on your hands."

"Like I said, he is Santona. But neither I, nor Barry, nor our informant have said anything to compromise his new identity. He's done that to himself."

Brookshire waved a hand dismissively over the file. "What? Because his name appears on some policy and as an officer of an obscure company no one's even looking for?"

"No. Because Robert Santona went back to Paterson, New Jersey, for his father's funeral. He tried to hide in a tree, fell out, broke his leg, and then escaped from his pursuing family members by the skin of his teeth."

"What?" This time Brookshire wasn't faking his bewilderment.

"Yep. Barry's wife's a doctor and she set the broken bone. So, Santona alone shot to hell any little rumors that the marshals or the prosecutors started about his being a vanished murder victim. The only blood on my hands will belong to my informant if word leaks out that we know Robert Sinclair's true identity." Tommy Lee pointed to the file. "An identity we could have discovered only through those documents."

Brookshire stood and paced the kitchen. "Let's say Robert and Joan Santona are protected witnesses. What do you want me to do about it?"

"Nothing," Tommy Lee said. "Absolutely nothing."

Brookshire stopped and threw up his hands. "Then why the hell are you brightening my morning?"

"Look, Luther. If we start getting close to your guy and he is dirty—"

"He's not my guy."

"Okay. Hypothetically, if he is your guy and he knows he's screwed up, I figure he'll come running to you for help. I don't want you whisking him and his wife away into another set of identities. I don't know what damning information he gave on his father, but your WITSEC witness brought organized crime from Jersey to Gainesboro. And created a pile of bodies in the process. Bodies whose blood is on the hands of the U.S. Marshals. So, when he shows up, you'll tell him he's imagining things. Or if he's admitting to a crime, you, as a sworn officer of the law, will have to arrest him and turn him over to the appropriate jurisdiction. In other words, you'll hand his ass to me."

"All right, hypothetically speaking. But from what I've heard from…how shall I say it?…from unnamed sources, your theory overlooks one important fact."

"What's that?" Tommy Lee asked.

"Your food stamp scam demonstrates a very clever and creative mind behind it. Robert Santona has never been accused of being the brightest bee in the hive. So there's a good chance he has nothing to do with this whole thing. I don't want his blood on my hands because I didn't make that clear. An IQ that hovers slightly above room temperature isn't going to mastermind such a complex operation. That fact I can unequivocally confirm."

"All right," Tommy Lee said. "Then we'll also keep our eyes open for other bees."

"You do that." Brookshire's words carried the tone of an order, not a suggestion. "And if any of this heads back my way, I'd appreciate being in on the sting."

Tommy Lee shook his hand. "Then I guess we're done."

"Yes," Brookshire replied. "And you were never here."

Chapter Eighteen

We returned to Gainesboro a few minutes after eight. Friday morning traffic was light since most vehicles were headed into Asheville. During the drive, Tommy Lee and I laid out our plans for going forward. I'd try to get in position to follow Robert Santona, aka Sinclair, as he left his home. I'd also check in with Roger Taylor, and although Ferguson and the SBI had given us his father's bank statements, Tommy Lee thought it wise to see the actual books and any files of payables and receivables that Roger might find as he immersed himself in the convenience store's business.

My undercover role as a food stamp recipient would begin as soon as my EBT card arrived from Commissioner James. Then my next step would be to approach Buddy Smith, the owner of Wilmer's Convenience Corner.

As we neared the department, I asked, "Why didn't you press Brookshire for more information on what Robert Santona had provided that enabled him to enter WITSEC?"

"Because I pushed him as far as I could. He went as close to admitting the Santonas were in the program as I could expect. The marshals follow a strict adherence to protecting their witnesses' anonymity. Luther now knows I found the information elsewhere. I'll first pursue anything I can get on the Santona family and their operations in New Jersey. Lindsay Boyce will be good for that. Meanwhile, I think we should continue to refer to them as the Sinclairs. Less chance anyone could overhear the name Santona."

Special Agent Lindsay Boyce was resident agent for the FBI's Western North Carolina district. She was also Tommy Lee's niece.

Tommy Lee pulled the patrol car into his reserved spot. "If I think I need more than Lindsay can provide, I'll circle back to Luther. He left the door open when he said he wanted in on any sting."

"You trust him to put our case first?"

Tommy Lee opened the driver's door and then leaned back toward me. "Hell no. I'll give him a heads-up just as we start to move on Sinclair. Minimal lead time with little chance for him to jump the gun. Once we've made our bust, Luther will want to keep his hands off and trust me not to embarrass him or the marshals. He knows we're friends even though I think the WITSEC program is a mixed bag. It has unleashed violent criminals on unsuspecting communities. Robert Sinclair's not the first one to have gone back to a life of crime. So, I'm not counting on any help from Luther, not when I've got ace detective Barry Clayton hot on Sinclair's tail."

"Thanks for putting it all on me."

"You're welcome. You know the old saying."

I groaned as I knew what was coming. "I do. So don't say it."

He did anyway. "Barry Clayton. Undertaker. The last man ever to let you down."

I pulled onto the edge of the side road and parked where I'd been the day before. It was eight-thirty and the ground was free of morning mist, giving me a clear view of the entrance to Arbor Ridge Estates. I placed a quick call to Mom's cell phone. She reported that Uncle Wayne had a good night and was being transferred to the rehab floor later in the morning. They'd do an evaluation, prescribe a course of physical therapy, and hopefully have him ready for discharge early next week.

She dropped her voice to a whisper. "Your uncle's in the bathroom but I want you to know we had a talk last night."

"About what?"

"I brought up the subject of moving to Alderway. I put the need more on me. The physical strain of going up and down the stairs. I told him I'd had some near falls."

"You've had near falls?"

"No. But you know how proud your uncle is."

"Yes. I also know you never want to be a bother, so I hope you'd tell me if something like that was happening."

"It's not. But why not take proper steps while I'm in control?"

"What did Uncle Wayne say?"

"That he'd think about it."

The answer surprised me. I'd expected my uncle to build up an instant defense like when Mom pushed him to sell his house and move into the funeral home. But then I remembered she'd used the same argument, that having her brother live with her would be better for her safety.

"So, he might mull it over for a while?"

"I don't think so. A unit's available the first of October. That's less than four weeks away. Another one like it might not be available any time soon."

I wasn't sure what to say. Things were speeding up and I hoped Mom wasn't rushing a decision because of Uncle Wayne's condition. Before I could respond, a reflected flash of sunlight swept across my jeep. I looked down the road and saw Robert Sinclair's SUV turn onto the highway and head away from me.

"Mom. Sorry, I've got to go. Let's talk this weekend."

"Okay. But don't worry, Barry. It's going to work out." She hung up.

I started the jeep and jammed down the accelerator, spinning the tires as the vehicle fishtailed onto the blacktop. Within a quarter mile, I had Sinclair's charcoal Infiniti QX80 in sight. I braked to slightly over the fifty-five-miles-per-hour speed limit so as not to come up behind him too fast, but I dared not lag too far behind in case a truck pulled in between us, obscuring my view. I didn't want a repeat of what had happened when I followed his wife.

Sinclair turned right onto a two-lane road leading away from Gainesboro. His logical destination was I-26 running west to Asheville or east toward Charleston, South Carolina. Tracking him on an interstate would be easier than navigating traffic on a county road. With no traffic, I would stand out; too much and I could get stopped by a school bus or slowed by some farm vehicle that cropped up between us.

I knew Sinclair's territory included counties in both North and South Carolina, and so I wasn't surprised when he took the eastbound access ramp. Once on I-26, I stayed about a quarter mile behind, only drawing closer as we neared exits. We crossed the state line and headed into the interchanges around Spartanburg. I pushed the jeep closer to make sure I didn't get trapped in a wrong lane. He left I-26 for I-85 and then took I-585 headed into downtown Spartanburg. Trailing him through the city could be difficult as I didn't know the street patterns if we became separated.

We were on the outskirts when he pulled into a strip shopping center and parked in front of a store with a sign reading ActiveStyle. The show window featured manikins outfitted in tennis, golf, yoga, and other light sportswear. The variety appeared to exclude extreme sports or heavy-duty hiking and rock-climbing in favor of garments with more fashion-oriented designs.

I pulled into a space in front of a nail salon with six empty parking spots between us. Since I'm not much for manicures and pedicures, I waited in the jeep, angling to look across at Robert Sinclair as he climbed out of the SUV.

Climbed was the word because his short height meant the step down was more of a jump. I, of course, attributed his successful maneuver to Susan's surgical skills.

Sinclair couldn't have been over five-four with a rotund body that made him a matching bookend for Mayor Sammy Whitlock. He wore a yellow polo shirt over khakis, probably lines of clothing he represented. His black hair was thin on top and the light breeze lifted the errant strands making his round head look like an upside-down jellyfish. This was the man who scrambled up a tree? It must have been more of an overgrown shrub. I thought about his very attractive wife, Janet Sinclair, and what an odd couple they made. Maybe he wasn't so short and tubby when he was standing on his wallet.

He went to the rear of his vehicle and I saw that the hatch door had already opened. He grabbed a hanging bag and a briefcase, fumbled with his key fob, and clicked the remote to close the hatch and lock the car. Then he disappeared into the store.

In addition to the nail salon, the shopping strip housed a yoga studio, a Chinese restaurant that probably wouldn't open for hours, and a dry cleaner. I had no clue how long it would take Sinclair to present his wares so I was stuck without an option other than to stay in the jeep. However, ActiveStyle was an end store and I spotted a few parking places along the side. Moving the jeep there would put me in a less-visible position where I could still see the rear of the Infiniti. I parked facing out and waited.

It was nearing ten o'clock. Roger Taylor was probably at his father's store. I dialed his cell.

"Yeah," he answered.

"It's Barry. I need you to do something for me."

"What's that?" He sounded wary.

"When you go through your father's business papers, bring me any files or ledgers that document his accounts receivable and payable. We need to match them to the bank statements."

"I'm at his office now. The one in the back of the store. He's got a couple of old metal file cabinets. You know, the vertical ones. I was just starting to go through them."

My plan to have him bring any ledgers to the funeral home changed on the spot. "Is the store open?"

"No. I put a sign in the window saying we'd be closed till at least Monday."

"Good. You can go through whatever you need to, but don't throw anything out. I'll come to you tonight. Say, eight?"

"Okay. But why at night?"

"I'd feel better if you weren't seen with me. I'll park behind the store. Have the back door open."

"It's your party, Deputy. Just keep me safe." He hung up.

Ten minutes later, Sinclair loaded up his samples in the rear of the Infiniti and drove away. I followed him to four similar stores, all specialty retailers that weren't affiliated with national or regional chains. During his sales calls, he visited only one convenience store and it wasn't on our list. He pumped gas, went inside, and was out less than five minutes later with a jumbo drink, Slim Jim, and a package of Twinkies. Lunch in search of a heart attack.

We were south of Spartanburg when he returned to I-26 and headed for Gainesboro. I stayed with him until he took the exit closest to his home. I drove on to the main exit for Gainesboro.

Tommy Lee was in his office reviewing budget figures. He looked up as I knocked. "How'd it go?"

"If you need a new jogging suit, I can find you the best deals."

He rolled back from his desk and patted his stomach. "Make it a jiggle suit and I'll take you up on it. So, nothing suspicious?"

"No. Looks like he was doing his job." I gave Tommy Lee a detailed report including the observation that Robert Sinclair must have looked like a giant pear if he was indeed in the tree in the Paterson cemetery.

When I finished, Tommy Lee sat thinking for a few minutes.

"He might have things so well organized that he doesn't make collections like some mafia bagman," he said.

"Or at least doesn't make those rounds every day. He has to be successful enough in his job to keep his manufacturers with him."

"So, what do you suggest?"

"Maybe he handles the food stamp fraud on the weekends. I'll stake him out one more day and then move on to my undercover role when the EBT card comes."

Tommy Lee nodded. "All right. What about Roger Taylor?"

"I spoke with him this morning. He said there's an old filing cabinet in the store office. I'm going to look through it tonight at eight."

"You want me with you?"

"No. He's keeping the store closed till Monday. I'm going to park my car around back."

"If you're worried about someone seeing your jeep, why don't you let me drop you off? You can call me when you're finished."

His plan had merit, and I also knew he'd be anxious to learn what I'd discovered.

"Thanks. But I'd prefer to have dinner with my wife. It's been a hectic week."

"Then take her someplace nice," Tommy Lee ordered. "And call me after you see Roger Taylor."

With a short window for dinner, I could think of no place nicer than home. I stopped at Fresh Market and bought two ribeye steaks, lettuce and other vegetables for a salad, and a carrot cake, which I also counted as a vegetable. Then I chose a bottle of Malbec that I knew Susan would enjoy. This weekend she wasn't on call.

I beat her home, fed Democrat at five, and started the charcoal. I was tossing the salad when she arrived at five-thirty.

"What's going on? What have you done with my husband?"

"That debonair fellow has to work tonight. I'm here to see that your evening isn't a total loss."

She kissed me on the lips. "And when does my debonair husband get home?"

"He's meeting Roger Taylor at eight and it might be close to midnight." I gave her the plan to go through Rufus Taylor's business files.

"So, I'm afraid we have to eat earlier than usual. I've opened a bottle of Malbec to get you started."

"Are you having some?"

"No. Not when I've got to work."

"Then let's both have sparkling water. A full glass of red wine and a voluptuous woman will be waiting for you."

"Where are you going?"

She gave me an elbow. "In search of that debonair man."

We ate on the deck, the evening air was fresh and cool, and I regretted setting the appointment with Roger Taylor. I told her of the brief conversation with my mother and my uncle's willingness to consider moving to the retirement community.

"What would you think about moving into the funeral home?" she asked.

"You're kidding?"

"No. Maybe we should consider it."

I looked around me. The forest was alive with crickets. Dusk deepened the shadows and the stars would soon be bright in the dark sky.

"Don't you like it here? Do you regret selling your condo?"

Before our marriage, Susan had lived in a condo close to the hospital. She'd sold it six months ago.

"It's beautiful here," she said. "And the condo wouldn't have made sense. Too small and you have no family connection to it. I'm just saying that if we need to do something like that for your mother and Uncle Wayne, I'm willing to discuss it. I could put the equity from my condo sale into helping buy the funeral home from your mother."

Her proposal caught me completely off guard. I was touched by her willingness to help in a way even I hadn't considered.

"I told Mom we'd talk about it this weekend. Let's see what she's thinking before we suggest any possible options."

She reached across the table and squeezed my hand. "Fine. But I want you to know we're in this together. As a family."

She sent me on my way at seven with a kiss and a promise not to run off with my debonair double.

A few minutes before eight, I drove my jeep behind Taylor's Short Stop. I knocked on the back door. Roger opened it immediately.

"You been here all day?" I asked.

"Pretty much. I ran out for a burger at lunch. Even though the sign says closed, people saw my car and kept stopping to give their condolences." He smiled. "Guess we should have had the funeral here at the store."

"That's the way everybody knew your father."

Roger led me along a back aisle to the office on the other side of the restrooms.

"Anybody seem a little strange?" I asked.

"No. I had a couple truck drivers stop. You know, the guys who deliver snacks and soft drinks. I told them not to start restocking till next week."

He stepped into the small office. There was a desk with one rolling metal chair and a battle-gray file cabinet. On the floor behind the chair stood a small safe.

I pointed to it. "You know the combination?"

"No. I looked through the desk drawers, even pulled them out and turned them over hoping he might have written it down somewhere. I tried his birthday, my birthday, my mom's birthday. No luck. Guess I'll have to get the lock drilled out."

"What if I get a warrant to authorize us to search the safe? We'll get it open for you."

"But will you take whatever's inside?"

"Not if it doesn't relate to our case."

Roger was probably thinking of the cash we'd found in his father's closet and the possibility that the safe held a similar stash.

"And I could get a court order without your cooperation." I realized when we thought the safe hadn't been robbed, we'd ignored what might be its contents.

"Okay," Roger grumbled. "When will that happen?"

"Maybe tomorrow. Maybe Monday. I'll talk to the sheriff." I moved closer to the file cabinet. "Anything unusual in here?"

Roger pulled out the top drawer. "Nah. He's got copies of all the invoices by vendor, and they're in order with most recent at the front of each hanging folder. The middle drawer holds his checkbook and bank statements, and the lowest drawer has taxes and payroll records. Take a look."

He slipped by me and I looked at the top drawer. The first two folders were payables and receivables. There were no receivables. I guessed since he sold everything over the counter, there was nothing that he sent in the way of bills to others. Perhaps he kept the file for any vendor credits that he might be due. Payables held about fifteen invoices for grocery and other products stocked in the store. These were yet to be paid. I pulled the front sheet from a folder labeled "Aimes Distributors" and saw the invoice was stamped "paid" and a check number was handwritten under the invoice total.

I closed the top drawer and opened the one beneath it. I found the most recent bank statement, looked up the check number and saw that the amount matched the amount of the Aimes Distributors invoice.

I handed the statement to Roger. "Okay, here's what we're going to do. I'll call out the check numbers on the invoices and you tell me the amount posted."

"What are we looking for?"

"Anything that doesn't match." I flipped to the folder after Aimes. "Appalachian Brewers. Check number 1508."

"Two hundred dollars, eighty-five cents."

"Correct."

We moved through the recently paid invoices one at a time, each check matching the billed invoice perfectly. Then I found an invoice for Staples Sources. No total was on the invoice and the description was for miscellaneous non-perishables. That could be anything—canned goods, a quart of oil, a bottle opener, or suntan lotion.

"Find the most recent check to Staples Sources," I told Roger.

"I'll need the actual checkbook and stubs," he said.

I passed him the three-ring book and he flipped through backwards from the first unwritten check.

"Here's one from August twenty-first for four-hundred seventy-five dollars."

I looked at the date of the invoice. August twentieth. Fast mail service, if the bill was actually generated that day. The billing address for the company was a post office box in Spartanburg. Not impossible. I looked at the second invoice in the Staples Sources folder. This one did have an amount. Three hundred eighty-six dollars, thirteen cents. The date was August thirteenth with the check written on the fourteenth. The purchased items were identified exactly the same as on the first invoice—miscellaneous non-perishables. I continued going back through the bills. Where most of the others had been a monthly itemized statement, these were weekly and sent every Monday with payment made the next day. Rufus was certainly moving a lot of non-perishable items, or they were sitting on the shelf, being sold and resold as they were fraudulently rung up on the register and swiped for payment through the EBT system.

Staples Sources certainly deserved scrutiny. But how were the amounts paid determined? Some EBT purchases would be legitimate. Rufus must have had some system for tracking the illicit money that came into the store's bank account via the electronic transfer. I looked down at the safe. Would it contain those records? Or had Rufus Taylor's killer forced him to turn them over and then executed him?

Chapter Nineteen

I phoned Tommy Lee as soon as I left Taylor's Short Stop and gave him the information about the safe and the unusual number of invoices from Staples Sources. He agreed to seek a warrant to search the safe's contents and would authorize drilling out the lock. While he took charge of that aspect of the investigation, I would stake out the Sinclairs and see if Robert's weekend pattern included making stops at convenience stores.

Having no clue as to when Robert Sinclair might leave home on Saturday morning, I decided I should drive by his house to make sure I didn't sit all day at my surveillance spot only to see him return in the evening. So, at seven-thirty, I cruised slowly by his driveway. Both Janet's Mercedes and the Infiniti were in the carport. The SUV's hatch was open and a golf bag leaned against the rear bumper. One or both of them appeared to be getting ready to hit the links.

I returned to my spot down the road from the entrance to their neighborhood. About twenty minutes later, the Infiniti emerged on the main road and headed toward me. I ducked and peered beneath the steering wheel as the vehicle passed. Robert Sinclair was the sole occupant. I followed from a safe distance until he turned into the main entrance of the Gainesboro Country Club. The manufacturer's rep business must be successful. A Mercedes, an Infiniti, and a country club membership. The funeral business wasn't so lucrative.

Since I was neither a golfer nor a member of the club, I couldn't just saunter in and checkout Sinclair's golfing partners. I also couldn't sneak along the fairways, scurrying from tree trunk to tree trunk like some demonic squirrel.

I drove to a second entrance closer to the tennis courts, looped back toward the bag drop-off zone as if I'd come from another direction, and saw Sinclair lift his clubs out of the SUV and place the bag in a rack along the sidewalk. He waved to three men sitting at an outdoor table, each one holding a steaming mug of coffee. Their outfits, including Sinclair's, looked like the designer had combined every color from a palette labeled "neon."

Sinclair climbed up behind the wheel and drove to a parking area about fifty feet away. I exited through the main entrance and then circled in again from the tennis courts. Sinclair and his three buddies were at the table, talking and laughing as they waited for their tee time. They paid me no attention as I went to the parking lot and cruised by the vehicles. I suspected none of the luxury cars cost less than forty-thousand dollars. The Jaguar next to Sinclair's Infiniti had South Carolina plates and the bumper sticker—"I do it in ActiveStyle." Clients, I thought. Sinclair's on an outing with his clients. I suspected they'd play a round of eighteen holes and top off the morning with lunch and a round of Bloody Marys.

I decided to return to the Sinclair residence and keep tabs on Janet. If there was an innocent chance I could run into her at a grocery store or downtown shop, I'd speak to her. She'd originally contacted me at the funeral home so exchanging a few words or even striking up a conversation would be a natural thing to do.

Again, I didn't want to be waiting in my surveillance spot if she'd already left. I made a slow pass by her home and received an unexpected shock. Parked in front of the carport was a green Ford Escape with the bumper sticker, "Semper Fi." U.S. Marshal Luther Brookshire was in the Sinclairs' house. Was he warning Janet that we were investigating her and her husband? Why hadn't he done that by telephone? Unless he didn't want a record of the call.

I couldn't simply park in front of the house and I didn't want to confront Brookshire without consulting Tommy Lee. The wooded lots in Arbor Ridge were large enough that the trees provided privacy between houses. I drove about a tenth of a mile, turned onto a second neighborhood street and found a pull-off by a bold stream cascading down a twenty-foot rock face. The topography of this small section of Arbor Ridge couldn't support construction and was tucked out of sight of the nearest house. I parked on the shoulder and walked back.

Along the way I met an older couple and their Schnauzer. My presence wasn't suspicious as I looked like a fellow neighbor out for a morning stroll. However, the dog barked like I was Attila the Hun. The couple waved, and the man said, "Sorry. Grady thinks he's a Great Dane."

As I neared the Sinclair residence, I left the road and angled through the woods to where I had a good view of the carport. I settled behind a rhododendron bush and waited.

And waited. An hour passed. My legs cramped. The ground got harder. My phone vibrated once. A text from Susan.

FEDEX delivered card from Raleigh.

Good. I could start my role as Barry Clayton, undercover cop. Another hour passed. I stretched as best I could and used the time to review the case.

We knew a fraudulent conspiracy existed that linked convenience stores into some kind of organized network. Toby McKay's EBT card found in Rufus Taylor's possession and the list of stores Sonny had secreted in his motorcycle saddlebag supported that theory. The murders of Rufus and Sonny appeared to be fallout from Toby McKay's attack on Commissioner James. Someone had acted quickly to sever any traceable connection between Rufus and the person or persons behind the scheme.

Tommy Lee and I were looking at the Sinclairs because Archie had told them he was going to talk to Sonny McKay, and then Sonny McKay died that night. As the second murder victim, Sonny could have been a marked man already, but the Sinclairs and their admitted involvement in WITSEC certainly raised their profile in the case. Now the marshal who had all but confirmed the Sinclairs' status was in the house with Janet Sinclair. Was he telling her our suspicions or doing an investigation of his own? Tommy Lee said the marshals don't want to be embarrassed by someone in WITSEC engaging in criminal activities. Maybe by breaking the case first, Brookshire would mute the impact of such a revelation.

And then there was FNS investigator Collier Crockett. His ongoing efforts to build his own case meant he wanted us to go away. I understood his concern. He didn't want to see his work destroyed by other law enforcement agencies who set off alarms that could drive his targets to ground. My undercover work would have to tread lightly around the investigation Crockett had already mounted.

I heard the squeak of a screen door. I edged around the rhododendron to see Brookshire coming out directly into the carport. Janet Sinclair stepped into the open doorway. She wore one of those thick terrycloth robes you find in the closet of a high-priced hotel room. It was loosely cinched and her bare legs and feet protruded beneath its hem. She said something inaudible and Brookshire laughed and turned to face her. He slipped his hands under the robe and kissed her on the lips. If his job was to handle the Sinclairs, he was going all out with Janet.

"Well, that certainly complicates things." Tommy Lee made the one-sentence assessment as we stood behind Taylor's Short Stop.

Roger Taylor and a locksmith were in the office. With the

whine of the drill masking my words, I'd told the sheriff what I'd witnessed.

"It could just be an affair," I said. "Brookshire might not be mixed up in anything else."

"I can guaran-damn-tee you that bedding your WITSEC charge isn't in the approved marshals' playbook. If Luther showed such a lapse in judgment, then what else has he compromised?"

"What are you going to do?"

"Only thing I can do. Confront him face-to-face."

"You want me with you?"

Tommy Lee shook his head. "No. That would only make him more defensive. I'm going to use one of my more unscrupulous investigative tools—blackmail. I don't want to pull you into it."

"But what if he does something desperate? You'll have no backup."

"Oh, he'll know you were surveilling the Sinclairs. I'll tell him. But I'll also tell him if I don't check in with you by a certain time, you'll go straight to the FBI."

The drill whine ceased.

"Lock's out," Roger yelled from the back door.

Tommy Lee and I entered the store and crowded into the office.

"All right, Roger," Tommy Lee said. "Open the safe."

Roger yanked open the perforated door and we peered over his shoulder. No cash. Just two items. A ledger book about the size of a paperback novel and, beneath it, a manila envelope.

"Don't touch anything," Tommy Lee ordered. He rolled on a pair of latex gloves.

Roger Taylor backed out of the way and Tommy Lee retrieved the ledger. I gloved as well and he handed the book to me. Then he took the envelope. The interior was now as bare as old Mother Hubbard's cupboard.

I flipped through the pages. "Dates and amounts. Not large amounts. Mostly thirty to fifty dollars."

"Probably what was paid for by EBT cards," Tommy Lee said. "An accounting for how much the bogus charges amounted to. Then they would know how to split the take." He opened the flap of the unsealed envelope. "This is interesting."

He handed me the top sheet of several pages. It was a blank invoice from Staples Sources.

The sheriff flipped through the other sheets. "They're all the same. Rufus must have filled out the invoice with the appropriate total each time he wrote a Staples Sources check."

"Do I need to know all this?" the locksmith asked.

"No, Ed," Tommy Lee said. "Thanks. Send your bill to the department. And, Ed, this is confidential police business. Not a word to anyone."

"Anybody asks, I was here because you locked your keys in your car." He laughed. "Everybody will believe that."

As soon as the locksmith was out of earshot, Roger whispered, "Are you going to take back the El Camino and the cash?"

"No," Tommy Lee said. "But for your own safety, don't talk to anyone about this." He raised the papers for emphasis. "Got it?"

"Yes, sir."

"So, we're going with the original plan. Operate the store, but let me know if anyone approaches you."

I followed Tommy Lee out the rear of the store.

"Let's talk in my car a few minutes," he said.

I slid into the front passenger's seat. The sheriff started the engine and turned on the fan to circulate the air.

"I'm going to call Alec Danforth," Tommy Lee said. "He's the manager of the Gainesboro Country Club."

"Why?"

"If Robert Sinclair played golf this morning, he might have played golf last Saturday. Alec can access the tee times."

"Right. And Sinclair could have an alibi for the time of Rufus' murder."

"Yes. I should have looked into that as soon as Sinclair became a person of interest."

"We didn't know he played golf, and we focused on his job that covers similar territory to the footprint of the stores."

"Well, we know now," Tommy Lee said.

"Okay. What can I do?"

"Take the weekend off. That's an order. I'll update you later, and I'll let you know when I catch Luther at home."

"I'll probably be at the hospital with Uncle Wayne. So I'll be close if you need me."

"I won't. Now get out of my car and go see your family."

At a little after one in the afternoon, I knocked on the door of my uncle's small room in a rehab wing of the hospital. I entered to find him sitting up in a chair next to the window. Beside him sat Reverend Lester Pace.

The old preacher got to his feet. "Barry, take this chair. I need to be running along anyway."

"No. I'm good here." I sat on the foot of the hospital bed. "And I need to ask you something before you go."

"All right."

"But first, how are you doing, Uncle Wayne?"

"I'll be doing better when they let me out of this place. Nothing wrong with me. My head's so hard there's probably a pothole on Main Street."

"So, rehab's going well?"

My uncle waved his hand dismissively. "I'm running rings around the other contestants."

"Contestants?"

"Well, patients. The nurses have us play these games. Like bowling with plastic pins. I beat everybody."

Nothing like a little competition to motivate my uncle.

"At least the doc's moved up my release date to Monday, if everything goes well." Uncle Wayne shook his head. "Hard to believe it was only a week ago. Seems like I've been here a month."

"Was my mother in earlier?"

"Yes. Susan came by and picked her up for lunch. She said you were working. You learn why Toby McKay went nuts?"

"Making progress."

My uncle winked at Pace. "Secret stuff. Nobody's more close-mouthed than Barry." Then he turned serious. "Your mother said she talked to you about this Alderway nonsense."

I glanced at Reverend Pace. He gave a slight nod to indicate he was aware of the situation.

"I wouldn't call it nonsense," I said. "Not to her. I think the funeral home's become a burden to her. The stairs, the visitations."

"Come on. We both know it's me she's worried about. This whole thing started because I'm in the hospital."

"That doesn't mean she's not right to be worried."

"I know. I know."

Reverend Pace cleared his throat. "I told your uncle she might think she's doing it for him, but actually is worried about her own condition. Unlike this champion contestant here," Pace patted my uncle on the knee, "some of us feel our age."

"But are you going into some retirement home?" Uncle Wayne asked.

"Yes."

The answer surprised both of us.

"Alderway," Pace said. "It's affiliated with the Methodist church and as a fifty-plus-year serving pastor, I receive special consideration. I didn't want to tell you because I knew you'd be afraid to move there. You know I'd show you up in all the activities."

My uncle laughed. "You. A man of the cloth. Lying through your teeth."

"You can have the chance to prove me wrong then."

"Thinking about it," Uncle Wayne said softly. "Thinking about it."

There was a knock at the door. A nurse stepped just inside. "Mr. Thompson. Time for your afternoon session."

"What is it? Mountain-climbing?"

"Close. We've got a little obstacle course set up."

My uncle stood quickly, and then lost his balance and fell back into the chair. His face went scarlet.

"Now remember, we stand up slowly and then pause to get our equilibrium." The nurse came over and offered her arm.

Uncle Wayne sighed and let her help him to his feet.

"There we go," she said. "Now, escort me to the gym. It's not often I have the pleasure of walking arm in arm with such a good-looking man."

My uncle looked down at Pace. "I bet they won't be saying that to you at Alderway."

"Probably not. Especially if you're there."

Uncle Wayne patted the nurse's hand. "Come on, honey. Let's go set a record for this so-called obstacle course."

When they'd left the room, I asked Pace, "Are you really going to Alderway?"

"Yes. A small one-bedroom unit. I'll still tend my churches as long as I can drive without being a danger to others. But if the good Lord gives us three score and ten, then I'm well into overtime. Alderway will provide me with a community when I no longer can get around on my own."

"And my uncle?"

Pace shrugged. "He'll come to a decision in his own time. He doesn't like to feel that he's being railroaded. But if I were a betting man, I'd say his train's headed for Alderway. Especially if he feels like he and your mom are leaving you in a manageable position." He reached behind his chair for his rhododendron walking stick. "Well, I'd better take off." He paused. "But you said you wanted to ask me something."

"Yes." I pulled a copy of the convenience store list from my pocket. "You know this area as well as anybody. Can you tell me anything about the people who run these stores?"

Pace took the paper and studied it a moment. "Well, Rufus' store obviously. The Smart Mart in Mills River is owned by the Harris family. They attend my Pigeon River church. The others are a little far afield for me. I do know Buddy Smith at Wilmer's Convenience Corner."

"Really?"

"Yes, his wife, Elaine, grew up in the Oak Hollow congregation. A small church I'd rotate into once a month. She met Buddy Smith at a Bible camp when they were teenagers. Tough story."

"What do you mean?"

"A couple years ago, Elaine got leukemia. The childhood kind. High cure rate in children, but devastating to an adult. The medical bills were huge and Buddy had some cheap insurance with a very high deductible. The church had some fundraisers. Bake sales, car washes. Buddy even had a donation jar on the counter of his store. But Elaine died back in the winter. Left Buddy with his daughter, Norie. She must be about ten. It's been a struggle. I've been by to see them a couple times." He looked back at the list. "This reminds me I should check on them. The other stores, well, nothing stands out." He handed me the paper. "What's this about?"

I told him our suspicions that Rufus Taylor and Toby McKay had been tangled up in some organized network of food stamp fraud. How we'd found the news article about the dead cat and Buddy's story about the underage kids. We didn't buy it, especially when Wilmer's Convenience Corner appeared on the list.

"When did the cat incident happen?" Pace asked.

"Back in April."

"A couple months after his wife died."

"You're thinking Buddy got involved because he needed money for her care, and then tried to get out?"

"You're the detective," Pace said. "But these are hard times for a lot of people. Between the opioid epidemic and scarcity of jobs, people are desperate for cash. What can I do?"

"Whatever you feel called to do, but I'd appreciate your not telling him about me. I'm not looking to bust him. I just need to find out who's behind the operation. I've got a plan to do that without endangering him or his daughter."

Reverend Pace studied me for a few seconds. "I'll pray that God will be with you and that you'll prepare like He won't be."

Strange counsel from a minister. Strange, but wise.

Pace rose from the chair. "Call upon me for anything and at any time."

I stood. He hugged me. I remained standing until the echo of the tap from his gnarled walking stick faded from the hall. I took the more comfortable chair to wait for my uncle. My phone vibrated and the screen flashed Tommy Lee's cell.

"Yes."

"I'm pulling up to Brookshire's house. His Escape is in the driveway."

"You want to check back in forty-five minutes, like we agreed for me?"

"No. Where are you?"

"In my uncle's rehab room. He's in a PT session. I'm alone."

"Good. I'm going to put the phone in my pocket with the line open."

"You recording?

"No. I want to be able to answer truthfully if he asks. Mute your phone so no sound comes from your end."

"Got it."

"Then do it now."

I hit the mute button and held the phone to my ear. My stomach tightened. If things went bad, I could only listen. Tommy Lee was on his own.

Chapter Twenty

I heard loud knocks. No doorbell for Tommy Lee this time.

"You again?" Brookshire's voice was muffled but understandable.

I boosted the level of my phone to the maximum.

"You asked me to keep you in the loop."

"So I did. Come in. You want a beer?"

"No thanks. I won't be staying that long."

Brookshire laughed. "Long enough to sit down?"

"Maybe." Tommy Lee's voice was devoid of any humor.

Springs creaked as the sheriff sat.

"Well, what is it?" Brookshire asked.

"We're staking out the Sinclairs. Robert played golf this morning. Janet, well, Janet had a visitor at home."

Silence. I thought for a second the call had been dropped. Then Brookshire spoke, his voice a deep rumble with a hint of menace. "What are you getting at, Tommy Lee?"

"I think you know. A green Ford Escape parked in her driveway, and a Semper Fi sticker on the bumper. 'Semper Fi. Always faithful.' At least it wasn't on her car."

"Knock it off. And I'll thank you to leave now."

"Would you care to give me an explanation for my report?"

"Okay, okay. She and her husband are in WITSEC. The Santona family would get to them if they could, so be damned careful what you spread around."

"And you're her, dare I use the word, handler?"

"I'm their contact. She called me. She's spooked by these murders that look like mob hits. She's been jumpy since Robert made the harebrained attempt to sneak back to his father's funeral. I tried to calm her down. When I left, she was feeling better. End of story."

"I see. So, that's your explanation? You calming her down? Does she always wear a white terrycloth robe over nothing but her new identity? Do you always say goodbye with a kiss and what appears to be a strip search?"

"That's your word against mine and hers," Brookshire barked.

"Not against my word. My deputy was the witness. It's your's and Janet's word against his...and the pictures."

Pictures? Tommy Lee was really playing hardball.

"Pictures?" Brookshire echoed my own question.

"Great thing about these new cell phones. They're also high-definition cameras, and the files can be stored in the cloud immediately. An easy download to the U.S. Marshals' office in Washington."

I mentally kicked myself for not having the sense to have actually taken pictures. Tommy Lee's lie carried such devastating consequences for Brookshire that the marshal would either cave or try to kill him.

I heard rough scratches as Tommy Lee evidently lifted the phone from his belt.

"And if I don't report to Barry within the next ten minutes, he's been told to send the photos on. Then it's out of our hands, Luther."

"You son of a bitch. You're threatening me."

"I don't like being lied to. You're much more involved than you told us. I want to know everything about the Sinclairs and everything about your relationship with Janet."

"And in exchange?"

"The pictures won't exist. You have my word."

I heard the scraping sound as Tommy Lee returned the phone to his belt. Then a moment of silence.

Finally, Brookshire cracked. "All right, damn you. Robert and Joan Santona were placed here about three and a half years ago. I wasn't involved with their flip in New Jersey. Prosecutors handled that. They were admitted to WITSEC after giving up documents proving Bobby Santona, Robert's father, oversaw a major fraud conspiracy in the state's tire-recycling program."

Brookshire's statement matched what I had learned from the news reports of the trial.

"So, Robert Santona didn't have to testify in court?" Tommy Lee asked.

"No. The evidence was presented to the grand jury with the story it had been confiscated in a raid of Robert Santona's home. Actually, Robert and Joan knew the raid was coming. They had alerted the FBI as to the existence of the records."

"Why would they turn on the family?"

"Because the family discovered Robert and Joan had been skimming off the top. Joan actually kept the books. They might spare Robert, but his wife wasn't blood kin."

I remembered Brookshire's earlier comment that Robert Santona wasn't the smartest bee in the hive. That would be the queen bee. Queen Joan. And I felt I had learned the source of the money that had gone into the single premium insurance policies.

"So, Robert and Joan went into WITSEC before the arrests and trial?" Tommy Lee asked.

"Yes. The marshals pulled them out at three in the morning. We put the word out on the street that they'd gone to join Jimmy Hoffa."

"Do you have any reason to believe the Santonas, aka Sinclairs, are involved in any way with a food stamp scam?"

"No. Frankly, I don't see how they could even set it up. They're outsiders. Who would trust them?"

"It might not be about trust. It might be about fear."

"Okay," Brookshire conceded. "But who would fear them?

Look at Robert. That human butterball's not exactly an intim-
idator."

"How did they wind up in Gainesboro?"

"Janet thought out west would be too alien, but she was afraid
to stay in the northeast. The North Carolina mountains seemed
remote enough with a small town less likely to attract any of the
people from their old lives. Then Robert had to go screw it all
up last July by sneaking back for the funeral."

"Any evidence that he was trailed back to Gainesboro?"

"No. But the dummy didn't have the sense to use a rental car.
He's pretty sure he got away from the cemetery before anyone
read the license tag. But they could have seen the colors of the
plate. And these two gangland-style murders have put at least a
regional spotlight on Gainesboro. That's why Janet's been upset."

"How long has your affair been going on?" Tommy Lee asked.

"Only a few months. And that's all it is. Comfort and com-
panionship. Tommy Lee, you don't know what it's like coming
home to an empty house every night." His voice choked. "Janet's
lonely too. Her husband's about as affectionate as a dead trout,
and she's afraid to make friends because of her history. She and
I...well, it just happened."

"All right, Luther. I'm taking you at your word, although the
cop part of my brain is screaming you've shoveled in a lot of
bullshit. Tell me this, and for God's sake, don't lie to me. Have
you told Janet Sinclair anything about our investigation?"

"No. Not a word. I have a cop brain too. I might have used
poor judgment in the affair, but I'd never compromise your case."

"How often do you see her?"

"When Robert plays golf. Sometimes during the week if he's
on a sales route that we're confident will keep him away."

"Was Robert playing golf last Saturday?" Tommy Lee asked.

"No. He wanted to watch the parade. He and Janet weren't
too far from the shooting. They left almost immediately. She
dropped Robert at home, and then made an excuse to run an
errand so she could phone me. She was worried she might show

up in some cell phone video if it made the news. That's the kind of footage that can go viral."

"Sid Ferguson headed up the SBI investigation," Tommy Lee said. "Talk to him if you're concerned."

"I've looked through YouTube and Facebook. Mostly posts of the first responders. You're in some clips, keeping people back. I looked carefully and Robert and Janet never appeared."

Another pause, and then Brookshire added, "Your deputy. Shouldn't you phone him?"

"Did you hear everything?" Tommy Lee asked me the question as soon as he returned to his car.

"Yes. Do you believe him?"

"For the most part. Unless he's withholding damning information, he doesn't offer anything that links the Sinclairs to the EBT scam. All we have is Archie's leak to them the night before Sonny's murder."

"Does that change our approach?"

"No. I'm going to look into this Staples Sources company. Next week I might have you sit in the post office in Spartanburg to see who collects mail from the P.O. box."

"I forgot to tell you. My EBT card came this morning. If Wilmer's Convenience Corner is open tomorrow, I might drop by."

"So much for your weekend off," Tommy Lee said. "But, yeah, go ahead and get underway. Monday afternoon, I'll be at the double burial for Toby and Sonny. Pauline McKay called the department and asked for protection. I'd promised that, so I'll do it."

"You also promised to feed her chickens. You been doing that too?"

"Reece is on that assignment."

"Reece? Didn't he take that as an insult?"

"Nah. I told him he could have the eggs."

Mom, Susan, and I attended church Sunday morning. Afterwards, we went to Rockwells' Cafeteria, a Gainesboro fixture
for over fifty years. Half our congregation was eating there and
a steady stream of diners came by our table to ask about Uncle
Wayne.

We took Mom back to the funeral home where she wanted to
get ready for Wayne's return the next day. I'd forgotten to alert
Tommy Lee that I couldn't stake out the Spartanburg post office
until we got my uncle settled. Given the way hospital paperwork
can be processed, his actual release time was anybody's guess.

I'd also wanted to have a conversation with Mom about her
intended move to Alderway. Fletcher's suggestion to get three
appraisals of the funeral home made sense, and Susan's offer to
use the money from the sale of her condo meant we might be
able to borrow enough funds for the shortfall with the existing
lease to the funeral business covering the monthly mortgage
payment. Fletcher's fiancée, Cindy, would be the first banker
I'd approach. Of course, the wild card was still Uncle Wayne.

My unannounced family conference was short-circuited when
Mom said she'd like to lie down for a few minutes. The barrage
of well-wishers at church and lunch had been exhausting. She
insisted that Susan and I should leave and enjoy our Sunday
afternoon.

After Mom retired to her bedroom, Susan said, "You wanted
to use that EBT card today, didn't you?"

"Yes. But I don't know if the store is even open. It's kind of
a long drive for nothing."

"Did you check the Internet?"

I laughed. "You think a place called Wilmer's Convenience
Corner is going to have a website?"

She pulled out her smartphone, rapidly thumbed the virtual keyboard, and then studied the screen. "No website."

"See."

"A Facebook page. 'Wilmer's Convenience Corner—If we don't have it, you don't need it.' They're open one to six, Sunday afternoons." She dropped her phone back in her handbag. "You can thank me tonight. And, Sherlock, you'd better change into some jeans and an old shirt if you want half a chance at pulling this off."

I found the store on the outskirts of Clyde, North Carolina, a small town two counties over from Gainesboro. Wilmer's Convenience Corner was indeed on the corner of Highway 23 and an unlined blacktop that wound through a warren of modest houses. It was the kind of place where kids would ride their bicycles for a Coke and a candy bar, and retired men would stop to chew the fat. There was one island of gas pumps and a single pump by the left corner of the white concrete-block building that dispensed kerosene.

A man in his mid-thirties was pumping gas into an old muddy Bronco. I parked along the side of the building, and, as I walked to the front door, he gave me a nod that was nothing more than an acknowledgment of my existence.

A thin man with tired eyes sat at the front counter. Behind him on a stool was a red-haired girl of ten or eleven. Her nose was in a Baby-Sitters Club paperback, and she didn't look up when the bells tinkling above the door announced my entry.

The man spoke the universal line—"Can I hep ya?"

"Just picking up a few things. Y'all take EBT cards, don't ya?"

"Yeah, for qualified purchases."

I glanced at the door to the man at the Bronco. "Oh, these will be qualified, all right."

I picked up a green plastic hand-basket and started walking the aisles. The Bronco's engine roared to life and the gas customer drove away. Now it was just the three of us.

I chose some bread, a box of breakfast cereal, a can of pork and beans, and then some items that weren't covered by SNAP benefits. I picked up a small bag of dog food, a roll of paper towels, dishwashing detergent, and then I hit the cooler for a six-pack of Budweiser.

I carried my purchases to the counter. "I'd like a carton of Winstons too. I flipped open my wallet and laid the EBT card atop the box of cereal.

"Some of these items don't qualify, sir."

I ignored him and turned to the girl. "How's the book, Norie? I hope it has a happy ending for everyone."

The child looked up at me with a smile that transformed into confusion when she saw a total stranger. She glanced at her father.

A tremor ran through his body. "Sorry, but they don't qualify." The words came out as a nervous whisper.

"Oh, Buddy, I'm sure they do. Go ahead and ring them up, and then they can find their way back to the shelves. The usual split is fine." I looked back at Norie. "Didn't mean to interrupt your reading. Your dad says you're a smart girl. He's very proud of you."

"Thank you," she said, obviously aware that something wasn't right.

"Oh, and I'll need the receipt, Buddy. You know, just a routine audit to make sure what you report and I report are the same."

He gave a barely perceptible nod and began keying in the prices. The total came to sixty-three dollars and seventy-six cents. I gave him my card and he swiped the stripe. A few seconds later the machine spit out an approved slip. The item prices matched but he'd changed the codes to nothing but approved products. I realized the normal procedure might have been nothing more than ringing up a phantom sale. On the other hand, Buddy Smith probably read my behavior as a test, a test he was desperate not to fail.

He handed me thirty-one, eighty-eight—half the purchase total. "Have a nice day," he murmured.

"Sorry to make you restock this time." I left him with the pile of groceries.

Once in the jeep, my stomach unknotted. Still, I felt godawful. Scaring that poor man and his child. I dreaded the next step which would put Buddy Smith in a vise. I'd be back with my deputy credentials, and after a repeat performance, threaten to take him into custody. But that could wait a day or two. I wasn't going to do that in front of his daughter. I'd make the bust while she was in school.

On the way home, I phoned Tommy Lee.

"You did well," he said. "Let's plan a return visit on Tuesday morning."

"Okay, but after the girl's at school."

"I understand."

"And then, after we get my uncle home tomorrow, I'll go to the Spartanburg post office."

"No, you won't," Tommy Lee said.

"I won't?"

"Funny thing about that post office. I'm on my way back from Spartanburg now. I decided to ride down and check it out. Even though the post office is closed, you can still get to the boxes. Except the P.O. box on the Staples Sources invoice, 8009, doesn't exist. The highest number is 8000. Those checks were either picked up at the stores in person or mailed to another address. I guess we're back to your new friend Buddy Smith and the hope that each week he's writing a check to Staples Sources."

"That's one avenue," I said. "Yet, the checks are being cashed at some bank, if not in Spartanburg, then it could be anywhere in the country. But if this is a local operation, they might keep it here. What do we need to do to get account names?"

"I can get a court order. Or I could first ask my lead investigator to use his winning smile and charm the information out of every bank contact he knows. So, be sure and brush your teeth, you charmer, you."

Chapter Twenty-one

Sunday evening, Susan and I sat in our customary chairs on the back deck with Democrat stretched out at our feet. I'd opted for a beer; she chose sparkling water over wine, citing seven o'clock surgery the next morning. I'd briefed her on my encounter with Buddy Smith and his daughter and she'd agreed with my efforts to shield the girl as much as possible.

"You think they're in any danger?" she asked.

"Not at the moment. I made my approach when it was just the three of us. He'll continue whatever the established practice is. If we succeed in getting his cooperation, then things could change. I'd want to make sure the girl was someplace out of harm's way."

"Did you have your gun with you this afternoon?"

"Snug in the small of my back. But I don't think I have anything to fear from Buddy Smith. The man was terrified by whom he thought I represented."

"I don't know about that," she said skeptically. "Don't underestimate what people will do to protect their children."

Democrat lifted his head and growled. I heard the crunch of tires on gravel.

"Who could that be?" Susan asked.

"I don't know." I laughed. "Archie's supposed to be out of town."

"Let's go see." She rose from her chair. "I'll put on a pot of coffee."

We went to the door, Democrat leading the way. Through the front windows, I saw a gray sedan behind my jeep.

"That looks like Sid Ferguson's car. He's with the SBI."

I was wrong. The driver's door opened and a man in a dark suit stepped into the glow of the front porch lights.

"It's the food stamp investigator, Collier Crockett. This is definitely police business."

"Then I'll put on the coffee and take Democrat and a book to the bedroom. Let me know when he leaves."

I stepped onto the porch. "Good evening, Collier."

"Clayton," he snapped. "Just what the hell do you think you're doing?" His jaw was tight and his eyes narrow slits. Whatever he thought I'd done was driving him to either slug me or have a coronary on the spot.

"Standing on my porch. On my property. And if you don't ratchet down that tone I'll have to charge you with trespassing."

He stopped at the bottom of the porch steps and looked up at me. "You think you're cute, don't you? We'll see how cute when I report you blew an undercover operation months in the making."

"Fine. Then we'll counter with how you obstructed a murder investigation by withholding information and leaving us to find our own way. If that screwed up your case, then you only have yourself to blame. Last time I checked, murder trumps fraud every time."

"I warned you to stay in your own county. I'm running a multi-state investigation. An investigation that you've jeopardized."

I realized what had set him off. "Buddy Smith. Wilmer's Convenience Corner."

"Yes. I've been working on him for several months. Since a terrible incident with the girl's cat. He's low on the food chain, but I'm sure he knows who's above him. He just hasn't gotten comfortable enough to talk. Now you've really spooked him."

"Were you tailing me?"

"No. Buddy called me right after you left. He thought you'd been sent to sniff out if he was turning sides. Now he's clammed up on me. If I bust him, it could send everyone else underground and we don't have all the players pegged yet." He stepped up on the porch closer to me. "So, do you understand how your fishing around is unraveling our whole operation?"

"We weren't fishing. We were targeting a very specific lead."

"Yeah? What was that?"

What the hell, I thought. He needed to know Tommy Lee and I weren't Laurel and Hardy. "A company we believe transfers the funds from the EBT deposits to whoever's running the fraud. A company called Staples Sources. I pushed Buddy Smith to sell me non-qualified items to get some leverage and see his accounts payables. See if Staples Sources was one of his suppliers."

"Why Buddy?"

"We found a list of stores tied to Toby and Sonny McKay. Buddy's was one of them. We also learned about the dead cat and thought that made him a more likely target."

Collier Crockett took a deep breath and seemed to calm down. "And why Staples Sources?"

"We found a number of blank invoices from the company in Rufus Taylor's store. He was evidently filling them in to pay whatever was the share of the week's illegal take that he owed his partners. We've confirmed the address of the company is bogus. Haven't they popped up on your radar?"

Crockett shook his head. "No. We've been concentrating on the EBT purchase side. I remember the company name but they seemed legit. This is the first I've heard about blank invoices."

"What did you tell Buddy Smith about me?"

"He gave me your name since it posted on your transaction. First time I've heard of an undercover operative not using an alias. Anyway, I told him to ignore you. I said if it was a test, then he'd passed and you wouldn't be back. I tried to leverage your visit as another reason he should trust me. I can protect him against you."

"Then if I see him again, I'll let him know I'm a deputy. That we're working together."

Crockett scowled. "He's my potential source. Whether you're a good guy or a bad guy, you're going to spook him. He's nervous enough when I dress down and drop by for a chat."

"We've got our own case to solve. I'll speak to the sheriff, but as far as I'm concerned, any lead is fair game. But thanks for the heads-up. We'll be careful."

He pointed his finger at me. "Be more than careful, Clayton. Buddy Smith is entangled with some bad people. You could get him and his little girl killed."

He pivoted on his heel and returned to his car. I watched him spin the tires on the gravel backing up, then lurch forward, spewing stones in his wake.

At seven-thirty the next morning, I phoned Tommy Lee and gave him the details of my confrontation with Crockett. "I told him I'd talk to you, but that I didn't see us limiting our investigation."

"I agree," the sheriff said. "But we should go easy. Crockett has a point about too much attention being paid to Buddy Smith. Let's see what we can learn about Staples Sources. I'll talk to Crockett and work out some information exchange. When are you headed to the hospital?"

"I'm leaving now. My uncle's supposed to be released at eleven. But don't count on me till mid-afternoon."

"Okay. And I'm tied up with the McKays' funerals. I'll ask Marge to do an Internet search on Staples Sources. Maybe we can come at them that way."

"Maybe, but the prospect doesn't seem very hopeful."

"I know," Tommy Lee commiserated. "We could be hitting a dead end and have to see where Crockett's case leads. I'm beginning to think the Sinclairs are a red herring. We're reading too much into them because of WITSEC."

"We're reading too much into them because we don't have anything else. Damn it, Tommy Lee, all we have to show for our efforts are three fresh graves in the Twin Creeks Baptist Church cemetery."

As I feared, Uncle Wayne's eleven o'clock discharge didn't happen till twelve-thirty. I offered to buy lunch from the cafeteria, but my uncle said he didn't want to spend another minute in the hospital. So, we made a run through a Wendy's drive-through and took food back to the funeral home.

I pulled to the rear entrance where there were fewer steps onto the back porch and into the kitchen. All was quiet. Fletcher and our assistant, Freddy Mott, were at the McKays' burial service.

Uncle Wayne didn't refuse my arm as he shuffled inside. Mom pulled a chair out from the kitchen table and he eased himself into it.

He looked around. "You know. This place is really quiet when nobody's here."

Mom and I looked at each other. Such an obvious statement was merely the preface to some other thought.

"Kinda sad," he continued. "When this place isn't a home. What will we call it? A funeral house? And the kitchen. I won't be cooking any more family meals here. Guess we'll have to call it the break room, like it's part of some office complex."

"Don't be silly," Mom said. "How many meals did you cook here?"

"Sandwiches, Connie. I made a lot of sandwiches."

Mom laughed. "Oh, Wayne, only you would lament over a home-cooked sandwich." She set the Wendy's bag on the table beside him. "Now eat your store-bought one."

My uncle chuckled and pulled out a cheeseburger.

After we ate, I helped Uncle Wayne upstairs. We had to stop on the landing a moment for him to catch his breath.

"I tell you, Barry, getting old ain't for sissies."

"No one ever accused you of being a sissy. The trick is to be sensible. Don't do too much too soon."

He tightened his grip on my arm. "Don't worry. I'll take the steps one at a time."

On the second floor, he dropped my support and walked down the hall to his room. It had once been mine. I followed him in and was surprised to see he hadn't changed it. The shelves still held the model ships and planes I'd built with my dad. Framed pictures displayed family vacations, some with Uncle Wayne, some without.

"I can box my stuff up and give you more space," I said.

My uncle sat on the bed and looked around. "No, I like it. Reminds me of when you were a boy." His eyes moistened. "Reminds me of when I was a boy. Not so long ago, Barry. You'll see. It all flies by in the blink of an eye."

I heard Fletcher's voice downstairs and left my uncle to rest. Mom was pouring him a glass of lemonade when I entered the kitchen.

"How'd it go?" I joined him at the table and Mom set a plate of cookies between us.

"As well as expected. Small crowd. Didn't have enough pall-bearers to bring both caskets out of the church at the same time." He shook his head. "If I never do another double funeral again, it will be too soon."

"And Pauline McKay?"

"She seemed numb. The sheriff stood with her and her sister Nelda. He was going to escort them back to Pauline's house. She's tired of hiding out in Canton and wants to return home. I think he was going to check the locks and give her some security advice."

I hadn't thought about Pauline McKay in a few days. Perhaps enough time had passed that she was no longer considered a threat. I hoped so. We couldn't force her to stay in hiding.

"I know you can't talk about a case," Fletcher said, "but are you making any progress?"

"We're finding some dots. Now we need to connect them."

My phone vibrated. I checked the screen. The number was for the Sheriff's Department switchboard.

"Sorry, I've got to take this."

I rose from the chair and walked rapidly out to the privacy of the backyard. "This is Barry."

"It's Carol. Are you at the funeral with Tommy Lee?"

"No. What's up?"

"Do you know a Luther Brookshire?"

"Yes. He's a U.S. Marshal."

"He called the department asking for Tommy Lee. I told him the sheriff was at a funeral and couldn't take a call. He asked for you. I can patch him through."

The phone clicked.

"Deputy Clayton?" Brookshire's voice was tense, the words clipped.

"Yes. What's wrong?"

"Janet Sinclair just called me. She arrived home to find Robert dead in the carport. I'm on my way there now."

"Dead? How?"

"Shot in the head. He was executed."

Chapter Twenty-two

I didn't bother to go to the department or change into my uniform. I sped to the Sinclairs as fast as I could, the jeep's hazard lights flashing and horn blaring in a desperate effort to clear the road. I called Carol our dispatcher back and told her to send EMTs to the Arbor Ridge address. I also asked her to make sure she saved the number that would have registered Brookshire's call. I wanted to know where he'd been when he phoned.

Then I called Tommy Lee. "Robert Sinclair's been shot and killed."

"Where?" he asked.

"His carport. Janet found him, called Brookshire, and he called for you. Carol passed him to me since you're with Mrs. McKay. I'm on my way. Carol's alerting EMTs and recording time and number of Brookshire's call, in case you want to pull a GPS location."

"Good thinking. I'll send out two deputies to help. Also, I'll contact Lindsay Boyce and request their forensics."

"You're bringing in the FBI?"

"Yes. We're dealing with WITSEC, and the marshals are going to go nuts. So much for never losing a witness. I want to deal with a friendly federal face. You secure the scene. I'll be there as soon as I can."

Janet Sinclair stood in the front lawn of her house and stared up into the trees. One arm was stretched across her chest with her hand clutching her opposite shoulder. The other hand held a cigarette that she puffed like it was a deep-sea diver's air hose. I appeared to be the first responder and parked the jeep on the narrow shoulder in front of the house, leaving the driveway clear for EMTs and forensic units. I got out and tucked the Kimber pistol in the small of my back.

Janet flipped the cigarette away and ran toward me.

"Mr. Clayton, Mr. Clayton," she cried hysterically. "They shot him. The family shot him."

She surprised me with a fierce hug, head against my chest. "I was afraid they'd come back for me. They left the White Rose of Santona."

"The what?"

"Their signature. By the body. Luther will know."

I let her sob a few minutes, and then took her shoulders and gently pushed her away. "I need to check the scene. Why don't you wait in the house? Luther Brookshire will be here soon. He's the one who called me." I hoped the mention of the marshal would calm her down, although at this point a dead husband, an adulteress wife, and her lover would be an unusual combination at a crime scene. I hoped my fellow deputies and Tommy Lee would arrive first.

I took her arm and steered her toward the front door and away from the carport. I couldn't see the body, but the trunk of Janet's Mercedes was open and a torn bag of groceries lay at the left rear corner of Robert's SUV. Several cans of food had rolled to the edge of the sloped driveway. To my eye, the story appeared to be that Janet had returned from the grocery store, lifted the brown paper bag from the trunk, and then rounded the back of Robert's vehicle headed for the door in the carport. I guessed the body was close to the front of the car on the driver's side. She didn't see it until clearing the large SUV.

We stepped up on the small front porch. The door was

unlocked and I opened it. "Wait here while I check inside." I crossed the threshold and pulled my pistol free.

The home had a formal living room, expansive kitchen, den, and a master bedroom on the first floor. Folded clothes were spread out on the king-sized bed where either Janet or a housekeeper had left them. Three bedrooms and two baths were upstairs. One of the bedrooms had been converted into a home office. Both a laptop and a desktop were on a credenza behind a wide desk. We would want to go through both and any external drives that might exist. I holstered my gun and returned to the front door.

"It's all clear," I said.

She sniffled and wiped her eyes with her fingers. "Is there anything I can do?"

"Whatever makes you the most comfortable. Brew some coffee. Have another cigarette. There'll be a lot of people here soon."

She nodded and withdrew into the living room.

I circled back and noted a dented can of corn and a shattered bottle of ranch dressing on the concrete driveway. Inside the ripped bag, I saw a box of elbow pasta and a jar of tomato sauce. Other items were underneath, but what I found most important was a receipt trapped under the pasta. I picked it up, noticed that the date and time stamp placed her in the grocery store less than forty minutes ago. I stuck the receipt in my pocket to add to whatever evidence might be forthcoming.

I moved into the carport. Robert Sinclair lay on his back by the front tire. The driver's door was closed, so he must have stepped out, shut the door, and was either surprised by or familiar with his killer. There was no way the scene I viewed distinguished between the two possibilities. What was indisputable was the bullet hole in his forehead and two red splotches on his blue polo shirt. Blood flow had been minimal, indicating he'd died instantly. The method was a classic hit—two to the body, one to the head.

Next to his face lay a long-stemmed white rosebud. A statement? A signature?

I returned to my jeep and pulled an evidence-collecting kit from the back. It included latex gloves and clear evidence bags. I also grabbed a small flashlight.

I went in the Infiniti from the front passenger's side. A supersized soda cup was in the center console holder. Some files with stores names on the label tabs were on the passenger's seat. A Snickers candy bar wrapper was wadded on the floor. I used the flashlight to peer under the seat. Nothing but wires for the position control.

The backseat was clear on the right side. I shone the light into the rear storage area. The golf clubs I'd seen on Saturday lay diagonally across the carpet. Spiked golf shoes were beside them.

Robert Sinclair's body blocked access to the driver's door, and I didn't want to move it even a few inches until forensics and the M.E. had cleared it. But I could get in the back door behind the driver. The floor mat was clean. I bent down, half in and half out of the car, and reached under the driver's seat. My gloved hand encountered a book and what felt like a tube. I placed my cheek on the rear mat and angled the flashlight so that the beam threw directly underneath the seat. It was a book. But the metal tube was a suppressor mounted to a semi-automatic pistol pointed straight at my face. I carefully lifted the gun and sealed it in an evidence bag. Through the clear plastic, I could identify it as a Beretta 92FS twenty-two caliber. The same caliber that killed Rufus Taylor and Sonny McKay.

I did the same with the book, but not before flipping through several pages. It was a ledger of columns filled with numbers. No words, no cursive handwriting. Sections were divided under five-digit headings. I suspected one of those five-digit codes stood for Taylor's Short Stop. Another for Wilmer's Convenience Corner. I was holding the master accounts for the network of stores engaged in the food stamp fraud conspiracy. I would probably become FNS Investigator Collier Crockett's new best friend.

I stood back from the car and looked down at the body sprawled before me. Robert Sinclair, aka Robert Santona, had received justice dispensed by his own family with bullets and a flower while his own weapon lay less than three feet away.

The sounds of sirens wailed ever louder. I turned and walked down the driveway, ready to wave the cavalry into position.

Deputies Reece Hutchins and Steve Wakefield had quickly established a perimeter. We knew the activities of police cars and vans would soon attract the neighbors.

Tommy Lee arrived about ten minutes ahead of U.S. Marshal Luther Brookshire, which gave me the chance to show the sheriff what I'd discovered beneath the driver's seat.

"For the time being, we keep these items to ourselves," he said.

"Robert's death is our case?"

He gave a wry smile. "Up until my niece yanks it away for the Bureau. I know Lindsay well enough that she's not going to let an interstate mob hit go to her Podunk uncle. She knows me well enough to know I won't back off until I'm sure we got the man who killed Rufus and Sonny."

I nodded, and then saw Brookshire's green Escape skid to a stop in front of my jeep. "Your buddy Luther's going to want a piece of the case as well. His protected witness got whacked."

"He's already had one piece too many. But I'll play nice. Let's go hear Mrs. Sinclair's statement before Luther has a chance to coach her. He can sit in, but it's our investigation."

Tommy Lee hurried to intercept the marshal as he ran up the lawn. I went in the carport door and through the kitchen to the living room where I found Janet standing in front of a bay window. If she'd brewed coffee, she wasn't having any. One hand held a cigarette, the other a glass of whiskey.

"We're going to need a statement now, Mrs. Sinclair."

She turned to me. "Can I give it to Luther?"

"He can sit in, but right now your husband's murder is our jurisdiction."

She sighed and took a healthy swallow from her glass. "Funny, isn't it? Me coming to you for those funeral arrangements. I didn't know you were a deputy. Guess you'll be doing double duty when we meet about getting Robert back to Paterson."

"We'll do that later." I glanced around the living room. There was a plush white sofa and expensive-looking wingback chairs in matching navy blue upholstery. I gestured to the sofa. "Why don't you sit with me? The sheriff and Marshal Brookshire can take the chairs."

She stubbed out her cigarette in an ashtray on an end table by one of the chairs and joined me on the sofa.

Tommy Lee and Brookshire came in through the front door. The marshal was clearly agitated and looked like he could barely restrain himself from running to her.

"Janet! Are you okay?"

"Yes," she said calmly. "I was at the grocery store. I guess the killers didn't want to wait for me. So, what now? Identity number three?"

"Yes. I'll get you out of here tonight."

Tommy Lee held up a hand. "Before anyone goes anywhere else, we need to learn what happened here. Marshal Brookshire," Tommy Lee said formally, "you're welcome to sit in, but right now this is our case and Barry and I will do the questioning. Why don't you sit over there?" The sheriff pointed to the wing-back chair farther from Janet.

Brookshire complied, sitting on the edge of the cushion and still clearly agitated.

Tommy Lee took a notebook and pen from his pocket. "Go ahead, Barry."

I angled myself on the sofa to face her. "Why don't you tell us what happened today? Walk us through from the time you woke up to when I arrived."

"Well, I slept till around seven-thirty. That's when I usually get up. Robert was already gone. He's an early riser and he had some appointments in Murphy."

Murphy was a town in the most western tip of North Carolina and nearly two hours from Gainesboro.

"Did you speak to him?" I asked.

"No. He's sweet to get up quietly and not wake me." Her voice caught. "I didn't even get to tell him goodbye." She glanced in the direction of the carport where her husband lay on the concrete floor. Then she looked at Brookshire. "Luther knows how close we were. How much I loved him."

Brookshire shifted uncomfortably. He knew that we knew the truth.

"And so you got up," I said, trying to keep her focused.

"Yes. Robert had started the coffeemaker. I turned on the *Today Show* and had a cup with a bowl of yogurt and fruit. Then I started some laundry. Now that I'm not working, I try to keep to a schedule and Monday is laundry day. Most of Robert's clothes are perma-press. They're samples of the casual wear and sports lines he represents. I touched up a few items with the iron and by then it was nearly ten. I was getting a little cabin fever and knew I had to buy a few things for supper. So, I decided to treat myself to an early lunch at the country club and then do my shopping."

"Did you meet anyone in particular?" I asked.

"I joined some women I occasionally play bridge with. Linda Albany and Chrissy Perry. They'll confirm my story. I ran by the bank, stopped at Ingles and picked up pasta, tomato sauce, greens for a salad, and a few other items I needed. Robert said he'd be back mid-afternoon, and we'd talked about squeezing in nine holes of golf so I didn't make the grocery shopping a prolonged affair. It was probably about two-thirty when I started for home. Robert had texted me that he was getting off the interstate. I replied that I was at the grocery store."

"What time was that?"

She thought a moment. "I was in the produce department. I guess around two-fifteen. The time stamp should be on my phone."

"So, you didn't speak to him."

"Correct. When he said he was exiting the interstate, I knew he was about ten minutes away. I expected to be home about fifteen or twenty minutes after him, change clothes, and then we'd take his car. His clubs were already loaded."

"All right. And did you come straight here from Ingles?"

She swallowed and then nodded. "It must have been around ten to three. As I expected, his car was here. I pulled to the right, where I always park. I popped the trunk and carried the single bag. Usually he'll come out to see if I need help, but I assumed he was probably changing back in our bedroom. I walked around his car..." She stopped and caught her breath. "I walked around the back of the car and saw him lying there. I dropped the bag and ran to him. I thought he'd had a heart attack. Then I saw it."

"It?" I prompted. "The bullet wounds?"

She shook her head. "The rose. The White Rose of Santona."

"Yes. You mentioned that. What is it?"

She looked at Brookshire. "I'd rather Luther tell you. He knows more than I do."

Tommy Lee and I stared at Brookshire, waiting for him to pick up the story.

He leaned forward in the chair. "First, I need to get something out in the open. Robert and Janet Sinclair were in WITSEC. Their former names were Robert and Joan Santona."

So, Brookshire was going to play it straight, I thought. He gave no acknowledgment that we'd already discussed their true identities.

"Thanks to their cooperation with the FBI, prosecutors were able to convict Bobby Santona and some of his key associates of racketeering. We took Robert and Joan into Witness Protection and spread the rumor that they'd been abducted and killed. You see, Robert is Bobby Santona's son and his role in the conviction of his father would be unforgivable."

"Why did he turn?" I asked.

Brookshire looked at Janet. She gave a slight nod.

"There were some funds that went missing," Brookshire said. "Accusations were leveled at Robert and Joan. Robert became fearful, especially for his wife's safety. We offered them a fresh start."

And in exchange for Robert's betrayal of his own family, Joan, aka Janet, started an affair with her handler. But I kept that thought to myself.

"And the rose?" I asked.

"It's never been proven, but the story is that whenever an informant or enemy of the family is killed, a white rose is left as a calling card. Some of the mob hits of the other families are more gruesome. Severed genitals, missing fingers, sliced-off ears. You get the picture. Warnings to anyone who would dare cross them." Brookshire sighed. "Looks like Robert didn't heed our warnings."

"What do you mean?" I asked.

Brookshire looked at Janet. "Tell him."

"Robert went back to Paterson for his father's funeral. He wore a disguise, if you can believe it. Fake beard. Glasses. I told him he was crazy. That was why I came to you about funeral arrangements. I was afraid his violation of the marshals' rules would lead Robert's family straight to us. I begged him not to go. When he insisted, I urged him to keep at a distance. I didn't mean for him to climb a goddammed tree."

"And he came back with a broken leg," I said. "My wife treated him."

"Yes. I wanted to contact Luther immediately. I thought we'd have to move again, but Robert insisted he'd gotten away before anyone saw his car." She looked at Brookshire. "I guess he was wrong. Dead wrong."

"Don't worry," Brookshire said. "We'll get you resettled."

I looked at Tommy Lee. He nodded for me to continue.

"When you found your husband's body, did you go in the house?"

"No. I was afraid. I called Luther and told him what happened. He suggested I get in my car and drive into town, but I couldn't just run away leaving Robert like that. Luther called back a few minutes later and said you were on the way. I waited in the front yard where you saw me."

"Why didn't you go to a neighbor's house?"

She shrugged. "I wasn't thinking that clearly. We really don't know our neighbors. And I thought if anyone was waiting for me, they would have shot me as soon as I got out of the car. Like they did Robert."

"But you didn't go into the house," I said.

"Well, I wasn't one hundred percent sure, was I?"

"But the doors were unlocked. Both the front and the one to the carport."

She gave me a humorless smile. "One of the nice things about living down here. We never lock our doors. Back in New Jersey, our house would have been stripped before we reached the main road."

"You left your doors unlocked, but your husband carried a pistol."

Her eyes widened. "He what?"

"I found a pistol under the driver's seat."

"That's news to me. Luther, did you know about it?"

"No," the marshal answered. "Maybe he carried it because he traveled so much."

"Did he have a permit to carry?" I asked.

"I don't know," Brookshire said. "It's the first I've heard of it."

"How much do you know about your husband's business?"

"He was successful. He liked his clients. We have a climate-controlled storage unit where he keeps his samples. We're not rich but we're comfortable."

"How's he paid?"

"He has a base salary and then a commission schedule."

"Is he ever paid in cash?"

"Not that I know of."

"A joint account?"

She shook her head. "He has a business account, then we have a joint account, and I have an account of my own. I pick up seasonal work with H&R Block. My background's accounting. That's how Robert and I met. A continuing education class."

"How long had you been married?"

"Had," she repeated, recognizing everything about her husband was now past tense. "Thursday next it would have been fifteen years. We were going to Kiawah Island to celebrate." She covered her eyes with one hand. A shudder visibly ran through her body.

"How much longer do we need to go on?" Brookshire asked.

"Till we've covered everything." Tommy Lee flipped through his notes. "Did you ever travel with your husband?"

"No. The mountain roads make me carsick, and there was nothing for me to do."

"Did you ever meet any of his customers?"

"A few times. Robert would have dinners or cocktails at the club. I attended when it was a spousal event."

"So, you were alone most days."

"Except during tax season. Then I go into the H&R Block offices. Sometimes here, sometimes Asheville. It depends on where I'm needed."

"And tax season is when?"

She smiled. "Longer than it used to be. Now they want me mid-January through April fifteenth. Three times they've asked me to take a full-time job." She paused. "Maybe I'll need one." She looked at Brookshire. "Wherever I wind up."

Not if Archie got the insurance policies changed, I thought. The woman could live anywhere in style as long as she collected before WITSEC gave her a new name.

"Barry also found a ledger book," Tommy Lee said. "It was under the seat with the gun. Do you know what it contains?"

Janet shook her head. "It would have to be for his work. Maybe orders or payments due. Do you think Robert was involved in something illegal?"

"We don't want to just assume that the killer came from the family. If Robert was involved in something illegal, then he could have had other enemies."

Her jaw clenched. "My husband is dead in the carport, the Rose of Santona by his side. He helped bring his own father to justice and now you're accusing him of a crime. Something like this food scam thing."

I glanced at Brookshire. His face turned red.

"They're not accusing you of anything," Brookshire said. "We're all trying to do our jobs. To protect you and to find your husband's killer."

Janet Sinclair buried her face in her hands. "I know. I know."

Deputy Reece Hutchins stepped into the living room. "Special Agent Boyce is here, Sheriff. She and her forensics team."

"Thanks. Barry and I will be right out."

"You brought the FBI?" Brookshire exclaimed.

Janet's head snapped up. "Why?"

"Because if this White Rose of Santona is the real thing, we've got an interstate murder of a federally protected witness. The FBI has resources way beyond our department. They're our best hope of finding your husband's killer."

Her eyes narrowed. "Then bring them on. If my Robert's going into the family plot, I want as many of his despicable relatives going into the ground with him."

Chapter Twenty-three

Tommy Lee told Reece to wait in the living room with Brookshire and Janet Sinclair while he and I briefed Special Agent Lindsay Boyce.

We found Tommy Lee's niece in the carport. She had gloved and booted and was bending over the body with a member of her forensic team.

"When you get a chance, Agent Boyce," the sheriff called, "Barry and I will be at my patrol car."

She looked over her shoulder. "Be there in a sec."

Tommy Lee and I walked to the bottom of the driveway to where he'd parked on the opposite shoulder. We both leaned against the front fender and watched the techs work.

"Are you going to hold anything back from Lindsay?" I asked.

"No. We'll give her everything, including Brookshire's affair."

"What does she already know?"

"I briefed her over the weekend about the Sinclairs and the potential that they could be linked to our food stamp scam. She wasn't that familiar with the Santona case in New Jersey, but she was requesting the file. If she's got it, I doubt she's had time to do much with it. But she'll run with this investigation. A dead, supposedly protected, witness will be high-profile in the Bureau."

"What happens to us?"

Tommy Lee shrugged. "Ballistics will either show Robert

Sinclair was killed by the same weapon as Sonny and Rufus, or it won't. The same can be said for the gun under the driver's seat."

"And if nothing matches the ballistics from Sonny and Rufus?"

"Then we press on. But Lindsay will take over Sinclair's murder because the non-match with our murders lends credence to a professional hit out of New Jersey. Likewise, if the gun under the seat isn't a match for us, then it means we've got another player in the game. If it is a match and Collier Crockett can get Buddy Smith at Wilmer's Convenience Corner to either confirm that Sinclair had threatened him or that a section of numbers in the general ledger matches what he was reporting, then I think we are done. The deceased Robert Sinclair will be our killer. Then Crockett can mop up his end as he identifies and arrests complicit cardholders and store owners."

Tommy Lee looked back at the carport. "Here comes Lindsay. Let me lead and you can fill in whatever I miss."

The Special Agent in charge of the FBI's Asheville resident agency cut an impressive figure as she walked toward us. Trim and fit, she wore her dark blue pinstripe suit like she was some Wall Street executive, yet her short brown hair was still long enough to bounce with each stride. Her pale blue eyes sparkled in the late afternoon sun, and with her back to her colleagues, she flashed us a brilliant smile.

"So, Uncle, you ask me to do a favor for you on Saturday and then dump a body on me on Monday. I can hardly wait till tomorrow. What's next?"

"What's next is you're wrapping up my case. Barry found a pistol and a potentially incriminating ledger book that were hidden under the driver's seat."

"Guns N' Roses. So, are you keeping the gun and giving me the rose?"

"No, you get the whole package, provided you run me an expedited ballistics report."

"Okay. That it? A gun and a ledger?"

"And a surviving WITSEC alum who's getting the ultimate in protective coverage."

Boyce arched an eyebrow. "Do tell."

For the next twenty minutes, Tommy Lee gave her a detailed briefing that ran from Toby McKay's assault on Commissioner James through our interview with Janet Sinclair. Then she walked with us to get the evidence bags locked in my jeep.

"All right. I'll keep the chain of custody secure on these puppies." She turned to me. "I may need a statement from you if Brookshire gets caught up in this mess. I'll also run a cell trace requesting the location of Brookshire's call to the Sheriff's Department."

"May I make a suggestion?" I asked.

"Please," she said. "Any suggestions from you are welcome. Now, from Uncle Tommy Lee, well, that's a different matter."

Tommy Lee ignored her.

I pointed to the clear bags protecting the gun and ledger. "I know you'll go over both of these for fingerprints, but when you do forensics on the victim's vehicle, check the floormat under the seat."

"What am I looking for?" Boyce asked.

"I'm curious as to the pattern of gun oil."

Boyce nodded. She knew what I was getting at. Every well-maintained firearm is frequently cleaned and oiled. Trace residue should appear on the Infiniti's carpet.

"So, if it looks like the oil pattern is fresh with no other trace, the gun was laid there," she said.

"Planted there," I corrected. "Odd that there's no holster, but not odd if Sinclair felt like he needed to be able to grab the pistol quickly. If you find lots of oil traces in a broad pattern consistent with the gun shifting during travel, then I'll feel better. Otherwise…"

Boyce looked at Tommy Lee. "Gee, I wonder who should be wearing the sheriff's badge?"

"What do you mean sheriff?" Tommy Lee said. "I was thinking the same thing about your FBI shield."

We left the scene about six as dusk was settling in. I phoned Susan from the jeep and asked if she'd started dinner. It was one of those nights where I felt like a pizza and a couple of beers. She'd just gotten home and said a pizza sounded wonderful. She'd make the salad if I'd pick up a plain cheese on one half and then whatever I chose to pile on the other. Mushrooms and pepperoni were my leading candidates.

It was another crisp fall evening and although we ate at the dining table, I slid open the sliding glass door to the deck and let the breeze blow through the screen. All the ambience of the outdoors without the bugs.

I devoured all four of my slices and looked longingly at one of Susan's plain cheese. "You know I've still got beer left in my glass. I try to make pizza and beer finish together. Like eating ice cream and cake. You, on the other hand, just have water, and after I bought you the nice bottle of on-sale Malbec."

She laced her fingers together and rested her chin on her hands. "Oh, poor dear, we can't have that. Go ahead and take the food out of our mouths." She gave a mysterious smile that signaled something else was going on.

"Our mouths? Who are we now? Queen Elizabeth?"

"No. You should make a better deduction than that." She picked up her wineglass of sparkling water and toasted me. "My Prince Charming."

My throat went dry. Clues clicked into place. Susan's sudden switch from wine to water. The Mona Lisa smile. "You're not?" My pulse quickened with unanticipated excitement. "We're having a baby?"

Her smile broadened. "No, silly. We're not having a baby."

And just as suddenly, my unexpected euphoria vanished, leaving only unexpected disappointment.

Susan kept her glass aloft. "We're having babies."

The rollercoaster of emotions within that ten-second span made the car jump the track. Maybe I blacked out. Maybe my mind soared to some other astral plane. The next thing I recalled was Susan standing beside me.

"Barry, are you all right?"

"All right? I'm ecstatic. But are you sure?"

Susan and I had decided the past spring we were ready for a family. We'd not done anything special but rather let Mother Nature take her course.

"I suspected it, but didn't want to say anything till I was sure. I got confirmation today."

"Two?"

She laughed. "Two strong heartbeats. That Mother Nature, what a sense of humor."

"How far along?"

"About eight weeks. I'd rather wait a few more before we start telling people."

I scooted back my chair and stood, my knees a little wobbly. "Shouldn't you sit down? How about the sofa?"

"Barry, I feel just as good as I did three minutes ago. Maybe you should sit. Finish your beer and the pizza."

"Beer? This calls for champagne."

"You may call for it but no champagne will answer. The closest we have is your beer and my sparkling water."

"Then that works for me." I lifted my beer. "To the most wonderful mother-to-be."

She raised her glass. "And to the calmest father-to-be. Either that or he might have to be tranquilized before these babies come."

We talked till midnight. When I was changing for bed and emptying my pockets, I found what I'd forgotten—the folded receipt I'd plucked from Janet Sinclair's torn bag of groceries. It should have gone in with the gun and ledger, especially since the time stamp could exonerate Janet by providing an alibi for the time of Robert's death.

I was careful to hold the receipt by a corner edge and take it to the kitchen where we kept zip-lock bags. Before securing it, I made a closer examination. The listed items included the elbow pasta, tomato sauce, ranch dressing, and produce I'd seen scattered on the concrete. And there was another purchase, one I hadn't seen, one that proved Janet Sinclair a liar.

Chapter Twenty-four

"Ice cream? You woke me up over a missing half gallon of ice cream?" Tommy Lee's gruff question warned me that he didn't view my discovery with the same "smoking gun" implications that I did. At least not a few minutes after midnight.

"She clearly lied," I argued. "She said she didn't go into the house but I bet you dollars to doughnuts she left the other groceries for show and put the ice cream in her freezer."

"Did you inventory the items in the dropped bag?"

"No," I conceded. "But I saw them scattered and I don't think there was enough room for a half gallon in what little space remained in the bag."

"That still doesn't change the time stamp on the receipt. Unless she had someone shopping for her, she could have come home, found her husband, and gone into shock. People do mundane things in traumatic situations."

"And people do calculated things when they can callously step over a dead body to enter their house to save a five-dollar carton of ice cream."

"All right," Tommy Lee said. "I'll cover Lindsay in the morning. She took possession of everything at the murder scene. Be in at seven and we'll sort out priorities. Anything else you want to tell me while I'm still awake?"

I wanted to shout I was going to be a dad twice over, but I

yielded to Susan's wish to delay. Besides, I didn't particularly want my news mingled with a conversation about murder.

"No. Sorry to bother you. It's probably nothing."

"What the hell, Barry. Everything starts from nothing. I'm just cranky in my old age."

"When were you not?"

He hung up on me.

At six-fifty the next morning, I walked into Tommy Lee's office wearing plainclothes and carrying a bag with two egg and sausage biscuits from Bojangles'. "Peace offering. No more late night phone calls."

He grabbed the bag. "Don't make promises you can't keep. Any more insights strike you during the night?"

"Nothing I can work on. I wonder if we're missing something and the WITSEC status and food stamp scam are more closely related than we thought."

"How so?" Tommy Lee mumbled, his mouth full of biscuit.

"There's a high degree of organization to this fraud operation. What if Robert Sinclair was still tied to the mob?"

"But he put his old man away."

"Yes. And there are competing factions within every family. What if someone in the family or more likely a rival family wanted old Bobby Santona out of the way? They entice Robert to give up the evidence. But they can't guarantee his safety so who better to protect Robert and Janet than the U.S. Marshals."

"That's a stretch," Tommy Lee said. "A lot of hypotheticals. And what's in it for Robert?"

"Right under the nose of Brookshire and the marshals, Robert runs the food stamp scam. The mob sets up shop in the mountains."

"So why the hit?"

"Robert generated too much attention. Not from his ill-conceived return for the New Jersey funeral but for the executions of Rufus and Sonny. They sever the ties by killing Robert."

"And walk away from the whole operation?"

"It was probably going down anyway. Collier Crockett's infiltrated the network. He might be able to turn Janet Sinclair. She'll claim ignorance, of course, but he might find some leverage."

"Like a missing half gallon of ice cream?"

"No. Although that does bother me. I was thinking more about money. We haven't followed that trail. We don't know where it leads."

"If the gun under Robert's seat matches the one that killed Sonny and Rufus, then I think our case is closed. But, share your theory with Lindsay. She can get to the financials."

I remembered Cindy's comments at Bank of America that Janet Sinclair also had accounts at Wells Fargo. Someone was cashing the checks Rufus had been writing to Staples Sources. Maybe that was Janet.

"What are you planning for this morning?" I asked.

"Back to paperwork and budgets. Nothing to do until Lindsay runs her tests and we get the M.E. report."

I pulled the zip-lock bag with the grocery receipt from my jacket pocket. "Pass this on to Lindsay."

"Give it to her yourself. Why don't you go to her Asheville office and have a sit-down? Frankly, I think your mob theory is farfetched, but no sense shutting down a line of inquiry over my misgivings. Besides, the expense won't be coming out of my budget."

"Thanks for your unwavering support."

He laughed. "Sure. Take an unmarked rather than your jeep. I'll spring for the gas. You still carrying the Kimber?"

"The pistol's in the jeep."

"Take it. We still might have a killer in the area who thinks you know more than you do. Keep your gun closer than Robert Sinclair kept his."

Tommy Lee called his niece at home and the special agent agreed to meet me at her office at nine. The FBI's resident agency was located in the Federal Courthouse in Asheville. Security was tight, and a little before nine I had to produce my credentials and declare the concealed Kimber before I could proceed to the second floor.

I'd been in the FBI office several times with Tommy Lee and knew his niece would give a fair evaluation of whatever I presented.

I accepted a cup of coffee and sat across from her in the small conversation area in a corner of her office.

She had exchanged her navy blue pinstripe pants suit for a charcoal gray one. Her blue eyes were bright and focused on me with undivided attention.

I pulled the zip-lock bag protecting the receipt from my jacket pocket. "I have a confession to make. I picked this up from the grocery bag yesterday and forgot to give it to you. I don't know if the medical examiner's time of death will be specific enough to clear Janet Sinclair, but combined with the time of her call to Luther Brookshire, there's a good chance this will corroborate her alibi."

"In your possession the whole time?" Lindsay glanced at the receipt and then laid it on the coffee table between us.

"Yes."

"Good. Since the Bureau is heading up the investigation, we'll get an official statement from you while you're here."

"There is one thing about the receipt that struck me as strange."

She picked it up and re-examined it. "What?"

I told her about the ice cream and that I suspected Janet had taken it from the bag and put it in the freezer. "That undercuts the statement she gave us," I said. "She claimed she never entered the house after finding the body."

Lindsay nodded. "That's what she told us in our interview."

"Why would she lie?"

"Who wants to be known as the wife more concerned with saving her ice cream than losing her husband?" She smiled. "Unless it was sea-salt caramel."

"Is Janet still in the house?"

"No. We took her into protective custody."

"With the marshals?"

"No. We have a safe house. I'm keeping her away from the marshals until we make sure Brookshire's not involved. As it is, he's on shaky ground because of your discovery of his affair with a married witness. He's being cooperative and I'm not looking to make him the centerpiece of a case without grounds. I've expedited the requests for cell records and ballistics, including Brookshire's service weapon. I'll also send someone by the Sinclairs' house to check the freezer for the missing ice cream. Then I'll raise the statement discrepancy with Janet Sinclair."

"What about the ledger?"

Lindsay Boyce set down the grocery receipt and picked up her cup of coffee. After a sip, she said, "Not sure what to do with that. We weren't involved in this food scam thing. FNS Investigator Crockett has already contacted us about needing that as evidence for his case. Given the white rose, odds are this is a payback hit from the Santona family. Joan Santona aka Janet Sinclair will get a third identity and the case will go cold. That's my fear."

"Let me float one other theory, but be warned," I said, "it's a stretch."

She laughed. "At this point, I'd even look at a theory involving aliens and a mothership."

So, I told her my thoughts that Robert Sinclair had betrayed his father for a rival faction, used the marshals as the best protection available, and then flagrantly set up his scam with the backing of mafia organization and expertise. "We never got a chance to trace the money trail of Rufus Taylor's checks to Staples Sources. You might want to explore that option."

"Isn't Crockett doing that?"

"I told him what we've found but I didn't hand over the Taylor ledger. I guess I should give that to you or him."

Lindsay pursed her lips as she thought it over. "Hold onto it till we get the ballistics report. If there's no ballistics match to the gun in Robert Sinclair's SUV, then you might need to follow that lead yourself. We should know a lot more by the end of the day." She took another sip of coffee. "How did you get interested in the Sinclairs in the first place?"

I told her about Archie Donovan's plan to enable the Sinclairs to access the cash values of the insurance policies that were still in their old names. And how, in true Archie fashion, he'd bragged about being in the cell next to Sonny McKay and that he was going to meet Sonny the next day.

"And then Sonny turned up dead," Lindsay said.

"Yes. Whether that was planned before Archie talked to the Sinclairs or as a result of that conversation, we didn't know. We had to check it out."

"And the ledger you found in Robert Sinclair's car is the missing link between him and the food stamp scam."

"And the gun might be the murderer's signature."

Lindsay Boyce looked out her second-story window and thought a moment. "Do you know if Archie Donovan's name-change paperwork went through?"

"I don't. He hoped by mid-week, so either today or tomorrow. You're looking at Robert's death in light of the benefits that can now come to Janet Sinclair?"

"Yes. There's a hell of a lot in the policies' cash values. I doubt she'll want a new identity until she gets that money. If there's no link between her and the crimes her husband might have committed, then she'll collect it all."

"Another layer of motive," I said.

"Too many layers. You're right about following the money. I guess we'll need to work with Collier Crockett and see where this food stamp scam takes us. If you're right, it could lead back to New Jersey."

"Any suggestions for what I should do in the meantime?" I asked.

"Assume your case is still going to be open and keep working it. We might intersect, but you go with your leads and don't worry about stepping on my toes."

It was good to hear her say those encouraging words, especially since that was my intent all along.

"Then can you photocopy the ledger book I found yesterday?" I asked. "And I'll have Tommy Lee send over a copy of what we discovered in Rufus Taylor's safe."

Special Agent Lindsay Boyce set down her coffee and offered her hand. "You've got a deal. I'll give you paper to write your statement while I take care of copying the ledger."

About twenty minutes later, I signed several handwritten pages documenting what I had discovered upon arrival at the murder scene. Lindsay Boyce handed me a thick manila envelope containing the photocopied ledger pages and walked me down the hall where we found a familiar face waiting in the small lobby.

"Deputy Clayton." Collier Crockett extended his hand. "I understand you broke open my case."

"That he did," Lindsay Boyce said. She and the FNS Investigator also shook hands.

"Well, I just happened to show up first," I said.

He laughed. "Most of the time, that's what it's all about." He eyed the folder in my left hand. "That for me?"

"No. It's some information for the sheriff."

"I'll go over what I have for you," Lindsay Boyce said. "And I want to share some interesting theories Barry's developed."

"All right." Crockett's tone became serious. "But the EBT fraud is still in my wheelhouse, just so we all understand."

"And I've got a dead federal witness," Lindsay stated. "I suggest we let Barry get on with his duties while you and I discuss how to move forward."

"No problem." Crockett turned to me. "I hope this wraps up

your case for you. If I come across anything relevant, I'll be sure and shoot it your way."

"Thanks." I left the two federal agents to battle over their turf.

I'd parked in the Otis parking garage across the street and before heading back to Gainesboro, I decided to follow up on the question Lindsay Boyce had posed about Archie and the paperwork. I hadn't spoken to him since he'd joined his wife and daughters at his mother-in-law's.

"Barry?" He answered his cell on the first ring.

"Everybody okay?"

"Yes, but I'm about to go crazy wondering what's going on. Janet Sinclair called me this morning about her husband. She's scared to death and wants to get her money before she goes into hiding."

"She's in a safe house," I assured him.

"Yeah. A room at the Renaissance Hotel in Asheville?"

"How do you know that?"

"She told me. She called from the bathroom while the shower was running."

"What's the status of the policies?"

"Everything is good to go. I got the confirmation the owner-ship has changed to the company. We'll drop the Santona names from the listed officers and leave only Sinclairs." He paused. "Now it will just be Janet. She wants the death certificate and the beneficiary and cash surrender forms."

"Beneficiary? Doesn't the name of the insured still have to be Robert Santona?"

"It does."

"How's she going to use a Robert Sinclair death certificate to collect on the death of Robert Santona?"

"She told me the marshals would straighten it out. I just need the death certificate and claim forms."

She's going to use them to create a forgery, I thought. Change the name from Sinclair to Santona.

"How are you going to get them to her?" I asked.

"I'm supposed to text her. She'll tell me where to leave them. A friend will pick them up."

A friend? I wondered if Janet was still in communication with Luther Brookshire. Was he the marshal that would enable Janet to collect the death benefit that would be much higher than the cash value? He certainly could arrange a name change on a death certificate.

"But I told her the documents haven't come back to the office yet," Archie said. "I didn't want her to know I'm in Weaverville. I expect to get them here later this afternoon."

"So, you could wait until tomorrow to deliver them?"

"Yes. And I need to get the death certificates from Fletcher. I spoke with him a few minutes ago and he expects them later this afternoon. I'll be so glad when this is over. All I want is to get the ten thousand dollars from Janet Sinclair for the Boys and Girls Clubs and be done with it. Barry, never encourage me to do something like this again."

Me? Encourage Archie? "I won't. You can count on it. But do me a favor. Let me know what Janet Sinclair arranges to get the death certificate and forms."

"Sure. You want me to give her your number?"

I took a deep breath and suppressed my better judgment. "No, Archie. This is our secret. It's even more important than when I told you not to tell anyone about your conversation with Sonny. Remember how that turned out."

"Don't worry. I've learned my lesson. Mum's the word."

We disconnected. I looked at the manila envelope on the seat beside me. Soon Collier Crockett would be trying to decode those records; Lindsay Boyce would be searching through Robert Sinclair's bank records. At the moment, both were still viable avenues for my investigation and I had no other leads. I pulled out of the parking garage and headed for Gainesboro.

Chapter Twenty-five

I found Cindy Todd alone in her glass-walled office in the Bank of America branch. She spotted me immediately as she must have been watching the lobby for any congestion in the teller lines. She waved and I beelined straight for her open door.

Cindy stood up from her desk, her face pale as parchment. "Barry, Fletcher told me about Mr. Sinclair. I can't believe such a thing would happen in our town."

"I'm afraid so. Can we talk a few minutes?"

"Yes." She motioned me to a guest chair.

I first closed the door and then sat across from her.

"Is this about the Sinclairs?" she asked.

"Yes. You're going to get a visit from the FBI."

Cindy's eyes widened. "Have we done something wrong?"

"No. But they'll come in with warrants for the safe deposit box, account records, and anything else tied to Robert Sinclair. Janet Sinclair is being held in protective custody for her own safety, but if she should come in here before the federal agents, I want you to call me immediately."

"She was just here yesterday. I waited on her myself."

"What time?"

"A little after noon. One of the tellers was on lunch break and another called in sick. I covered a window for about thirty minutes."

"What did she do?"

Cindy wet her lips, uncomfortable with my question.

"Cindy, this is a murder investigation. You're going to have to cooperate with the FBI, so you may as well start with me."

"She got a cashier's check for nine thousand dollars from the Sinclairity Sales account."

"How much did that leave?"

"I think it was around a thousand dollars and some change."

"So, she could have deliberately kept it under a ten-thousand-dollar withdrawal."

"I guess so," Cindy said.

"Had she ever withdrawn that much before?"

"Maybe. I don't wait on her that often. We'd have to go back through the records. I think most transactions are commission deposits and then transfers to the Sinclairs' personal account. As I said before, sometimes there are cash deposits as well."

"Who was the payee on the cashier's check?"

"She wanted it made out to cash. That's a little unusual. Most of the time the payee is someone who wants to know the check is good."

"Anything else?"

"She also went to her safe deposit box. I saw her leave with a couple of manila envelopes under her arm."

"Taking things out, not putting them in like the other day?"

"That's correct."

Janet Sinclair's actions didn't necessarily mean she was involved in her husband's murder. She had a history of reacting to perceived threats. Her July visit to the funeral home and her concern for the life insurance policies had been triggered by her husband's ill-fated, secret attendance of his father's funeral. She also could have been aware of Robert's criminal enterprise and been spooked by the spate of killings, anticipating the jeopardy created for her and her husband. Was she organizing a financial life raft for both of them, or was she bailing out on her own? Or with someone else?

"You said Janet had an account at Wells Fargo," I said.

"Yes. Where my friend Tina works."

I looked at my watch. It was a few minutes before eleven. "Do you think she would meet me for lunch?"

"Maybe. She usually goes early. Sometimes she skips the meal and runs errands."

"Would you do me a favor and call her? An introduction from you might put her at ease."

Tina Logan didn't have time for lunch but agreed to meet me at eleven-thirty for a cup of coffee at the Cardinal Café. I used the extra time to phone Tommy Lee and brief him on my conversations with Special Agent Boyce and Cindy.

When I'd brought him up to date, I asked, "Do you want me to report to Lindsay?"

"No. Let's wait till she gets us the information from her forensics team. If Janet's at a safe house, then she's not a flight risk. What's your plan after you meet Tina?"

"I thought I'd make an unannounced visit to Buddy Smith at Wilmer's Convenience Corner. I hope he'll have some records like Rufus Taylor did. Lindsay gave me photocopies of what we think is Robert Sinclair's master list. Can you also scan and send a photo of Sinclair that I can show him? The one on his driver's license is certainly preferable to anything taken at the crime scene."

"You're stepping on Crockett's toes," Tommy Lee warned.

"Crockett never said he'd successfully flipped Buddy. Maybe showing the photo to the man and telling him that Sinclair is dead will take away his fears. At this point any other stores in the fraud network are of no interest. Crockett's welcome to them all."

"All right. Go ahead. We've got a pair of murders. That's two aces in my book. Lindsay's got one, while Crockett's only holding an EBT card. He's not even in the game."

At eleven-twenty, I slid into the back booth at the Cardinal Café. I wanted to beat the lunch crowd and claim the spot that offered the most privacy. I'd told Tina Logan what I was wearing so she had no trouble finding me as soon as she entered.

Tina looked to be in her mid-twenties, an attractive African-American woman with a bright smile and slim figure.

I stood to greet her.

"Deputy Clayton?"

"Yes. But I'd prefer you call me Barry."

"And I'm Tina."

I gestured for her to sit on the booth bench across from me. Helen Todd, owner of the cafe and Cindy's mother, immediately came to us with a pot of coffee and two cups.

"Well, Tina," she said. "Couldn't find a better lunch date?"

"I'm a new diet," I said. "Women see me and lose their appetites."

They both laughed.

"Oh, Barry's not so bad," Helen said. "And he's married. His wife's trained him well." She set the pot on the table. "I know y'all want to talk, so I'll leave you to it. If you decide you want something else, just holler."

She left and Tina grabbed two packets of Sweet 'N Low.

"How long have you known Cindy?" I asked.

"A couple of years. I moved here from Asheville for my job. I met Cindy through our book club."

"As she told you on the phone, I'm working on an investigation tied to yesterday's murder of Robert Sinclair. Cindy told me his wife Janet also has an account at your branch."

She nodded, and then shook her head. "I can't believe it. Mrs. Sinclair must be devastated."

"Yes. Right now the best thing we can do is find out who killed her husband."

"Why do you want to know about their banking?"

"Standard procedure." I tried to make it sound like it was no more unusual than finding out their age. "And you might be asked some similar questions by the FBI."

"I'd much rather talk to you."

"Thank you. Let me assure you the agents will be very courteous. But I thought this would be a more relaxed setting."

She took a sip of coffee. "I don't know how much help I'll be."

"Did you know Mr. Sinclair?"

"No. I never met him. I only knew his signature."

"His signature?"

"The endorsements on his checks. Evidently, Mr. Sinclair set up the account over three years ago. That's before I came. It's in his name along with a DBA name."

"DBA?"

"Doing Business As. The account number that is tied to Mr. Sinclair receives deposits to a doing-business-as company name."

"Sinclairity Sales," I said.

Tina shook her head. "No. His account was for Staples Sources."

Her words struck like a flash of lighting, illuminating the path from Rufus' records of bogus EBT charges to the master ledger in Robert Sinclair's car to the deposits in a bank account named Staples Sources. We could potentially trace funds from Rufus to the final deposit, but the stronger case would come from Buddy Smith and his testimony as to exactly how he was threatened into participating.

"Did these checks always come made out to Staples Sources?" I asked.

"Yes." Tina thought a moment. "Although once Mrs. Sinclair brought in several checks in an envelope that was addressed to that Sinclairity Sales you mentioned. The double S caught my eye."

"Double S?"

"Sinclairity Sales—Staples Sources."

Barry, you idiot, I thought. I'd never noticed the alliteration.

"Do you remember the address on the envelope?"

"No. But I'm pretty sure it was their home address. I could look it up."

So, the dummy invoices that transferred money from fraudulent EBT card purchases had a phony address, but the stores mailed their payments to the Sinclairs in envelopes addressed to Robert Sinclair's legitimate company. A double layer of insulation. Staples Sources sounded like some grocery supplier. A simple audit probably wouldn't look past the invoices and canceled checks.

"What payments went out of the Staples Sources account?"

"A few times Mrs. Sinclair made withdrawals by a check her husband had written to cash. I can review the statements when I get back to work."

I remembered Cindy Todd said Janet sometimes deposited cash into the Sinclairity Sales account at Bank of America. Something Janet denied. Were the cash withdrawals an untraceable way to get money from Staples Solutions into their personal accounts?

"Yes," I said. "Please review the statements."

Tina looked at me with concern. "This is okay, my talking to you?"

"Yes, but I wouldn't want to cause any internal policy problems between you and the bank. When the FBI comes, don't mention we talked unless they ask. Believe me, they'll find your information very useful." I handed her my card with my cell phone number. "Call me once you've checked that account."

"And if Mrs. Sinclair comes in again?"

"Help her. You've got no reason to treat her differently."

She nodded, reached for her purse, and opened it.

I held up my hand. "Coffee's on me. Thanks for making the time."

"You're welcome." She slid out of the booth and left.

Helen came over and I ordered a grilled ham and cheese sandwich. I needed to eat and to chew over what Tina Logan had told me. We now had the provable link between Rufus Taylor's checkbook and Janet Sinclair's deposits. Also, Rufus' itemized list of the amounts of the fraudulent EBT purchases could be examined against Robert Sinclair's master ledger. I wanted to find those connections, and then, armed with that confirmation, visit Buddy Smith at Wilmer's Convenience Corner where I hoped he'd confess to a similar setup. If he could identify Robert's face as the person who intimidated him, our circle would be complete.

I returned to the Sheriff's Department and booked one of the conference rooms where I could work undisturbed. I spread out the ledger we found in Rufus Taylor's safe, his checkbook stubs, the photocopies of the book from Robert Sinclair's Infiniti, and a legal pad for jotting down any notes.

I started with the last page of Rufus' entries and then worked backwards through Sinclair's ledger looking for a match. Each page had a five-digit number as a heading, a list of dollar amounts, and their total sum. About five pages in, I found a page with numbers identical to Rufus' last page, including the total amount of four-hundred-seventy-five dollars. I noted the heading number 00027. I flipped forward till I found the number recurring again. This page total was three-hundred-eighty-six dollars and thirteen cents. Both numbers matched checks Rufus had written to Staples Sources.

I flipped through the master ledger and found twenty-four unique coded headings in all. Probably the identifying numbers for the individual stores in the fraud network. We had store names from the list I'd found in Sonny McKay's saddlebag, but without the key, I had no way of knowing which store corresponded with which heading without going through each store's fraudulent purchase records. And those records might be destroyed once Sinclair's death went public. If there was a key sheet, it wasn't in any of the materials I had. Could Special Agent Lindsay Boyce have missed it when the book was copied?

I called the Asheville office of the FBI and was put through immediately.

"What's up?" she asked.

I told her I'd matched sums on Rufus Taylor's checks to records in the book from the murder scene, but that I couldn't decrypt how the heading numbers identified the stores.

"Sorry I can't help you. I express-shipped the book to Quantico for analysis right after I made copies for you and Crockett."

"Where's it going after that?"

"If nothing seems relevant to our case, it will go to Crockett. Maybe he can figure out that key."

"Do me a favor," I asked. "If the lab results yield something promising like prints or DNA, have the book come back to me. We are talking about a double homicide."

"You know Crockett's a federal investigator. He won't want it going to a local sheriff. He wasn't too thrilled when I told him I'd given you a copy."

"Why?"

"Because he's a tight ass who fears you'll screw up his case. I told him he's lucky I held onto the book long enough to make him a copy and that it didn't go to Quantico last night."

I shared her assessment of the FNS investigator, but I had an ace to play. "All right. Who would you rather face? Tight ass Crockett? Or your hard ass uncle, Tommy Lee?"

She laughed. "Okay, you'll get your damn book when we're through with it. I did send the gun and Sinclair's floor mats to Quantico last night. I expect to hear something back this afternoon. A murdered federal witness gets everyone's attention."

I thanked her for her help and disconnected. No sooner had I laid my cell phone on the table than it rang.

"Barry Clayton," I said.

"Deputy Clayton. It's Tina Logan."

"Yes, Tina."

"Sorry to be late getting back to you. We were slammed after lunch."

"No problem. Have you had a chance to look at that account?"

"Yes, sir." Her voice dropped to a whisper. "It's empty."

"What?"

"The funds were wired out yesterday afternoon. Nearly half a million dollars."

I stood up from the table, too agitated to sit. "Wired where?"

"The Cayman Islands."

Chapter Twenty-six

"And you're sure about the time?" The speakerphone in the middle of the table vibrated as Special Agent Lindsay Boyce asked the critical question.

Tommy Lee had called her from the conference room where I'd spread out the ledgers, check stubs, and Staples Sources invoices from Rufus Taylor's store.

"Yes," I said. "The bank employee told me the funds had been wired out at four-fifty-five yesterday afternoon. We know Janet Sinclair was with you. Did she slip into the bathroom with her phone or have access to a computer?"

"No," the FBI agent insisted. "You handed her over to us at four-fifteen, we interviewed her for approximately an hour, and then took her to a safe house."

"The Renaissance Hotel in Asheville," I said.

"How did you know that?"

"She called her insurance agent, Archie Donovan. She's getting the death benefit and the cash values out of some insurance policies."

"Not if she murdered her husband," Lindsay said sharply.

"And your evidence to charge her?" Tommy Lee asked.

"From what Barry says, we've got her fingers all over the Staples Sources bank account, whether she wired out the money or not."

Tommy Lee shook his head, a fruitless gesture in front of a speakerphone. "She can say she thought the checks were all part of her husband's businesses. He signed them, she deposited them. She had no idea he was doing anything illegal. And she has an alibi for when the funds were transferred."

I thought of another argument. "If Janet was guilty, why let me discover the ledger book in the car? That's what her attorney will profess."

"But we know it was to take you off the case," Lindsay said. "You have your killer and your investigation is closed. The gun and ledger tie him to the murders."

Something began gnawing at the back of my brain. "Who told her we were investigating food stamp fraud?"

"What do you mean?" Tommy Lee asked.

"Yesterday, when we spoke with her in her living room, she said, 'Something like this food scam thing.' It was when she thought we might be accusing her husband of a crime. We hadn't mentioned it, but Brookshire looked uncomfortable as hell when she said it."

Tommy Lee drummed his fingers on the table. "When did Brookshire leave the scene?"

"He left around four-thirty," Lindsay said. "I pulled him aside, told him I knew about the affair, and that we would be handling protection for Janet. We argued and he left in a huff."

"I guess we were with the techs in the carport," I said. "I don't remember him going."

"That gave him twenty-five minutes to either use his smartphone or access a computer," Lindsay said. "If he and Janet are not only lovers but also conspirators, then he could have had all the passcodes and account numbers to facilitate the wire transfer."

"What do you suggest for a next step?" Tommy Lee asked her.

"Do Janet and Luther know we know about the bank accounts?"

Tommy Lee looked at me.

"I haven't told them."

"Then let's do nothing about the accounts," Lindsay said. "I'll put a tail on Luther Brookshire and we'll give Janet freedom to use her phone and move about. I'll even tell Brookshire he can start the process for putting her back in WITSEC. We'll see if they start communicating with one another."

We heard someone call Lindsay's name.

"Hold a second," she said, and she muted her phone.

"That's not a bad plan," Tommy Lee whispered. "If Brookshire is involved, he'll want those store owners to get rid of any records of the fraudulent payments so there's no way to match the master ledger. We might not be able to tie him to Sinclair's murder, but some of those store owners might be able to identify him."

The speakerphone clicked on.

"I've just gotten results in from Quantico," Lindsay said. "I'll fax the report, but here's the basic information."

I grabbed a pencil and my legal pad.

"The ballistics test confirms the gun matches the one used in the murders of Sonny McKay and Rufus Taylor. However, the bullets retrieved from Robert Sinclair's body are from a nine millimeter."

"What about prints on the gun?" I asked.

"They match Robert Sinclair's. However the lab tech added a note. The preponderance of the prints are from the left hand."

"Do we know if Robert was left-handed?" Tommy Lee asked.

"Yes," Lindsay said. "I asked Janet Sinclair that question yesterday, anticipating we'd want to make sure someone hadn't tried to place the prints after he died. But the key word is preponderance. The tech notes only left-hand prints—on the gun, on the magazine, and on the cartridges. Have you ever tried to load a magazine with one hand?"

"Someone knew he was left-handed and overdid it," Tommy Lee said. "Obviously, Janet knew her husband was left-handed, as would Luther Brookshire, given his close connection during their relocation in WITSEC."

"And, Barry, your concern about the floor mat paid off. The only gun oil was on the spot where the pistol lay. That's a pretty unlikely circumstance given curvy mountain roads. Both the ledger and gun would have slid around to some measurable degree."

"So, Janet Sinclair is either a hapless pawn or a coconspirator," I said.

"Well, she couldn't be her husband's killer," Lindsay declared. "We ran down the surveillance video from Ingles and confirmed she was in a register line at the time on the grocery receipt."

I thought how Luther Brookshire had described Robert Sinclair. That an IQ hovering slightly above room temperature isn't going to mastermind such a complex operation. "Sounds like Robert Sinclair could have been a dupe in this whole thing. And if the murderer was a hitman from the Santona family, why bother to plant the pistol with Robert's prints? He'd just want to waste the guy, leave the rose, and be gone."

Tommy Lee leaned closer to the speakerphone. "Lindsay, have you tracked Brookshire's location for when Janet called him yesterday?"

"Yes. He was on your side of Asheville. He could have removed the battery from his cell phone, traveled undetected to kill Sinclair, and then powered back up in time to receive Janet's call when he was safely away from the crime scene."

Tommy Lee sighed. "Well, if nearly a half million dollars is now out of the country, is there a danger Brookshire's a flight risk? Either solo or with Janet?"

"I don't know about Brookshire," I said, "but I don't think Janet's going to walk away without collecting the money from the insurance policies. If she can get the death benefit as well as cash values, we're talking more than a million and a half. As far as she knows, she's not a suspect."

"Then let's leave it that way," Lindsay said. "We'll let her stay in the safe house, but give her a loose rein. I'll tell Brookshire I've reconsidered and that as soon as we check out a few things from her statement, the marshals can have her back."

"Sounds good," Tommy Lee agreed. "Barry, what's your next move?"

"I think if Brookshire's part of the EBT conspiracy and he planted the ledger book, he'll want to make sure the store owners destroy the matching records. He might instruct them by phone, or if he's concerned about being tapped, visit them in person. I'd like to see Buddy Smith at Wilmer's Convenience Corner and show him a photo of both Robert Sinclair and Luther Brookshire. I've got Sinclair's. Lindsay, can you e-mail me one of Brookshire?"

"Sure," she said. "And I'll throw in one of Janet. Never underestimate a woman's deceitfulness."

Tommy Lee laughed. "That's my niece. Calls 'em like she sees 'em."

"And what I want to see is this case closed," Lindsay said. "Especially if we've got a dirty federal marshal."

I remembered that Wilmer's Convenience Corner wasn't convenient around the clock. Buddy Smith closed at seven during the week. If I was going to have a confrontation with him, I preferred to arrive nearer closing time and wait till we could talk in private.

As it was late afternoon, I phoned Susan at her clinic to let her know I'd be late for dinner.

"How are you feeling?" was my opening question.

"I'm fine, Barry. I don't want you treating me like I'm sick for the next seven months."

"I know. I know. I guess I'm just getting used to the idea."

"Don't worry. I'll whine when I want to. What's up?"

I gave her the status of the case and told her I'd be home late. Wilmer's Convenience Corner was about forty-five minutes away.

"Is this undercover?"

I realized I wasn't sure. Collier Crockett had come to the cabin angry at what he saw as my interference, but he said that he hadn't given away my identity. Maybe I could demand

Buddy's records claiming to represent Sinclair or Brookshire. If that didn't work, I'd show my creds and tell him I was working with Crockett and the FNS.

"I'll play it undercover at first," I told Susan.

She took a deep, audible breath. "Please be careful. Two little ones are going to need their father."

Her words hit hard. I wasn't one for taking unnecessary risks, but now the prospect of leaving Susan a widow with two infants shocked me with its unanticipated magnitude.

"I will, dear. We're close to wrapping this up. In a few days, everything will be back to normal."

"Barry, you know our normal will soon be changed forever."

"And I can hardly wait. Love you."

"Love you too." She hung up.

I sat for a moment, second-guessing my plan. Buddy Smith had his own little girl to protect and she'd be home from school. So, I'd play my role easy on the threat level, either as a criminal or a deputy.

Next I phoned Fletcher at the funeral home and learned he had the death certificates for Robert Sinclair.

"Have you told Archie?" I asked him.

"No. I just picked up ten copies from the town hall fifteen minutes ago."

"Good. I'll call Archie. Leave them on my desk in case he wants me to run them by tonight."

I immediately dialed Archie's cell phone. "Have you heard anything more from Janet Sinclair?"

"Yes," he said. "She called at noon asking for the insurance forms and death certificates."

I could hear Archie's young girls laughing in the background. "Where are you?"

"Still with Gloria and her mother. Do you think it's safe for us to return home?"

"Not yet. A day or two at most. And I have the death certificates from Fletcher and you can contact Janet Sinclair. But,

Archie, tell her you'll just drop them off at the Renaissance Hotel. Don't meet her or this unknown friend alone."

A few seconds of silence passed. "You think she killed her husband?" His voice sounded like he was being strangled.

"No, I don't. She has an ironclad alibi. But there are things and people still at play. Someone might be watching her, so I'd rather you keep your distance."

"So, should I drive into Gainesboro now?"

Weaverville was an hour away on the north side of Asheville. That meant Archie had to come in and then turn right around. Wilmer's Convenience Corner would be a much closer rendezvous. "Archie, do you have all the policy information with you?"

"You mean like the companies and the numbers?"

"Yes."

"Of course. I downloaded the forms and I've pre-filled everything out. All Janet has to do is sign and either mail or FedEx them and the death certificate."

"And where will the checks come?"

"To that company. Sinclairity Sales. The one we rolled the ownership into when we added their Santona names. The address of record is their home."

Janet had left the Sinclairity Sales bank account open, which meant she would need to collect her mail, or, if there was an accomplice, have that person pick it up. Then the checks could be deposited, and if our theory was correct, wired to the Cayman Islands.

"Good. We'll meet near Asheville. I'm interviewing someone at Wilmer's Convenience Corner." I gave Archie the address. "Just be there around five to seven and wait in your car. Maybe pump some gas if you need it, and then park at the edge of the lot if I'm not there yet. Try not to be late. They close at seven."

"And where do I drop the forms off at the hotel?"

"At the front desk. Phone her after you're back in your car. If she wants to change the mailing address, tell her she can't because it's not the address of record."

"Okay. Then I'll see you at Wilmer's Convenience Corner. Six fifty-five."

"Yes. Just do everything exactly as I said and you'll be fine."

Archie laughed. "When have I ever not listened to you, Barry?"

Only whenever I'm talking, I thought.

Chapter Twenty-seven

I was in the jeep, headed for my rendezvous with Archie and a possible confrontation with Buddy Smith at Wilmer's Convenience Corner. On the seat beside me were two folders: one with three copies of Robert Sinclair's death certificate and the other with individual photos of Luther Brookshire, Robert Sinclair, and Janet Sinclair. I felt confident that if Buddy recognized any of the three people, he would break and I could get Lindsay Boyce to place him and his daughter Norie in an FBI safe house.

The drive gave me an opportunity to review the scenes of the case, one by one, like placing pieces of a puzzle together when you're not sure what the final picture is going to be.

Toby McKay had had a failed apple crop and gotten in debt to Rufus Taylor. He'd forfeited his EBT card as a forced method of repayment. All of the cash generated by its fraudulent purchases was either being kept by Rufus or split with the organizers of the scam food stamp network. Then Toby lost a second crop and suffered an emotional breakdown. But instead of going after Rufus and the conspiracy, he targeted Commissioner of Agriculture Graham James, whose department had destroyed his tainted apples and forced him into his dire circumstances.

Rufus was murdered less than an hour later. One certainty—his death wasn't a coincidence, not when Toby's EBT card was discovered in his wallet. Toby's son, Sonny, showed up drunk at the hospital that night, trying to see Commissioner James, ostensibly to explain his father's actions. He wound up in a jail cell next to Archie, who took on the ridiculous alias of Brad Pitt and learned that Sonny believed his own life was in danger. Reluctantly, Tommy Lee agreed to let Archie continue his charade with Sonny, but Archie, being Archie, bragged to his clients, the Sinclairs, that he was playing a crucial role in the investigation of Toby McKay's attack on the Commissioner of Agriculture. Sonny was murdered that night, and with the same gun that killed Rufus Taylor.

We had statements that Janet Sinclair left the Apple Festival parade soon after Commissioner James was attacked. She could have called someone, like her lover Luther Brookshire, or gone after Rufus herself. She knew Toby's action would trigger an investigation that could lead back to Rufus. With him dead, ties to the large-scale fraud would be severed.

But we found cash and articles in Rufus' closet that pointed to a broader conspiracy, and the newspaper report of the slaughter of a little girl's cat led to Wilmer's Convenience Corner, a store on a list that Sonny McKay must have intended to share with Archie, aka Brad.

We also had the definitive link between checks Rufus Taylor wrote to Staples Sources and the deposits Janet Sinclair made on behalf of her husband. Or the more likely scenario that Janet had been forging his name from the start. Once the possibility arose that Janet Sinclair killed Rufus, then her execution of Sonny McKay became an easy leap to make. The gun was the same. And the likelihood existed that Sonny would have let down his guard if a pretty woman knocked on his trailer door late at night claiming to have car trouble. But Sonny had drunk himself into a stupor and a simple break-in was all she needed.

If we assumed Janet's guilt brought her lover Brookshire into the picture, then he could have killed Robert, or all three, for that matter. He'd been close to Janet and her husband, guarded their identities in WITSEC, and could have been both seduced and enticed by Janet and the food stamp conspiracy. She'd probably witnessed the Santona family organize something similar in New Jersey.

Planting the gun and ledger on Robert pegged him with both the murders and the food stamp fraud. The signature White Rose of the Santonas diverted the focus from North Carolina to the New Jersey mob and created the impetus for Janet to be given a new identity within WITSEC. She and Brookshire could then follow the money out of the country. Between the insurance and the wire transfer, they could live very well, indeed. It was all an impressive plot if we hadn't had the breakthrough with the bank accounts and the overreach of making sure the gun in Robert Sinclair's car reflected his left-handedness. They'd been too clever for their own good. And now the potential testimony of Buddy Smith would be the final piece of the puzzle.

My cell phone vibrated. I glanced down to see the call was from Tommy Lee.

"Where are you?" he asked.

"About fifteen minutes out from Wilmer's Convenience Corner. What's up?"

"You and I had a visitor come by the department who wanted to talk to both of us."

"Who?"

"Luther Brookshire."

"Really?" I felt my heart rate jump. "A confession?"

"Partly. A confession of stupidity for getting involved with Janet Sinclair. But his main concern was that we believed him when he said he would never undercut our investigation. Yesterday, he picked up on what you did. That Janet Sinclair knew we were investigating the EBT scam. He realized he would be the first person we zero in on as the leak. He swears he never mentioned anything to her about our case. And he thinks she killed her husband."

"And you believe him?"

"Let's say it gives me pause. I've known Luther a long time, but sex and money are powerful motivators. He claims Janet made the first move and the affair's been going on only a few months."

"Isn't that what you'd expect him to say? It's a preemptive move because we know he's tied to her."

"Yes, but because we know he's tied to her, why would he say he thinks she killed her husband? Why even go there?"

Tommy Lee's question stopped me. If Brookshire accused Janet, she'd only drag him down with her. And we hadn't put any leverage on Brookshire yet. It wasn't like he was copping a plea. "I don't know. It's something to think about."

"Here's hoping your conversation with Buddy Smith sheds some light. If he identifies Luther, then his mea culpa about the affair is nothing more than an attempt to throw us off. But the timing of the affair is interesting."

I understood what the sheriff meant. "It started about the same time as Robert went to his father's funeral and when Janet first sought to change the insurance policies. She wanted to keep Brookshire close. He was her WITSEC guardian."

"And the source of a new identity," Tommy Lee added.

"But if not Luther Brookshire, then who? We know she had to have an accomplice."

"Unless Robert really was hit by the Santonas."

"But that makes no sense with a planted gun and ledger."

"I know. I wanted you to have this information before you talk to Buddy Smith. Keep open the possibility that Luther is innocent of everything except being seduced."

We disconnected. I quickly ran through the scenes I'd constructed. If Janet hadn't learned of the EBT investigation from Brookshire, would she have brought it up herself? It wasn't common knowledge. A switch threw in my brain. A perspective shift projected the case from a whole new angle. The EBT scam wasn't common knowledge. Sid Ferguson of the SBI and Lindsay

Boyce of the FBI hadn't been aware of it. That was odd because an FNS investigator was usually paired with one or the other as a case progressed.

What had Collier Crockett said about his background? Chicago, New York, New Jersey. A tingle started in the back of my neck. Was Luther Brookshire the first person Janet Sinclair had seduced? Crockett had broken up rings in eastern North Carolina, but only the occasional single store in western North Carolina. He could have come across the Sinclair operation, but instead of busting it, he could have joined it. The network would have been protected. Even the ledger book from Robert's SUV would have been handed back to Crockett. Or if Janet and Crockett went as far back as New Jersey, he could have set the whole thing up down here. Brookshire said Janet was the one who wanted WITSEC to locate her in the North Carolina mountains.

I was only minutes away from Wilmer's Convenience Corner. It was too late for me to get a photo of Crockett e-mailed to me. I had to meet Archie. I had to intercept Buddy Smith as he was closing the store. But I'd give him a verbal description of Crockett and maybe get a positive ID from a photograph later tonight.

The other businesses near Wilmer's had closed for the evening. The small grocery store was open but as I drew closer, the light on the gas pumps went out. It looked like Buddy might be closing a few minutes early. I drove by and then made a sharp turn into the lot out of sight of the front windows. Less than a minute later, Archie pulled his Lexus next to me headed in the opposite direction and we lowered our windows so we could talk without getting out.

He gave me an okay sign. "I got here early, bought some gas, and then parked at a tire store one building over."

I handed him the folder with the death certificates. "There's three in there. Wasn't sure if she needed one for each policy."

He shook his head. "Just the one for the death claim, but good to have the extras. I guess she really is going to try to change the name from Sinclair to Santona. If I'd known they were crooks, I never would have suggested the whole plan."

"And we might never have known what was going on."

Archie sighed. "Yeah. That's some comfort. Just so you know, there's a little girl in the store. Looks like she's doing her homework."

"I know. She's the owner's daughter. Thanks. I'll check in with you later."

Archie hesitated. "You sure you don't need me?"

"It's just a conversation. You go on to Asheville."

He raised his window, gave a wave through the glass, and eased back onto the two-lane highway.

I slipped the Kimber pistol into the back holster, waited for an oncoming car to pass, and then stepped out of the jeep. I checked my phone to make sure it was still silent, and then opened the app I needed.

Bells tinkled as I opened the store's front door.

"We're closing in a few minutes." Buddy Smith's voice came from one of the aisles. He stepped into view, a broom in his hand. His face went pale when he saw me and he laid the broom against a display of Hostess snacks. His gaze went immediately to his daughter, who was writing in a notebook at the end of the checkout counter.

I held my hands out, the folder in the right one. "I don't want any trouble. I just want to talk and show you some pictures."

Buddy Smith held up his own hands as if to push me away. "No. I've been told not to talk to you." He sidestepped around me and went to his daughter.

The girl looked up from her homework, fear plainly visible in her eyes.

Buddy put his hands on his daughter's shoulders. "You're trying to muscle in, and we won't be intimidated. Not anymore."

"That's what you were told? I was muscling in?"

"Yes. So get out and I won't tell that you came back. It's for your own good."

"I'm a deputy sheriff."

He eyed me skeptically. "Right. Then you'll let Norie go." He stepped back. "Leave your books, honey. Run up to the house. I'll be there shortly."

The girl hesitated, clearly reluctant to leave her father.

"Go!" he ordered.

She scooted off the stool and hurried by me. The bells jangled and the door slammed. Buddy Smith moved closer to the cash register.

"I'm with the Laurel County Sheriff's Department. All I want is for you to look at these photographs." I stepped toward him.

His hand disappeared beneath the counter and then reappeared gripping an old, tarnished thirty-eight revolver.

"Whoa," I said softly. "There's no need for that. I can show you my ID."

Buddy pulled back the hammer. "Keep your hands where I can see them." His voice quivered and the gun shook. I hoped there was a lot of play in the trigger.

"Whatever you say. But at least take a look at what's in the folder. Why would I bring pictures if I meant to do you harm?"

"Spread them out on the counter and then step back."

I did as he ordered. He looked at them in short glances, afraid to take his eyes off me for more than a few seconds.

"Nope. I don't recognize none of them."

His own facial reactions supported his words.

"Then tell me this. Do you know a man named Collier Crockett?"

Again, the blank stair.

"He's about forty. Black hair going gray at the edges. Sharp dresser."

His eyes widened slightly. "No. I don't know no one by that name."

I nodded. "Fine. I'm done here. I didn't mean to scare you or Norie. She's a lovely girl." I smiled. "My wife and I are having twins. I hope they're as nice as she is."

Buddy Smith's chin trembled and his eyes teared. He lowered the gun as the tension left his body.

The door burst open, ripping one of the bells from its mounting. Sheer panic flared on Buddy's face. I turned around.

Little Norie stumbled into the store, her arm wrenched behind her back. A pistol was jammed against her temple. A pistol held by Collier Crockett.

"Mr. Callahan, no!" Buddy wailed.

"Set the gun down, Buddy." The menace in Crockett's voice curled my blood. He kicked the front door closed.

Buddy uncocked the revolver and laid it on the counter. Norie whimpered.

"Slide it to the far end," Crockett ordered.

Buddy complied.

"I have to congratulate you, Buddy. You've caught yourself a real fish." He turned to me. "And you, Deputy Clayton, you just couldn't keep your nose out of my case, could you? That's why I've been following you."

He moved the pistol away from Norie's head and pointed it at me. "Buddy. Frisk him. Run your hands up each leg and check under his shoulders and his waist."

"There's a gun in the small of my back."

Buddy pulled the Kimber from the holster and set it on the counter.

"Frisk him anyway," Crockett said.

I spread my legs and held out my arms to make it easier.

"It's over, Crockett. We've found the bank accounts, we've got the money trail, we've got the evidence that you murdered Robert and then overdid it with the prints and placement of the pistol. Whose gun was that? Janet's?"

"She freaked out when Toby McKay went nuts. First killed Rufus and then Toby's son."

"And if she went down, you'd go down. So, what are you going to do now? Kill us all?"

Crockett didn't answer. He looked at the photos on the counter. "What are those?"

"Pictures. I was hoping Buddy could make an ID. He couldn't. He didn't give you up."

Crockett kept his grip on Norie's arm and motioned with the pistol. "Hold them up one at a time, Buddy."

The store owner lifted Robert Sinclair's photo, then Janet's, followed by Brookshire's.

"What's Brookshire doing with them?" Crockett asked.

"We thought he might be part of it."

"Why?"

"Because he's having an affair with Janet."

Crockett flinched like I'd slapped him. "He's what?"

"Having an affair. Do I need to spell it out? Janet wants to make sure she gets her new WITSEC identity. After all, everyone's supposed to think the Santona family is after her. Then she and Brookshire will leave the country and catch up with the wired funds and the insurance money. I guess you'll be left here holding the bag. And after you wired the money for her. I tell you there's no justice, is there?"

His eyes narrowed. "What insurance money?"

"You mean you didn't know about the million and a half dollars she's walking away with since you so conveniently murdered her husband?"

Crockett's face turned nearly purple with rage. "You're lying, you son of a bitch."

"Really? Didn't she tell you she met with an insurance agent? Archie Donovan. That's where she heard Sonny McKay was about to talk about your little EBT card fraud. That's what set her off again, right?"

Crockett's jaw clenched. I knew I'd pushed the right buttons, but I'd overplayed my hand. He knew that I knew he'd been played for a fool. In a flash, I saw what was coming.

My fear was confirmed when he said, "Bring me your revolver, Buddy."

"Don't do it. He's going to shoot me with your gun and then murder you and Norie with mine."

"Shut up." Crockett moved the barrel of his semi-automatic back to Norie's temple. "Bring it, Buddy. Hand it to me butt first and I'll let your daughter go."

Buddy walked like he was about to collapse. He picked up the old revolver, holding the barrel in his left hand.

"Daddy, don't," Norie whispered.

Buddy's face went hard. He grabbed the gun with his right hand. Crockett whipped his pistol from the girl's head and aimed it at her father.

The explosion was deafening. Not from the gun, but from the front door and wall exploding as a car smashed through it. Glass and splinters flew from broken windows and boards. Crockett spun around and fired shots indiscriminately into the windshield of the vehicle. Norie fell to the floor as I jumped for the Kimber and racked the slide just as Crockett wheeled back around. I fired three shots as fast as I could pull the trigger. The impact of the forty-five caliber slugs into Crockett's chest drove him back like he'd been hit by a train.

Dust hung in the air like fog. I ran to Crockett and kicked his pistol clear. His eyes were open, seeing nothing.

I turned back to Buddy. He was kneeling, embracing his daughter in a smothering hug. Both were crying.

I stepped over the debris to the driver's side of a mangled Lexus. Archie Donovan fought through a deflated airbag and practically fell out of the car. He looked up with blood streaked across his face.

"Archie, are you hit?"

He coughed. "I fell across the seat after the airbag smacked me." He looked up at the windshield. Bullet holes showed where Crockett's shots had penetrated just above the steering wheel. "Sorry, Barry. I didn't do what you told me."

I helped him to his feet and did the unthinkable.

I hugged him.

Chapter Twenty-eight

Wilmer's Convenience Corner looked like a war zone. Blue, red, and orange lights flashed from vehicles filling the parking lot and running along the highway's shoulder for a hundred feet in either direction. EMTs, Buncombe County deputies, and firemen dotted the scene. Buddy Smith's neighbors from the houses on the ridge behind the store stood on a perimeter the police had cordoned off. The murmur of their whispers was like a steady buzz of insects.

Archie had had the presence of mind to call 911 before his crash and a horde of Buncombe County law enforcement quickly arrived on the scene. I'd raised Tommy Lee, who in turn contacted Lindsay Boyce. She and her FBI team were nearer and it seemed like no more than twenty minutes before she appeared, making it clear to the Buncombe County Sheriff that this was a federal investigation.

Buddy Smith and Norie were together in the back of an ambulance. Both had suffered minor cuts and bruises from flying debris. Archie's nose had swollen from the airbag's impact and he had a gash on his forehead that required a few stitches. Miraculously, I was unscathed.

Lindsay Boyce requested Tommy Lee, Archie, and me join her in her SUV for a briefing on what happened. She would speak with Buddy Smith and Norie after they'd been removed from the trauma of the scene.

Lindsay and Tommy Lee sat in the front seats with Archie and me in the rear.

"Okay, Barry," Lindsay said. "walk us through what happened."

I opted to let my story be told directly. I retrieved my cell phone, opened the record app I'd started before entering the store, and we heard Crockett convict himself and Janet with his own words.

"This is good," Lindsay said when I stopped the recording with the sound of Archie's car crashing through the store wall. "Really good."

"Yes," Tommy Lee agreed. "But it would be better if we could get Janet Sinclair incriminating herself as well."

"Any ideas?" Lindsay asked.

"Have the agents who are minding her said anything about this event?" I asked.

"I don't know. Why?"

"We get Crockett's phone and see if he had any e-mail or text correspondence from Janet. If so, we contact her as Crockett. Arrange a meet. If she comes to him, we've further nailed down that they had a relationship. Maybe even have Archie drop off the insurance forms as originally planned. She might pick them up and try to give your agents the slip. I mean, she knows the Santona family didn't kill Robert, so she's got nothing to fear."

"Worth a shot," Tommy Lee said.

"I'll check my agents," Lindsay said. "If Janet doesn't know, I'll make sure she's isolated from any news." Lindsay twisted in her seat to face Archie who sat directly behind her. "Why did you stay?"

Archie nervously wiped his palms on his pants. The magnitude of his action was beginning to sink in. Especially the bullet holes in the driver's side of the windshield.

"I pulled out of the parking lot and about fifty feet down the road a car passed me going the other way. I wondered if the driver would think it suspicious if he saw Barry going into the store as it was closing. So, I slowed and checked the rearview mirror. The car kept going but then suddenly turned into the lot of the closed tire store. That's where I'd been waiting for Barry. I pulled onto the shoulder and killed my lights. In a few minutes I saw a man walking near the gas pumps. A little girl ran out the front door of the grocery store and the man grabbed her. He dragged her inside. I turned my car around and eased back with the headlights off. I stopped out of sight of the front window and got out. I crept up beside the front door and could hear everything. You heard what Crockett said. It was clear to me he could start shooting at any time. I ran back to my car, made the 911 call, and then used the only weapon I had. My Lexus."

"That was quick thinking," Lindsay said. "Are you still game for taking the insurance forms to the hotel?"

Archie looked at me and shrugged. "Yeah, but what if she happens to come down to the lobby and I look like this?"

"Just leave them at the front desk," I said.

"Okay, but there's another problem?"

"What?" I asked.

"I need a ride."

Archie rode to Asheville with me in the jeep. I'd placed a quick call to Susan to tell her I was okay and Archie did the same with his wife Gloria. We weren't sure what names the news media might be mentioning, but we didn't want our families worrying.

Special Agent Lindsay Boyce had been assured by her agent at the hotel that Janet had no knowledge of the incident at the store. She was watching a movie on HBO. Lindsay had found a text message on Crockett's phone that read,

at 302 Renaissance.

The number matched Janet's hotel room and Lindsay verified that the sending cell phone belonged to Janet. It was the same number from which she'd contacted Archie. We would send the ruse message from Crockett's phone after Archie delivered the forms to the front desk. Since she was expecting them, we didn't want any delay to alarm her.

We'd just entered Asheville on I-240 when I had a call from a number I didn't recognize. I started to let it go to voicemail, but with all the actions swirling around us, I decided I'd better take it.

"Barry, it's Luther Brookshire."

"Yes, Luther. I'm kind of tied up right now."

"I understand. I'm watching the news. Are you okay?"

"Yes. Thanks. Tommy Lee said you came by the department."

"So you know I had nothing to do with this."

"I do."

"Did she kill Rufus and Sonny?"

"That's what Crockett said. He was in it with her."

"That's the FNS investigator, right?"

"Yes. We think they were in it together from the very start. And they were lovers."

Brookshire's voice choked. "She played me for a fool. And I made a fool out of the marshals."

I didn't say anything. My unspoken thought was that Brookshire was correct. She had played him for a fool, she'd played Robert Sinclair for a fool, and I felt certain she was planning to ditch Crockett and take all the money. *La femme fatale.*

"Don't worry, Luther. We'll get her. I've got to go." I hung up before he could say anything else.

I parked the jeep in a ten-minute loading zone at the hotel. "On second thought, Archie, don't leave the forms at the front desk. Ask that they deliver them to room 302. We don't want her coming down where she might see a newscast in the bar."

"Got it." He grinned. "This time I'll listen to you."

He was back in five minutes. "Now what?"

"Now I take you to Weaverville and your wife and girls."

After Archie was reunited with his family, I phoned Tommy

Lee. It was nearly eleven, but he was still with Lindsay at the FBI office.

"What's the plan?" I asked.

"Why don't you head home and get some rest?" Tommy Lee said.

"Oh, no. You made me your lead investigator on this thing and I'm seeing it through."

"Okay. I'm staying at the Aloft. I'll book you a room. Lindsay and her agents will take Janet into custody in the morning. We'll be observers."

"Did you send Janet the text?"

"Yes." Tommy Lee chuckled. "My niece is quite devious. She wrote, 'trouble with the wire transfer. Need to see you! Over Easy Café. 8AM.'"

The Over Easy Café was a popular breakfast spot a few blocks' walk from Janet's hotel.

"Good," I said. "She might not come for Crockett but she'll come if she thinks there's a snag with the money. Are you going to make it easy for her to slip out?"

"Yes. Lindsay has one female agent with Janet. She'll just happen to take a shower around twenty to eight."

"And we'll be where?"

"Lindsay's sending a van for us at seven-fifteen. We'll be watching through its tinted windows from across the street."

"All right. I'll see you in the lobby of the Aloft at seven-fifteen."

The room was available when I arrived. I was afraid I'd have trouble falling asleep, the way my mind was racing. I stripped, tried to shake the dust from my clothes, and then took a hot shower. I set my phone alarm for six forty-five and put my head on the pillow. The next thing I knew the alarm was chirping.

The van was in position by seven-thirty. Lindsay had brought two thermoses of hot coffee and some sweet rolls. The plan was to take Janet at the front door. But the concern was that as vicious as she'd proven to be, we didn't want any altercation to break out that could injure an innocent bystander. The Over Easy Café was so popular that a line usually formed about fifteen minutes before opening time.

Around ten till eight, an Asheville police car, siren blaring and lights flashing came speeding past us. We didn't think much of it until two minutes later when a second cruiser raced by.

"Uh, oh," Lindsay muttered. "I don't like this." She turned to an agent in the front passenger's seat. "Henry, walk back toward the hotel along the route Janet should be taking."

Five minutes later, his voice crackled over the comm set. "A woman's body's been found behind the hotel. I believe she's our target."

"Copy that." Lindsay slid open the side door. "Gentlemen. Shall we?"

We showed our IDs to the police officers who were setting up a perimeter around the body. They were very curious how the FBI had showed up so quickly, but Lindsay offered no explanation other than the victim was a federal witness.

Janet lay on her back along the single-lane road that ran between the hotel and the historic Thomas Wolfe House. Blood splotched the front of her light-blue coat. An oozing wound marred the center of her forehead. Even in death, her face held an expression of total surprise.

Beside her head lay a single white rose.

"How could the Santonas find her?" Lindsay asked.

"Check her phone," I suggested.

Lindsay borrowed a pair of latex gloves from one of the officers and rummaged through the purse beside Janet's waist. She found the phone.

"What am I looking for?" she asked.

"Any text containing the hotel information. Like what we found on Crockett's phone."

Lindsay thumbed through the texts as Tommy Lee and I huddled around her. "Here's the one to Crockett," she said. "I recognize the number." She continued to scroll. "Here's another."

"That's Archie's phone," I said.

"And here's a third."

I pulled my own phone from my belt and checked my messages. The number matched. "That belongs to Luther Brookshire."

"How will we prove it?" Lindsay asked.

"You won't," I said. "You can canvas every flower vendor in the area to see who bought a white rose, but I suspect he might have just paid someone to buy it for him. What's the time on that message?"

"The night before last. When we first booked her into the hotel."

"Or maybe he tipped off the Santona family," Tommy Lee said.

"Maybe," I conceded. "Ironic that the marshals never lost a witness in WITSEC and here's the second within three days. And possibly shot by the marshal handling her."

"No," Tommy Lee said. "The marshals will claim they voided their protection the day Robert Sinclair went to that New Jersey funeral. Their record's intact."

Lindsay nodded. "So, what now?"

I looked down at the body. "Now I call a cemetery in Paterson, New Jersey."

Chapter Twenty-nine

"Then on Friday afternoon, Commissioner of Agriculture Graham James announced the formation of a task force involving his department, the SBI, the FBI, and FNS to track down and prosecute all who might be part of the fraud ring Collier Crockett and Janet Sinclair created." I picked up the wineglass by the leg of my chair and took a sip. "And now you're up to date."

Melissa Bigham leaned over and turned off the digital audio recorder on the low table between us. She, Susan, and I sat on our back deck. Democrat lay at Melissa's feet. It was late Sunday afternoon. Janet Sinclair had been shot the previous Wednesday, and Melissa had returned from her vacation in the Caribbean yesterday to find one of the biggest stories in Gainesboro's history happened while she was gone. To say she was as angry as a wet hornet doesn't begin to describe her wrath.

As an attempt to pacify her and the *Gainesboro Vista*, Tommy Lee had authorized an exclusive interview with me. I'd suggested drinks and dinner at the cabin. I was counting on Susan to prevent any bodily harm. Bodily harm to me.

"Okay," Melissa said flatly, "so, off the record, who do you think killed Joan Santona, aka Janet Sinclair?"

The sheriff and I had agreed there would be no speculation on Luther Brookshire's guilt while the FBI investigated Janet's murder. And I'd kept Brookshire out of my story because his affair had no bearing on the key events.

"All I can say is we found a white rose beside her body. Whether it was a Santona hit or someone else casting that suspicion, I don't know. Anyway, that case is out of our jurisdiction."

She frowned. "Come on, Barry. Surely you have an opinion."

"Well, I will say that we've learned Collier Crockett had investigated food stamp fraud in New Jersey when the Santonas were suspected of being involved. My speculation is that Crockett and Joan Santona met then. She was already skimming from the family, and that's why she turned over evidence that got her and Robert into WITSEC. Robert was so infatuated with her that she could manipulate him to do anything. As far as we know, he was happy repping his sportswear lines and playing golf. His signature that the FBI found on checks and deposit slips appears to have been consistently forged by Janet. I believe Robert really didn't have much of a clue as to what was going on."

"And you think Janet and Crockett planned to leave the country?"

"I think Janet did. Crockett could have wound up someone she used and discarded along the way."

"Any update on Buddy Smith and his daughter?" Melissa asked.

"He's turning state's evidence. I expect he'll get a light sentence and probation. His store was barely making ends meet and when his wife got cancer, he got involved with Crockett, only Crockett called himself Callahan. Lindsay Boyce believes Crockett used a false name with every store owner as another layer of protection. In his investigations, he'd find ones who were taking cash out of customers' EBT cards and threaten to report them if they didn't start splitting the take. Staples Sources was the shell company and the corrupt store owners wouldn't be audited since Crockett was the lead investigator."

"Did he kill the little girl's cat?"

"Yes. After Buddy Smith's wife died, the medical bills ceased. Buddy wanted out. The dead cat was a message. I think a judge will be sympathetic to what the poor man went through."

"And it sounds like at the end, he was going to defend you, rather than give his gun to Crockett."

I flashed back to the grim look of determination that transformed Buddy's face from fear to resolve.

"Yes. But I'm afraid Crockett would have shot first."

Melissa smiled for the first time. "Except for Archie."

I nodded. "Except for Archie."

"And here's my threat to you, Barry Clayton. If something like this ever happens again, promise me you'll track me down even if I'm on Mars."

"Or what?" I asked.

"Or I'm running this story under the headline, 'Archie Donovan, Junior, saves Buryin' Barry.'"

Susan laughed and raised her glass of sparkling water. "To Archie."

"To Archie," I repeated. For once, the words didn't stick in my throat.

Over six weeks later, Thursday, the first of November, dawned chilly and clear. At eight o'clock, Susan and I stood on the front porch of the funeral home and watched the moving van turn off Main Street into our parking lot. I put my arm around her waist and patted her tummy. The baby bump seemed to be growing daily.

We'd loaded the truck the previous day after getting Uncle Wayne and Mom settled in their apartment at Alderway. Both had been over the moon when we'd told them about the twins. Mom was already anxious about what the grandchildren would call her, and Uncle Wayne regaled us with tales of how they needed a set bedtime like when he grew up on a farm and had to get up early for chores. My bachelor uncle, the expert on child-rearing. Our only livestock was going to be Democrat.

"Your mom called a few minutes ago while you were out back," Susan said. "She and Uncle Wayne are on their way with ham biscuits and orange juice."

"Did you tell her we're fine?"

Susan laughed. "Now what good would that have done? She said she wants the movers to have something to eat. You saw how they loved those cookies yesterday."

That was my mom. See a person, feed a person. The local movers were doing triple duty: moving Mom and my uncle, moving Cindy and Fletcher, and moving Susan and me.

Not since high school had I lived in the funeral home. Susan and I agreed the two-bedroom cabin would be cramped quarters and it was Susan who convinced me that the funeral home with four bedrooms was a ready-made option. We took the money from the sale of her condo, also sold the cabin, and paid Mom a fair appraisal. Fletcher and Cindy bought the cabin before it went on the market and the movers got all the business, plus cookies and biscuits as a bonus.

Trailing the van was a Chevy Malibu of several years vintage.

"Oh, no," I groaned. "I wonder what this is about?"

"Who is it?" Susan asked.

"Archie. He bought a used car because his insurance company says he wrecked his Lexus on purpose."

"But he saved three lives."

"Don't I know it. Lindsay Boyce and the FBI are getting involved. They're working the angle that Crockett and Janet caused him to total his car. The FBI may manage to have the Sinclairs' assets impounded. Archie could wind up with Janet's Mercedes or Robert's Infiniti, if Archie doesn't die of old age before the government paperwork is completed."

Archie parked on the far side of the moving van. He got out, waved, and then pulled two wrapped boxes out of his backseat.

He stacked them under his chin and walked toward us without being able to see his feet.

"You'd better go help him," Susan said. "We don't need to test our new homeowner's policy if he trips."

I met Archie at the edge of the sidewalk and took one of the packages.

"Thanks, Barry. I can't stay, but Gloria and I wanted to get you something for your first day in the funeral home. Can't believe you're living here. It's like old times."

He stepped up on the porch and smiled at Susan. "And how are you doing, little Momma?"

"I'm good, Archie. How's the family?"

"Terrific. Everything's terrific."

"Well, that's terrific," I echoed.

"Come on in," Susan said. "Have some coffee."

"Thanks. These are for the kitchen anyway." Archie stepped around her and led the way into the house.

Susan and I looked at each other. She shook her head as if to say, "Only Archie."

He set his package on the kitchen table and I placed the second one beside it. They were wrapped in pink and blue paper.

"Go ahead. Open them."

Susan took one and I took the other. In less than a minute, we were looking at identical boxes with a picture of a yellow booster seat on the sides.

"What do you think?" Archie asked. "We got this color because we don't know the genders, but you'll need them for when the twins are old enough to sit at this table and eat their peanut butter and jelly sandwiches."

Archie punched me gently on the arm. "Huh, buddy? Just what this funeral home needs. New life." He laughed at his own joke. "And if they're boys, I've got the perfect names."

I cringed.

He punched me harder. "Archie and Barry."

Author's Note

Secret Undertaking is a work of fiction, but elements of the story are based in fact.

The U.S. Marshals Service is charged with operating the Federal Witness Protection Program, or WITSEC, as it is known. In contacting the U.S. Marshals for information, one quickly learns that all aspects of their procedures for relocating their witnesses are closely guarded. "Neither confirm nor deny" is their prevalent answer. However, they referred me to the book, *WITSEC: Inside the Federal Witness Protection Program* by Pete Earley and Gerald Shur, the man credited with creating WITSEC. Although the Marshals neither confirm nor deny its accuracy, the book is a fascinating revelation of the program's history.

WITSEC was instrumental in decimating the mob, but an unintended consequence has been those occasions when relocated witnesses have used their new, squeaky-clean identities to return to a life of crime. Local law enforcement is not made aware of their presence in their communities. That tension between invaluable testimony for the prosecution of major criminal enterprises and the protection of those witnesses who are criminals themselves is real and created the underlying conflict for my story.

Likewise, the urban and rural abuse of the Supplemental Nutrition Assistance Program (SNAP Food Stamp Program) is also documented fact, but I wouldn't want the crimes depicted in my story to undercut the tremendous benefit that SNAP provides. Although fraud exists, it is a very small percentage of an overall program that offers vital assistance to millions of low-income individuals and families. It is a key component of our social safety net, and the USDA aggressively investigates and prosecutes those who would subvert it.

Acknowledgments

Special thanks to retired Mecklenburg County Sheriff Chipp Bailey for his insights into the U.S. Marshals' insulation of relocated witnesses from local law enforcement. Also I'm appreciative of what information the U.S. Marshals Office of Public Affairs was able to share regarding WITSEC. Thanks to my brother Arch de Castrique, insurance and investment guru, for devising the Sinclairs' policy scheme.

I'm grateful to my editor Barbara Peters for her guidance in developing the story and to Robert Rosenwald and the staff of Poisoned Pen Press, who turn stories into books. Thanks to the many librarians and booksellers who introduce my stories to readers and to all who spend time with my characters.

Finally, I'm grateful for my family—Linda, Melissa, Pete, Charlie, Lindsay, Jordan (and canines Grady, Belby, and Norman), who make reality even more fun to experience than fiction. Thanks for creating such a wonderful world.

To see more Poisoned Pen Press titles:

Visit our website:
poisonedpenpress.com
Request a digital catalog:
info@poisonedpenpress.com